Paul Heyse

Barbarossa

and other tales from the German by L.C.S

Paul Heyse

Barbarossa
and other tales from the German by L.C.S

ISBN/EAN: 9783337089306

Printed in Europe, USA, Canada, Australia, Japan

Cover: Foto ©Andreas Hilbeck / pixelio.de

More available books at **www.hansebooks.com**

BARBAROSSA

AND

OTHER TALES

BY

PAUL HEYSE.

FROM THE GERMAN
BY
L. C. S.

Authorized Edition.

LEIPZIG 1874

BERNHARD TAUCHNITZ.

LONDON: SAMPSON LOW, MARSTON, LOW & SEARLE.
CROWN BUILDINGS, 188, FLEET STREET.
PARIS: C. REINWALD & Cⁱᵉ, 15, RUE DES SAINTS PÈRES.

CONTENTS.

BARBAROSSA.

BARBAROSSA.

I HAD only intended to spend one day up in the
mountains, and this one day grew into two weeks, which
I found pass more rapidly in that high-perched ruinous
nest on the confines of the Albano and Sabine range—
the name I will not give—than was often the case in
the whirl of great cities. What I actually did with myself during the sweet long days I hardly know how to
tell. But in Rome a mighty hunger after solitude had
fallen on me. I could satisfy it here to the full. It was
early spring-time, the leaves of the chestnut trees shone
in luxuriant freshness; the ravines were filled by the
song of birds, and the murmur of brooks; and as of
late a large body of banditti who had rendered this
wild district insecure, had been in part captured, and in
part driven into the Abruzzi, it ensued that a lonely
wanderer might without any apprehension climb the re-
motest crags, and there give himself up undisturbed to
profoundest meditations.

From the first I declined all intercourse with the
German artists, a good number of whom had taken possession of both miserable inns the village possessed, and
as to the desire of every now and then hearing one's
own voice, which impels hermits to converse with their
domestic animals, I could gratify it quite sufficiently
within my own walls. For as it happened I lodged with
the apothecary, and he had the utmost indulgence for

my very defective Italian. True he indemnified himself for his outlay in patience by not unfrequently taking advantage of mine, for as soon as the first shyness had worn off, he showered a whole cornucopia of his own verses on me, confessing that despite his fifty and five years he was still unable entirely to shake off this childish malady. "What would you have?" he pleaded, "when at evening I step to my window and see the moon coming up behind the rocks, and the fire-flies on the wing about my little garden,—why I must be a brute if it does not set me off poetising." And indeed he was anything but a brute this good Signor Angelo, whom owing to a natural tonsure—a rim of black hair still circling his smooth bald head—his friends were wont to nickname Fra Angelico. He had never indeed left his native place more than twice in his life, nor on either occasion gone further than Rome. But then Rome is the world, he would say. He who has seen Rome, has seen everything. And forthwith he proceeded to speak of everything, partly according to the very miscellaneous and chaotic knowledge he owed to a few books accidentally picked up, partly from the audacity of unbridled poetical fancy. Of all the worthies who according to old Italian custom were wont to gather at evening in his apothecary's shop: priest, schoolmaster, surgeon, tax-gatherer, and a few unofficial well-to-do proprietors, whose faces beamed with the profits of their rich olive and vine yards,—of all these notabilities not one ventured to contradict Fra Angelico, not at least, when previous to one of his longer harangues, he polished his large silver spectacles on his coat-sleeve and began, "*Ecco signori miei*, the matter stands thus." But all the same he was the best and most harmless creature in the world, and the most amiable landlord one could desire, provided one had no wish beyond a hard bed, and two ricketty arm-chairs! He was certainly fond of me, although, or perhaps *because* he had not the faintest idea that I was a brother poet. I was discreet enough to confine myself to playing the part of a grateful public, and it was not until after the four-and-twentieth sonnet that I would gently lay my hand on his arm and say, "Bravo, Signor Angelo! But I fear this is too much of a good thing. Your poetry, is you know, potent, and flies to the head. To-morrow you shall fill me up a new flask from your Hippocrene." Whereupon with the most good-humoured look imaginable he would close his volume and say, "What avail if I read you to sleep, night after night a whole year through? I should still not have come to an end! Here we have another Peru!" And tapping on his bald forehead he would sigh, offer a pinch of snuff, and wish me a good night.

The majority of these poems were of course devoted to love, and when the little man recited them with sparkling eyes and all the pathos common to his nation, it was easy to forget his five and fifty years. Nevertheless, he lived a bachelor's life, with one old maid-servant and a boy who helped him with his salves and potions, and it seemed strange that with all his love for the beautiful and his comfortable means, he should never have married, nor even now in his sunny autumn seem inclined to make up for lost time. One evening, when we sat smoking together over the good home-grown wine, and I jokingly asked him why he took his monkish nickname so much in earnest, and whether none of the pretty girls that daily passed his shop had contrived to touch his heart, he suddenly looked up at me with a strange expression, and said, "Pretty girls? Well, I dare-say they are not so far from it either, and marriage

may be better than is reported. But I am too old for a
young man, and too young for an old one, or rather let
me say too much of a poet. The older the bird, the
harder to catch. And then you see, my friend, I was
once devoted to a girl who did not care for me—one I
tell you the like of whom will never be seen again. So
now I am too proud, or whatever it may be called, to
be flattered even if some common-place creature—of
whom there are twelve to the dozen—were to fancy me.
I prefer to dream myself happy in my verses, and to
shape myself a perfect beauty out of a hundred incomplete ones, like the Grecian painter—was his name
Apelles?—who took for his Venus the eyes of one
neighbour, the nose of another, and thus got the best
together bit by bit. But as for her who really did unite
all perfections, and was so beautiful that you would not
believe me if I tried to describe her, she paid dear for
her beauty, and many know the story as correctly as I
do, though if you were to ask any of the older people
in the place about Erminia, they would all bear me out
that she was a wonder of the world, and that during the
twenty years that have passed by since then, nothing has
ever happened that made such an impression as her
fate and all connected with it. Come now, I will tell it
you, as you already know the sonnets to her—I allude
to the sixty-seven that I keep in the blue portfolio, of
which you said that they really had much of Petrarch's
manner; they all date from the time when the wound
was still fresh; and when once you have heard the story
you can hear them over again. It is only so that you
will thoroughly understand them."

After which, with a sigh that sounded to me rather
comic than tragic, he snuffed the candle, leant back in
the arm-chair behind his counter, half-closed his eyes,

and buried his hands in the side-pockets of his worn-out paletot. It was about nine o'clock in the evening. The Piazza before the house was still as death, one heard only the prattling of the brook, and the heavy breathing of the apprentice asleep in the next room. Then after a long pause he began with his usual exordium.

"*Ecco amico mio*, the matter stands thus. Somewhere about the year '30—you are too young to remember so far back—this said Erminia lived here in the village with a mother and sister who are also dead and buried long ago. If when you leave this door, you turn to the right up the little street leading to the old ruin on the summit of our hill, you will come to a small house, or rather hovel, roofless now except for two worm-eaten beams, and even then it was not much better protected from sun and rain; only that the great fig-tree that is withered now, used at that time to spread its broad thick-leaved branches over it just at the season when shade was most needed. In those bare stone walls that had formerly served as a shelter to wild creatures, Erminia lived. Her father had been dead for years, her mother had no idea of management, so that the family had come down wofully, and were glad enough to be allowed to nestle down in those ruins. There were, indeed, many who would have been glad to support the widow for her husband's sake. But you know how the proverb runs:

> 'Sacco rotto non tien miglio.
> Pover uomo non va a consiglio.'*

It was all in vain. The girls who were thoroughly well-behaved, might work their fingers to the bone, spinning

* Sack that's torn will not hold grain.
To poor men good advice is vain.

and lace-making, and the neighbours might do their part as well as they could, the old woman drank everything up, and if she was not raging like a fury, she would lie on the hearth and sleep, and leave her daughters to find food and clothing for all. I do believe if their next neighbour, the fig-tree, had not done its part so gallantly, that Erminia and her sister Maddalena would both have died of hunger, for they were too proud to beg. Raiment, indeed, the tree could not afford them, since we no longer live in Paradise. Consequently everybody was astonished to see the poor things come to church so neatly dressed, the more that there was not a word to be said against them. True the younger of the two, Maddalena was thoroughly safe from temptation, for she was as ugly as sin, a short, unkempt, club-footed creature, with long arms and short legs, having a gait much like that of a toad, and frightening the children in the street if she came upon them unexpectedly.

"But she knew quite well how unsightly she was, and for the most part kept at home, doing, however, no harm to anyone, which is not often the case with such afflicted creatures, who are generally envious and spiteful by way of revenging themselves for their misfortune. She, on the contrary, seemed to look upon it as in the order of things that her mother, after bringing into the world one child so boundlessly beautiful as Erminia, should have had nothing but nature's refuse left for a second. Instead of looking askance at her elder sister, and wishing to poison her, she made so perfect an idol of her, that none of the young men about were more in love with Erminia than the poor fright Maddalena. And indeed Erminia was one that to see was to love. I for my part had seen all the statues in Rome, Muses, Venuses, Minervas, no small master-pieces, but such triumphs of art as the world cannot equal. And yet, between ourselves, utter failures compared to what nature had done. Look you, friend,"—and so saying the little man jumped up and raised his arm—"she was so tall, about a head taller than I am, but so beautifully formed; her little head so gracefully set on her magnificent bust, that no one found out how tall she was. And then her face, chiselled as it were, with large eyes richly eyelashed, and an expression proud and sweet both; a mouth red as a strawberry, or rather the inside of a white fig, and her brow crowned with thick blue-black curly hair, which she bound up behind into such a heavy nest of ringlets that it needed as stately a throat as hers to bear their burden. And then when she moved, walked, raised her arms to steady the basket she carried on her head, with her taper fingers turned, as it were, out of ivory; and her little feet in their coarse wooden shoes—*amico mio*, if I had not been a poet, that girl would have made me one. As for the others who had not a drop of poet blood in their veins, at least she made them mad, which is half-way to the Temple of Apollo. There was not a young fellow in the place who would not have had his left hand cut off, if only he might have worn her ring on the right. But she would listen to none of them, which was the more surprising when you considered the poverty she lived in, and that of the offers made to her, the very worst would at least have saved her, her mother, and her sister from any further distress. Of myself I will not speak. Madly in love as I was, I had still sense enough left to see that I was not worthy of her, and after I had in some degree got over the pain of my rejection, I told her that I would at least be her friend at all times, and she gave me her hand, and thanked me with such a smile. Sir, at that moment I was more crazy than ever! But there was another that everybody thought would outbid us all, and although we might have grudged her to him, still we should not have had a word to say against her choice. This was the son of the landlord of the *Croce d'oro*, a handsome fellow, rolling in money, and about two-and-twenty, a couple of inches taller than Erminia; generally called Barbarossa, or merely *Il Rosso*, on account of his having with light curly hair, a fine red beard of his own; but his real name was Domenico Serone. He paid his court to Erminia in such a way that nothing else was talked of, went on like one distracted, while she dismissed him just as she had done the rest of us, without positive disdain. She only gave him to understand that he might spare himself any further trouble, that she could not marry him, for a good girl like her would not awaken any false hopes. Many thought that her own country-people were not distinguished enough for her, that it must be some foreigner, a milord, or a Russian, and that her mind was set on distant lands and fabulous adventures. But no, sir, that too was a bad shot. I myself knew a rich English count, or marquis, or whatever he might be, who told me that he had thrown a couple of thousand pounds or so into her apron, and implored her on his knees to accompany him to England. But she just shook off the bank-notes as though they had been dead leaves, and threatened if he ever spoke another word to her, to strike him across the face, even if it were on the public market-place. And so we went on exhausting ourselves in conjectures as to what her motives could be; whether she had made a vow to die unmarried; and I even once summoned up courage to ask her—such was the friendly footing we stood on—whether she had a hatred to men in general. Not so, she quietly replied, but as yet she had not found one whom she could love. In this way two years passed, she still with the same calm face, Red-beard looking more and more gloomy, and it was plain to see how consumed he was by the fire within, for the handsome youth went creeping about like a ghost.

"One day, however, a stranger came here, a Swedish captain, who had left the service because his promotion had been unfairly delayed, and who, since then, having means of his own, had travelled by land and by sea half over the world, shooting elephants and tigers, crocodiles and sea-serpents, and carrying about with him half-a-dozen most beautiful guns and rifles, and a great Newfoundland dog, who had more than once saved his life. If I remember rightly this stranger's name was *Sture*, or something of the sort, but I myself called him Sor Gustavo, and the village-folk just "the Captain." He took up his quarters here because he liked my little garden, had the very room you now occupy, and he and I were soon as thick as thieves. He was not a man of many words, nor indeed would he listen to my verses, for he cared only for one poet, Lord Byron, whose adventures he had set himself to emulate. Well, and he was quite up to the task. He was as brave as a lion, with more money than he knew what to do with, and as for the women, they ran after him go where he would, for he was wonderfully stately in his bearing and figure, and yet had so good-humoured an expression that they all thought it would be easy to play the part of Omphale to this Hercules. In Rome he seemed to have been pretty wild, at least so this one and the other pretended to know; he himself never touched on his love-affairs, and here in our village, he never appeared to care whether there was any other race in the world than that of men. With these he went about continually; would sit—if he were not prowling along the ravines with his rifle—whole afternoons at the café, playing billiards to perfection, and when he had won everybody's money, he would order a barrel of the best wine, and insist upon everybody partaking. So all began as with one mouth to sing his praises, and to rejoice that such a travelled gentleman should have taken such a craze for our little spot above all others, that he even talked of buying a vineyard, and of yearly spending a couple of months among us.

"Domenico Serone was the only one who kept aloof from our captain, would get up as soon as ever he saw him enter the café, and pass him by in the street as a thief does the gallows. No one wondered though at this, for to see himself eclipsed by a foreigner—he who was accustomed to be cock of the walk—must naturally have mortified him. It never even occurred to me that Erminia might have something to do with it. I had been present when Signor Gustavo met the fair creature for the first time. 'Now look here, *amico mio*,' I had said, 'never—if only you will honestly admit it, never have you seen anything like her in either of the Indies, Turkey, or Golconda.' But he after a mere glance, without a look of surprise, merely said, 'Hum!' biting his blonde moustache so hard, you heard the crunching of the hair. 'Not amiss, Sor Angelo, not amiss indeed.' '*Possareddio*,' said I to myself, 'this is the only man who can look without blinking at the sun.' It crossed me that I would engage Erminia in conversation, that he might see more of her, and be punished for his cold-blooded 'not amiss,' by falling over head and ears into love. But she, usually so calm and unembarrassed when she met any one, turned strangely red, and hurried away, so that I thought at once, 'Hollo! at length her hour has struck,' but I said not a word, and the meeting went out of my head.

"But about a week later, I stood before my shop-door in the twilight deciphering a letter I had just received, in which a friend in Rome told me he had read aloud my sonnets at a meeting of a poetical society— the 'Arcadia'—and that amidst general approval I had been elected honorary member, which so surprised and pleased me, that for the moment I was not aware of what was going on about me, till I heard *Il Rosso's* voice so loud and threatening that it woke me out of all my cogitations. Looking up I saw him standing by the fountain not ten yards from my door, pale as a corpse, and quite unlike the smart fellow he used to be, and not far from where he was,—the pitcher that she had intended to fill left standing on the edge of the fountain, and her left hand pressing her side,—stood Erminia, and as it happened no one else was in sight. I wondered what both could be about, as they had avoided each other for months past. But *Il Rosso* did not keep me long in suspense. 'Hear me, Erminia,' he said, as though he were reading out a sentence of death to some convicted criminal in the hearing of all the world: 'It is lucky that we have met here. True we have no longer any dealings with each other, but as I once loved you, even though you trampled my love under your feet, I would still warn you. Take heed to yourself, Erminia, and be careful what you do. I know one who has sworn your death if any stranger ever carries off what you have refused to your own people; and if we are not good enough to make you an honourable wife, we are at least men enough to help a lost girl out of the world; and so tell your fine gentleman to look out against accidents, for the bullets we cast hereabouts can hit as well as those

of Swedish lead; and so God be with you, Erminia. I
have nothing further to say.'

"He pressed his hat on his brows, threw a glance
around, and went off with a quick step. The girl said
not a word, and as for me I was so bewildered by his
passionate outburst, that not till she had lifted her
pitcher to her head, and was preparing to leave, did I
regain the power of speech. 'Erminia,' I said, going close
up to her, 'who does he mean by the stranger?' 'He is
a fool,' she replied without looking at me, but blushing
deeply. 'I hope so indeed,' said I, 'for if there were
any meaning in his words I should be sorry for you,
Erminia.' 'I want no one's pity,' was her curt reply; and
then she went off without so much as good night, and
from the defiance of her manner I first discovered that
she was really implicated. And being sincerely her well-
wisher I hurried after her, so as to walk on by her side.
'You know me to be your friend,' said I, 'if you will
not believe Domenico, believe me Erminia, it will be
your ruin if you have anything to do with the captain.
He is a fine fellow, but he will not marry you, Erminia,
for all that; indeed, he cannot, for he is a Lutheran,
but, in addition, he would not wish it. Therefore, even
if Il Rosso did not make good his threat, nothing but
mischief could come of the affair,' and so on, according
as my friendship for the girl inspired me. She, meanwhile, walked straight on in silence without once raising
her eyes. So at length I left her with a faint hope of
having made some impression on her mind. The great
dog came to meet me at the door of my house, which
told me that his master was returned from shooting. I
went up to his room at once, and found him with his
English rifle in his hand, having taken it to pieces to
clean, and a couple of dead birds before him. 'You

have lost something, Sor Gustavo,' said I, 'there on the market place your secrets have been discussed so loudly, that all the gossips in the village are acquainted with them.' And I went on to tell him of Redbeard's threats, adding that he did not know our people if he supposed they were not in earnest, and that if he really had triumphed and won Erminia's coy heart, he ought for both their sakes to be on his guard and break it off, and get out of the scrape the best way he could. And being once fairly started I could not refrain from taking Domenico's part, and declaring that all friendship would be at an end between us if he made Erminia unhappy. There were plenty of others who would be no great loss. But to see the Pearl of the whole Sabina trampled in the mire was what I could not endure, and so I told him to his face that if I discovered him going after Erminia, I could no longer be his host, and that he might look out for some other quarters. To all this he answered nothing further than what Erminia had once told me, 'You are not over wise, Fra Angelico,' and continued polishing up the locks and barrel of his rifle, and puffing the blue smoke of his cigar through his fair moustachios. At last I left him even more disgusted with his cunning cold-bloodedness than with the affair itself, and I did not see him till the noon of the next day, when he entered my room with a letter in his hand which he told me necessitated his immediate departure, and as it was too late for the mail, he requested me to lend him my little vehicle. There was nothing I was more glad to do, not indeed that I laid much stress upon the letter, but rather believed that it was my own eloquence that had induced him to leave us, and to break off that luckless love-affair in good time. And so I let him have my apprentice, as I myself had no time to drive him to Rome, and we parted the best of friends.

"It was his intention, he told me, to travel to Greece in order to visit Lord Byron's grave, and he promised to write to me as soon as he got there. The rogue! He thought as little of Greece as I of a journey to the moon. But what would you have? A mighty spell was on him, and held him down with a hundred meshes in the Evil One's net, so that he could look me, his best friend, in the face and tell me so confounded a lie as this!

"That evening I went to bed with the consciousness of having done my duty, and saved two human lives. Nay I was even planning a lyric on the subject, which would have been by no means one of my worst, though a convincing proof that poets are no prophets. For would you believe it, on the following afternoon my lad returned home with the vehicle, and the first thing he did after taking the horse to the stable and feeding him, was to ask me if Signor Gustavo had told me they were to take a stranger with them, for that about two miles from the village, where the evergreen oak stands near the old tomb, this stranger had beckoned to them, and then jumped so quickly into the conveyance, that he, Carlino, never got a good look at his features. But in spite of that alacrity, and of the manly attire,—which by the way belonged to Signor Gustavo's wardrobe,—he was ready to take his oath that this stranger was no other than Erminia.

"I will not detain you by describing the effect this discovery had on me. I bound the youth down most solemnly to hold his peace about it. But what could that avail! The very next day there was not an old woman who entered my shop for a penny-worth of any-

thing who did not inform me that Erminia had gone off
to Rome with the captain, and had sent a message to
her mother to the effect that she should not indeed return, but would never forget that she was her daughter.
And, moreover, she had left behind for her sister Maddalena whom she must have taken into her confidence,
all her clothes and other effects, and a bag of money—
probably from the Captain—so that their mother might
want for nothing.

"That this news should work upon the young village-
folk like valerian upon cats, you, my friend, will easily
believe. Had we been in the old times of Greeks and
Trojans, Domenico would easily have assembled an
army to pursue and recover his lost Helen. But in spite
of all that was said and shrieked, spite of fury and
curses, nothing came of it, and soon it seemed as though
these braggadocios were ashamed of even uttering the
name of the girl who had refused them all to go off at
last with a heretic and barbarian. There were only two
who could not forget her. I was one, and it was in
vain I sought consolation from the muses. The other
was Domenico Il Rosso, in whose eyes anybody with an
insight into human nature might easily have read that
he was brooding over desperate deeds.

"And too surely before a month had elapsed since
Erminia's flight all my fears were realised. I remember
the day as tho' it were yesterday: it was on a Thursday
—and the heat was such that the flies on the wall were
giddy, and at noon no Christian soul ventured out. I
had closed my shop-door, and all the shutters, and lay
between sleeping and waking in this very chair where I
now sit. There was nothing to be heard but the sleepy
drip-drop of the fountain, and the rustling of dry herbs
on the counter, over which my tame canary-bird was

hopping to-and-fro. Suddenly I fancied I heard some one knock at the shop-door, and call my name, and annoyed at being disturbed, I rubbed my eyes awake, and prepared to see whether any one had really been taken suddenly ill. The knocking was repeated, louder and quicker, as if in urgent haste, and I had my hand on the door-handle when I heard a dreadful scream, 'Jesus, Maria, have mercy on me!' I tore open the door, and saw a woman sink on the threshold, from whose breast there gushed such a stream of blood, that while I stooped to raise her I was reddened from top to toe. Three steps off with a face like ashes stood Domenico, with eyes wide-opened as though his crime had killed him too. 'Domenico,' I cried, 'what hast thou done? Cursed be thy hand which has wrought this horrible deed.' 'Amen,' he replied, 'it was her fate. Now let *him* come.' And so saying he turned round—for some horror-stricken faces began to appear at the windows— and slowly traversed the sun-lit piazza till he reached the gateway, where he disappeared like a spectre.

"Meanwhile I held the poor gasping frame in my arms, almost swooning myself from grief and terror. I called to my maid-servant, the neighbours rushed out, and so we carried her in, and laid her on a bed. But I saw too plainly that there was nothing to be done, and so I sent the lad off as fast as he could go to fetch a priest. I scarcely hoped though that she would live long enough to see him, so bending down I asked her if she had anything to communicate. She husbanded her last breath to ask me how her mother was. 'Just the same as for a month past,' I replied. Then her dying breast heaved a deep sigh, and she gasped out: 'Then he deceived me!' 'Who?' said I. She felt for her pocket, and drew out a letter, the tenor of which was that if she

wished to find her mother still alive she must set out
without delay, for that the illness was a mortal one.
This letter bore the priest's signature, but was not in his
handwriting. I made out from the few words that she
with difficulty whispered, that a youth from our village
had secretly delivered it to her the evening before. How
he had found out her lodging in Rome she had no idea,
for she was living most privately, and not in the same
house as her lover, who had been to see her as usual in
the evening, and on reading the letter had forbidden her to
go home, saying that it was only a plot to allure her to de-
struction, and she herself had taken that view of it, and
promised him not to go. But in the morning when she was
alone, a fear came over her that it might after all turn
out to be true, and if so, her mother would die and
would curse her own child on her death-bed. So she
took a carriage, and promised the driver a double fare if
he would take her in half the usual time. She got out,
however, at the foot of the hill, wishing to reach her
mother's house alone and unobserved. But as soon as
she neared the first houses she had a sense of some one
following her, and for protection she ran rather than
walked towards my door, when suddenly Domenico appeared behind her, and called out, without however
looking at her: 'What, Erminia, do we see you here
again? That is well, it was time you should come
to your senses!' 'What have you to do with my senses?'
she replied; 'you have no hold upon me for good or
bad.' 'Indeed!' said he, drawing closer and closer, 'all
the same one does not like the disgrace to attach to our
village of having no young man worthy of such a jewel.
Probably you have now found out that your foreigner
was but a poor make-believe, like the rest, and that you
would do better to remain at home.' And she. 'What

2*

I think of him is *my* affair. Why do you always come after me? You knew long ago what I think of you.' Then seizing her arm he said in a hoarse voice, 'For the last time, Erminia, I give you warning. Renounce him, or both you and he will have to rue it. I cannot prevent your loving him, but that he should rob you of honour and happiness, that as sure as GOD lives I *will* prevent and that shortly. Do you understand me?' Then she stood still, looked him full in the face, and said, 'You and no one else wrote that letter.' And he, without answering, went on as before: 'Will you give him up and remain here?' Then when she continued silent, and shook her head resolutely, he three times repeated the same question. 'Will you, Erminia, give him up and remain here?' And when she pretended not even to be aware that any one was speaking to her, but quickened her steps fearing that he might do her some violence in the deserted piazza, she suddenly felt his hand grasp her arm as in a vice, heard the words, 'To hell, then, with your Lutheran,' and in the same moment fell down mortally wounded close to my door.

"And now she had no wish, she said, but that her lover should forgive her for leaving him against his will; she expiated it dearly enough. He had meant to make her his wife, and take her to his own home. Instead of that she must go down into the grave, and who could say whether the Virgin Mary would intercede for her; and whether she should ever pass out of the pains of purgatory into the Heavenly Paradise!

"That was the last sentence that crossed her lips, then her head sank back, and she was dead!"

When the little man had got so far, he stretched

himself back in his arm-chair, and closed his eyes with a deep sigh. After some minutes so spent he sprang up, walked several times to and fro in his dark shop, and seemed to make a strong effort to recover his self-control. At length he stood still beside me, laid his hand on my shoulder, and said, "What after all is human life, *amico mio!* A fleeting nothing! grass that is green in the field to-day, and to-morrow dry and withered. Hay, that the insatiable monster death crams his maw with! *Basta!* There is no waking the dead! She was a wonder of the world while she lived, she was wondrous still when her fair silent form was no longer warmed by a drop of life-blood, and her soul no more susceptible of joy or of sorrow. There she lay in the room yonder, and until she was buried I never left her night or day. When sleep overcame me, I still held a corner of her dress in my hand, and thought myself highly favoured in that at least in death I was nearer to her than any other. But by the second night another came. The door opened, and the captain stole in on tip-toe, as though he might still run a risk of disturbing her sleep. We did not exchange a word, only I began to weep like a child when he so mutely, and with such a look of despair in his eyes, approached the bier. Then he sat down beside her and gazed steadily upon her face. I went out, I could not endure his presence any more than if I myself had been her murderer.

"The next day when the funeral took place and the whole village was gathered in the church-yard, even before the priest had blessed the coffin, there rose a murmur and a stir among the dense crowd. And the captain, whom no one knew to be in the place, was seen striding through the people with a look on his face that terrified them all. He took his station close beside the grave, and threw two handsfull of earth on the coffin. Then he knelt down, and every one else was on his homeward way while he remained prostrate on the newly-made grave, as though he would force himself through the earth, and make his bed there. I was obliged to drag him away into my house, where for some days he remained as though in a trance, and I could hardly get him to take a spoonful of soup or a drop of wine. Four days passed before he seemed to come to himself at all, but even then he continued silent, and it was only in bidding me farewell, before he went off again in my little conveyance, that he begged me to oblige him by buying for him the house with the vineyard that he had once before looked at. In eight days he said he should return, and then make his home with us for life.

"I did not dare to remonstrate, although I could not approve the plan—partly because of Domenico, of whom it was known that he had fled to the mountains, and joined a party of banditti, and partly because I had always been fond of the Swede; and could have wished that he should not by living near this grave keep the wound in his heart for ever bleeding. But, however, I knew well that he must have his own way, let Heaven or Hell oppose him, and so I laid myself out to render him any service that I could, for her sake who had been dear to me too, and to whom even beyond the grave I could still prove my good-will by befriending her beloved.

"And in a week's time he actually came and took possession of the house which stood about a mile from the village in a tolerably large vineyard, not far from the ravine where the chestnuts are; a lovely, solitary spot for a man at least who had no fear, good weapons at hand, and a faithful dog for companion. But the latter was not the only living creature that joined him. Erminia's sister Maddalena insisted on doing so, that she might wash and cook for him, and keep his house while he was on his rambles. Nothing could have suited him better, though people in general shunned her. But he knew that her dead sister had bequeathed her own love and fidelity towards him to this poor creature. And so the singular pair lived on in their solitude, and never seemed to concern themselves about the rest of the world.

"I went to see him a few days after his arrival. The house had once belonged to a Roman noble, and was still in tolerable condition, though the old furniture was covered with dust and cobwebs which Maddalena never disturbed. She had been used to worse in her mother's ruinous hovel under the roof of the fig-tree. But in the neglected garden she had somewhat bestirred herself, and planted a few beds with vegetables, and the locks of all the doors had been repaired and new bolts added. 'She insisted upon it,' said the captain; 'she is continually dreaming of an attack upon us.' 'Dreams are not always mere moonshine,' returned I, but he paid no attention. He went before me up the stone steps, and opened the door of the familiar salon, the balcony of which looked on the garden. This was the only room that he inhabited; he had made a bed out of an old divan, and cleaned the rubbish out of the corners single-handed, but he could not stop up the countless holes in the walls through which bats and squirrels went in and out. My first glance fell on a stand against the wall, from which his beautiful fire-arms shone out, and as I was always fond of them I fell to examining these master-pieces one by one. 'Just turn round Angelo,' he said; 'there is something in the room that will interest you more.' It was a life-size picture of Erminia, and so strikingly like, that it gave me, as it were, a blow on the heart. During their early days in Rome, a first-rate painter and friend of his had begun this wondrous picture, and finished it with the exception of one hand and part of the dress. The head, which looked over the shoulder with an indescribable expression of proud bliss —actually beaming with love and beauty—was highly finished, and as I said, one fancied one saw the exquisite creature breathe. I could not speak a word, but I stood a full half-hour motionless before it, from time to time wiping away the tears which obscured the picture. It was then he told me for the first time, that on the very day when she left him he had received a letter from an old uncle, his only remaining relative, on whose consent to his marriage he had laid great stress. Then he tried to tell me something about those happy weeks in Rome, but his voice suddenly gave way, and he went into the next room. I could not venture to follow him, and as he did not return I concluded I was not wished for any longer, and quietly crept down the steps accompanied only by the great dog, who looked into my face as much as to say that he knew all about his master's grief.

"I now resolved to wait until he should seek me out, but I might have waited long! However, I sometimes saw Maddalena in the market or one of the shops, and twice I spoke to her, asked for Signor Gustavo, and heard that he was well, and if not out shooting was always reading books, and allowed no one to enter, not even the priest, who had felt it his duty to enquire for the mourner. In our village, where everyone had been so enraged against him, the tide turned gradually in his favour. People remembered the merry evenings over the wine-barrel, and his courteous and sociable ways, and in time the women who had been the most violent were quite conquered by his solitary sorrow. Many a one, I suspect, would not have required much pressing to lend him her company in that lonely villa, if he had only held up a finger. But month after month passed by, and all went on in the old way.

"One night towards the end of August I had a headache, having drunk more wine than usual, and the mosquitoes were more unconscionable than ever: so that I sat up in bed, and began to think whether I had not better strike a light and write some verses. All of a sudden through the stillness of night I heard two shots, then again others, and from the direction in which they came I judged that they must be somewhere near the captain's villa. '*Corpo della Madonna!*' thought I, 'what can he be about! Is he shooting bats or owls?' But they did not sound like the English rifle of Signor Gustavo, and they succeeded each other too rapidly and irregularly to be fired by any one man, and all at once I jumped horrified out of bed, for I no longer had any doubt about it,—what I had long silently feared had happened: Il Rosso and his banditti had fallen upon the lonely man, and they were fighting there in the vineyard for life and death. I got on my clothes, snatched a pair of old pistols from the wall, wakened up my apprentice, and told him to run through the streets, and call out 'help! murder!' as loud as ever he could. I myself knocked up a couple of neighbours, and encouraged all who were already roused to follow me. When we came down from the village we were a party of ten or twelve, each armed with rifle or pistol. And to be sure the firing did come from the vineyard, and we to whom the

moon fortunately served instead of lanterns, scrambled
over hedge and ditch towards the house, where we saw
firing going on from the windows. That comforted me
somewhat. He had withdrawn then into his fortress, and
those rascals had to content themselves with firing into
the room at him at random. I was just about to explain
my plan of operations to our party,—how we were to
form four divisions, surround the enemy, and attack him
in the rear; but some out-post must have observed us,
for there was a shrill whistle, and at the same moment
the attack came to an end, and here and there where
the moon shone on the open space between the rocks
and the wood, we saw the band scatter, some of them so
lame that we might have captured them if that had been
our aim—over and above defending the captain—to
take Il Rosso, our own fellow-citizen, prisoner. But we
wished to spare his father the pain of that, and thanked
God that we had come just in time, for at our loud call
we saw Signor Gustavo step out on the balcony into the
bright moonlight, and wave a white handkerchief to us.
But when we saw the handkerchief nearer, it proved by
no means pure white, but had large spots of blood, from
a bullet having grazed his temple. It was nothing of
any consequence, and did not prevent the captain sitting out of doors with me the next morning when all
the rest had gone to their homes. Only Maddalena in
her passionate way, besotted with the man in spite of
her sister's story, could not be tranquillised, and went
on searching for one healing herb after the other, and
he had to apply them all to prevent her becoming quite
frantic. The good creature, whose sleep was like a cat's,
was aware of footsteps creeping about the house even
before the dog heard them; and she ran up to wake her
master. On the first bandit who placed a ladder against

the balcony, she bestowed such a blow on the head with the barrel of a gun, that he fell backwards, and the ladder with him. And so there she was at hand to load one rifle after the other, and indeed every now and then she herself took a shot through the window, and swore with might and main that she had sent a ball through the coat of the murderous villain Il Rosso himself, and that he gave a great start but went on firing. As for the room, it had a ruinous aspect, not a pane was whole, the plaster had fallen in great sheets from the ceiling, and Erminia's picture had been struck in two places, but fortunately only the dress and the frame were injured. When the day began to break, the Captain and the dog too did get a few hours sleep, but Maddalena would not hear of it, although for the present the cut-throats had been scared away.

"I spent the next day at the villa, and kept imploring my friend to leave the district. Indeed all the reasonable people from the village who came to see the battle-field gave the same advice. He most obstinately refused to do so. It was only on the following day when the Roman Prefect of Police came over to keep up appearances, and draw up a protocol, by way of doing something, that he let himself be turned from his foolhardy resolve. 'I most earnestly advise you,' said the official, a monsignore N——, 'as soon as possible to leave the mountains, and indeed the country itself. A youth who witnessed the attack of the bandits —if indeed he were not one of them—has told me that more than one bullet has been cast for you; that Il Rosso has sworn upon the host that he will pay you off. Were I to remain here I could only protect you so long as you kept by my side. But if you took again to your lonely wanderings through the ravines you might expect

out of every bush a shot that would consign you to another world.'

"And so at last he made up his mind to leave, and
that at once, in the carriage of the Prefect of Police.
When I pressed his hand at parting, 'Now then, Signor
Gustavo,' said I, 'this will certainly be the last time we
two ever meet on earth.' 'Who knows?' he replied.
'After all I am half a countryman of yours, and have
no other home.' Then he gave me some directions with
regard to Maddalena. She was not to leave the villa,
nor did the captain think of selling it. If he failed to
return within a certain number of years, she was to consider the house and garden her own property, and
meanwhile to appropriate their profits. To the priest he
gave in token of gratitude for the assistance rendered
him by the villagers, a considerable sum for the poor.
On me he bestowed a small picture of Lord Byron,
which he had always carried about with him. The portrait
of Erminia he had rolled up in a tin cylinder, and that
and his fire-arms were all that he took away with him.
So we parted, and as I believed, never to meet again,
and Maddalena, who insisted upon going with him, and
clung like a wild cat to the carriage, had to be forcibly
dragged off and locked into the house till it had rolled
far away.

"However that very night, so soon as they left off
watching her, she vanished, and for days ran up and
down the streets of Rome like a maniac, looking in vain
for her master. At last she returned, and hobbled about
the villa alone, but she let everything go to waste; the
grapes might rot on the vines, and the fruit on the trees,
rather than she take the trouble of gathering them and
carrying them to market. She had always been idle,
indeed, as a toad—a creature she resembled in appear-

ance too—and it was only when it concerned the captain that she could work and bestir herself like three people in one.

"Of him, however, we heard nothing more; of his mortal foe Barbarossa we heard far too much. Since that night he and his band had lingered about our neighbourhood, and he seemed to have conceived a hatred against his countrymen, because they had gathered to the assistance of the foreigner. But for the company of papal gendarmes who were sent us as a permanent support from Rome, I do believe he would have fallen upon his own native village and taken a bloody revenge.

"Accordingly no one who had been present on the occasion, ever ventured himself a rifle-shot from the last houses without taking his fire-arms with him, and such as had to go into the mountains always begged for two gendarmes as escort. Those were sad times, *amico mio*, and I even lost my pleasure in rhyming, for I knew that he had a special spite against me. Twice there were great expeditions undertaken against the bandits, but not much came of them, for they had their scouts posted everywhere; they knew every crag and cranny of the mountains as intimately as the devil does his own den, and they were merely driven for awhile a little further back into the Sabina.

"However when in the winter old Serone, Domenico's father, died from grief on his son's account, we had an interval of peace. Il Rosso, whom of course the fact reached, may perhaps have felt some remorse, for by nature, as I have said, he was not bad-hearted, only his unfortunate love had hardened and frenzied him. It really seemed as though he meant to keep quiet during his year of mourning, and until midsummer we heard no more of banditti. Whether they were at work further south, or how they kept themselves alive during this holiday, God knows. But when we took it for granted that our deliverance from them was final we reckoned without our host. Our neighbourhood began all of a sudden to be haunted again. My neighbour, Pizzicarlo, who had been one of us that night at the villa, was captured by these villains while riding his donkey to Nerni, dragged off into their haunts, and only released on payment of a considerable ransom. And so with others, whom they sadly maltreated. This could not go on. The gendarmes obtained reinforcements, the razzia into the mountains began anew, but not with much better success. At that time Barbarossa seemed to be everywhere and nowhere, terrible as a basilisk, and slippery as an eel, and far and wide mothers quieted their screaming children by saying: *Zitto*, Barbarossa is coming! But other stories were told too, more to his credit; how he behaved to the poor and defenceless like a knight in a legend, intent mainly on righting the defective justice of the world, though every now and then robbing the egregiously wealthy just to supply his own needs. As I have before said, he was to be pitied, and if he had not run up so heavy a score that the law could not possibly wink at it, perhaps an amnesty would yet have changed him back into a peaceable honest citizen.

"Under these circumstances we lived wretchedly enough, much like shipwrecked sailors on a plank, with a shoal of sharks around. Thirteen months had now passed since the captain's departure, and no one spoke of him, at least no one said any good of him, fearing to be overheard by somebody who might repeat it to Barbarossa. Imagine, therefore, my horror one afternoon,

I had just opened a bottle of castor oil, and was thinking of nothing worse, when Signor Gustavo his own very
self entered my room as though nothing had happened.
'*Corpo della Madonna!*' I cried, 'What wind has blown
you here? Are you so weary of life that you determine
to make your villa your mausoleum?' Then he told me
that he had not been able to endure either the East or
West. Nowhere had he found any flavour in the wine,
everywhere the women were tedious, and since he had
fired at men, the chase of lions and hyenas had become
insipid. And always too he had been pursued by the
feeling that he had, like a contemptible coward, left the
field to his foe, instead of waiting to measure his strength
against him. And a short time back, when staying at
some German Spa, he read a newspaper account of the
Sabine mountains being again ravaged by banditti, and
of Papal carabinieri having for months pursued the va-
gabonds, who seemed as inexterminable as toadstools
after rain: why then he had found the monotonous
elegant world in which he was living, simply intolerable,
and taking an extra post, he had travelled day and night
without halting, crossed the Alps, and got here. And
now here he was again settled in the vineyard. Maddalena had been actually wild with joy, and he himself felt
more at home than he had done for a year and a day.
'And what then was he going to do here?' asked I in
horror and amazement. 'Oh!' said he, 'I shall have no
lack of occupation; I shall join the patrol of gendarmes
that are constantly on the mountains, and so as a volun-
teer and dilettante face my man. When I come to consider it, it was I who hung this mill-stone about your
necks, and so it is only fair that I should try to help
you off with it. Good-day, Angelo, pay me a visit in
my mausoleum.'

"And away he went: he had grown so strangely restless—quite unlike his former self—that he could not stay long in any one place. What I felt about the whole affair, I leave you to imagine. Meanwhile it had never been my wont to play the coward, and indeed here it behoved me to take the initiative, on account of my old acquaintance with Signor Gustavo. So I boldly visited him in the villa, and found everything just as though he had never left it. Maddalena hobbling about as before, and busy enough now, gathering the grapes with her long arms; the dog, who had grown old and blind of one eye; and in the salon the marks of the bullets still visible, but the holes in Erminia's portrait had been carefully repaired. When I went in, the captain was walking up and down, smoking and reading, but on seeing me he laid aside his book—as usual verses by his English poet—and heartily shook my hand. He had spent the whole night between the rocks and woods, lying out to stalk his game, and only slept a little in the morning. At midnight he was going out again with three stout fellows who did honour to the Pope's uniform. If I liked I might go with him.

"I declined with thanks on this occasion, and did not remain long, for his manner, half fierce and half reckless—as though he were playing a game of chance—gave me an uncomfortable feeling. On my way home, I laid a kind of wager as it were with myself—that if seven days passed without his coming to a bad end, I would print my sonnets to Erminia at my own expense; if otherwise I would leave them in manuscript. And an end did indeed come, but whether it could be called good or bad, God knows, and so to the present day I am in doubt whether I won the wager or not.

"It was he himself who circumstantially related to

me the way things fell out, so that you can receive my narrative as though you had it from his own lips. He began to wonder much, he said, that Barbarossa did not confront him, for his return was nothing else than a direct and open challenge. Twice when on his rounds with the gendarmes, he had stumbled upon suspicious-looking characters, but they had not held their ground —dived out of sight like frogs when the stork appears. He fancied they did this with the intention of drawing him on further into the mountains in order to attack him with less risk. So he was glad when an expedition on a large scale into the Sabina was planned, although not for the next night, but the next but one, for the soldiers were determined to get their fill of sleep first, so as to be all the fresher.

"But the captain could not remain so long inactive, and as he had no companions—his usual escort preferring a good night to an aimless ramble—he loaded his double-barrelled gun, called his dog, who seemed disinclined to follow him, and left his vineyard just as the moon rose.

"Fool-hardy as he was, he yet guarded himself against any unnecessary exposure. He wore a dark coat, and dark trowsers which he pushed into his high boots, and also a grey hat, one of those called, you know, *Comecipare*, in which attire, so long as he kept in the shadow of the oaks and chestnuts, it would have been hard even in the day-time to distinguish him from the trunk of a tree.

"Now it so happened that the night was still and beautiful, and he told me he had never so much enjoyed the gloomy forest, and had never had Erminia's form and face so vividly present and near to him as they then seemed. The dog silently and wearily crept on after him, and he himself was lost in dreams, having never hoped that on this occasion he should meet with his enemy, but being led on and on merely for the sake of exercise, and by the exquisite coolness of the night.

"He had he thought wandered thus—creeping and climbing alternately—for more than an hour, when the dog suddenly stood still and growled. Instantly the captain's hand was on his gun, but before he could look round, two shots were fired close to him, and he felt that he had received a wound in the leg. At the same moment he saw a fellow stand out from behind a great ilex and level a pistol, but he was beforehand with him, and took such good aim that he shot off the lock of the pistol and two fingers of the hand that held it; whereupon the villain took flight, and ran along the steep path with such speed that neither the dog—who to be sure was no longer so agile as he had been—nor the second barrel of the English gun reached him. The captain had paid dear for his night walk. The wound in his leg bled so much that the bandage he improvised with pocket and neck-handkerchief was of little use. So having re-loaded both barrels, he set out homewards, but contrived to lose his way, the moonlight confusing him, and it was only after much fruitless wandering about that he saw the roof of his villa shining above the vineyards, and he was then so exhausted with loss of blood and fatigue, that he sank down on a stone, and was obliged to rest awhile before he could rise and drag himself over the last hundred yards.

"But one there was past rising, and that was the dog. The second shot had wounded him more seriously than the first his master, and having limped after him thus far without a whine of complaint, his strength was spent, and he moaned away his faithful life. The cap-

tain told me he felt his blood run cold when he saw
his old ally feebly wag his tail and then stretch out his
four legs stiffly. He himself was hardly able to stand,
yet he could not find it in his heart to leave his dead
comrade there in the open plain where vultures would
soon have found him out next morning. He wished to
give him the honourable burial he had so well earned,
in the vineyard at home, and so he took him up, supporting the weight with the stock of the gun—that gun
itself being heavy enough for him in his present condition—and with tottering steps he reached the vineyard, and found the iron gate as usual locked from
within. He opened it by a trick known only to him and
Maddalena. But he was surprised that the sound of his
steps should not have roused the wakeful creature:
thought she had perhaps been drinking some strong
wine which he had just had from the village, and as he
passed the door of her room did not care to disturb
her. The dog he laid down in the kitchen, and covered
with an old straw mat, then he tottered up the steps
that led to the upper room, feeling as if he should
hardly live to reach his couch, and re-bandage his burning wound.

"But when he opened the door of the salon, he
stood motionless on the threshold, turned to stone by
what he saw. The moon was shining full upon the balcony and through the windows, and lit up the stand of
fire-arms in the corner. In the middle of the room, his
back to the light, erect and stiff as a marble pillar, arms
crossed, and contemplating the picture of Erminia, stood
Domenico Serone, Il Rosso. He no longer deserved
this nick-name, however, for he had cut off his beard,
and his long wild hair looked ashy grey against the old
yellow straw hat that so shadowed his face nothing was

to be seen but the white of his eyes. But Signor Gustavo knew him at a glance.

"They looked full at each other for a moment, those two deadly foes, Domenico, however, without changing his position, while the captain leant upon his gun, and called up his last remnant of strength to play the man, spite of his wound.

"'You are come at last then,' said Il Rosso, and his voice trembled. 'I have waited for you here, since I did not find you at home. You know that I have sworn to reckon with you, and the time is fully come. To-morrow night you are going to make a great sally and surprise my band. Bravo! Set to! Only what you and I have to settle could be better done, I thought, by ourselves. Let your gun alone,' for the captain was about to stand on his guard. 'If I had chosen, you would have drawn your last breath long before this. Do you suppose I did not hear you outside when you were opening the iron gate, and had I wished for your blood I had but to shed it then and there. I own I was very near doing so. But I was not able. *She* would not suffer it,' and he hurriedly pointed to the picture. 'If you have still the heart to love your life you may thank *her* for it.'

"'Domenico,' said the captain, 'let there be an end to this. You are in my house, and I cannot tolerate your playing the master here, and acting as if I was at your mercy. I will have no gift from him who plotted to deprive me of the dearest thing I had on earth. You had no right to the girl, none—that she herself assured me. And as nevertheless you murdered her, and are now seeking after my life, why you are nothing better than a wild beast, and whoever renders you harmless does a good work. It is pure mercy on my part not to avail myself of my advantage, and shoot you down before you can lift your gun from the floor. But I feel sorry for you. I can understand how one might lose one's reason for that girl's sake, and not recover it after her death. Therefore I offer you honourable terms. Take up your gun. When I have counted three—one or both of us will have ceased to live.'

"Domenico never stirred. 'Do as you will,' he said, 'I shall not fire. If I were to kill you, what better should I be? I am a miserable man. I have murdered the fairest woman in the world, like a wild beast that I was; you do well to call me one. I thought I should be happier if I got you too out of the world. I was a fool. If you were to meet her again up yonder, rage and jealousy at not being able to part you any more, would devour my heart till I went down to hell damned beyond redemption. No, make an end of me as you said. See, I stand quite still. This gun,' he pushed it away from him with his foot, 'I will not touch. Fire, captain, and with my last breath I will forgive you. For by God's holy blood the life I have led was purgatory, and now it would be hell itself since I have seen *her* again, and *you* whom she loved.' While so speaking, his strength seemed to fail him, he fell on his knees before the picture, and hid his face in his hands, his whole body, as it were, convulsed.

"At last the conflict ended. He sobbed aloud, wailed and writhed like one mortally wounded, then trying to rise he groaned out, 'My God! My God! She is dead! Lord have pity upon her murderer!' and down he fell again as in a swoon and pressed his sobbing lips against the cold flags, and seemed to have utterly forgotten that any one stood by and saw it all.

"And meanwhile there was the picture on the wall

standing silent and stately, and in its bloom of bliss and youth looking down upon the poor sinner.

"'Domenico,' said the captain, gently drawing near, bending over him, and laying a hand on his shoulder, 'neither of us can call her back, and what we have to do is to get through our remnant of life. If you will take my advice you will leave this country and cross the seas. There is war going on in Africa, and the French need brave men. Your crime—I forgive it, and there is One who weighs with other scales than we do, who sees your heart and knows how you repent and suffer. If I can help you in any way to get off, and fling your past behind you, tell me. You shall find a brother in me.'

"Il Rosso had meanwhile risen, and was now standing with face averted from the picture, gazing hopelessly into the night. At these last words of his rival he vehemently shook his head. 'It is over,' he replied. 'You and I are quits. The rest is my affair. You and I shall never meet again, that I swear to you by her shadow. But leave this house in which I can no longer protect you. With the others it is an affair of your money and your fire-arms, they hanker after them. If they hear that it was in my power to give you up to them, and that I have not done so, they will never forgive me, and there are some of them who still carry about the tokens of that first tussle we had. Take care of yourself, and good night to you. You have seen the last of me.'

"He bent down, picked up his gun, and with one last look at the picture that in serene beauty shone out in the moonlight, glided from the room.

"The captain heard him go slowly down the stairs, step by step, and when outside, open the iron gate and lock it again. Then the night was once more still as death. He required some time to collect himself. He felt, he said, as though he had been thrown down from a high tower and had reached the ground without broken limbs indeed, but unable to move from sheer giddiness. For awhile he lay half fainting on his couch, but the streak of blood on the moonlit floor reminded him of his wound. He roused himself to call Maddalena to bring him water and help him with his bandage. But no one answered, call as he would. So at last he tottered down the stairs and entered her room. There in a corner he saw the poor creature lying huddled up, bound hand and foot, and with a gag in her mouth. When he had unloosed her she fell half dead at his feet, and only recovered when he had sprinkled her well with water, and poured a little wine down her throat, and then crying and laughing, she began to kiss his hands and his coat. But there was no getting a single rational word from her; her fright when Il Rosso surprised her, and then her agony when she heard her master return and go up the steps at the top of which his enemy was awaiting him—these upset her poor mind completely, and during the remainder of her life, the years followed each other without her being conscious of any alternation except of heat and cold, hunger and repletion.

"I took the captain to my house, and nursed him for a week until his wound had pretty well healed. The sortie against the banditti had to take place of course without him, but nothing more decisive was effected than the procuring us peace for about a couple of years. The only prisoner taken was a small boy whose father was one of the bandits, and who himself had sometimes joined them. Nothing could be made of him, so he was let go again. However one fact he did have to tell us: on the morning after the night in which Il Rosso had that reckoning with his enemy, a quarrel arose, and some of the party accused Domenico of being a traitor. At last knives were drawn, and before the cooler-headed could interfere, Domenico lay dead on the bare rock, the knife in his breast, almost on the very spot where he had met Erminia.

"As for Signor Gustavo he went to Naples, and thence sailed to Greece. Later I heard from an artist that he had been drowned there, swimming in the open sea. Possibly the wound in the leg was imperfectly healed, or it may have left some weakness behind it, for once he could, as he told me, have swum a match against that great Lord himself. But as to what became of the picture of Erminia, which the artist well remembered to have seen, I could learn nothing. I would gladly have given half my substance if only I could have got possession of it.

"And now, *amico mio*, you know the history of Barbarossa and Erminia."

END OF BARBAROSSA.

THE

EMBROIDERESS OF TREVISO.

EMBROIDERESS OF TREVISO.

Iт was our third day of rain, and the wood and garden walks around the country house we were staying at, were turned into water-courses. On the first and second day, the party of guests had made it a point of honour to be as inexhaustible in good humour as the sky in clouds, and within the large five-windowed saloon, with the oleanders blooming before it, jests rained, laughter rippled, and witty repartees flashed uninterruptedly as the drops pattered on the terrace outside. On this third day, however, even the most genial in our ark became dimly conscious that the deluge might prove more persistent than their good spirits. True no one ventured to break the vow of enduring this visitation *in common*,—made the day before yesterday,— by slinking off to his room and sulking there on his own resources. But general conversation, games, spontaneous play of intelligence and wit, had somewhat failed since the professor who passed for a great meteorologist, had confessed that instead of the change to fair which he had promised, his glass actually showed a fresh fall of the mercury. He had procured a second barometer, and was now seriously investigating the causes of this discrepancy between two prophets. His wife meanwhile was silently painting in body colours on grey paper her sixth water-lily; at a second table, Frau Helena was setting up her men for a seventh trial of skill at chess, while Frau Anna sat in a corner beside her baby's cradle, fanning away the flies from it, while trying to guess the conundrums and charades in the old almanac open on her knee. The young doctor with whom Frau Helena was playing chess, saw in this interval of silence an opening for doing justice to a rustic anecdote, but suddenly broke off, remembering that he had told it the day before. The husband of Frau Anna, mindful of the elder Shandy's sagacious dictum, that all manner of mental distresses and perplexities are best endured when the body is in a horizontal position, had stretched himself out full length on an old leather sofa, and blew the smoke of his damped cigar up in slow blue circles to the ceiling.

In the midst of these more or less successful efforts to adapt oneself to one's fate, the off-hand cheery way in which a middle-aged man with arms locked behind, continued slowly pacing up and down the room, naturally arrested attention. Sometimes he would stand for an instant beside the chess-table, or look over the shoulder of the painter, or gently wave his hand in passing over the little brow of the sleeping child, but all this he seemed to do unconsciously, as if absorbed in some train of thought quite unconnected with the rainy Present, and fixed either on a sunny Past, or sunny Future.

"What can you be about, dear Erminus?" enquired Frau Eugénie, who had just returned from a housewifely excursion into the kitchen and store-closet. "Here we all are pulling faces in keeping with this horrible wet, and on yours there is actual fine weather, nay even a kind of sunshine, as though you had secretly got betrothed, or had written the last page of a book, or felt a toothache of four-and-twenty hours subsiding. Come now, confess at once what this means, or we shall suspect that it is nothing but most unholy exultation over us who do not—like you—come to the country for the exact purpose of shutting ourselves up in a room with books."

"I can satisfy you on that point, my good friend," answered, with a laugh, the one thus addressed. "This time there is no malice in the case, although I am enjoying myself; and your other hypotheses are, thank God, equally groundless, nay, one of them actually impossible; since I could hardly show a cheerful face if, after so long a freedom, I had pledged myself to submit once more to petticoat government. No, that which keeps up my equanimity, spite of our condition, is neither more nor less than a pretty story on which I accidentally lighted yesterday as I was looking over my old papers, and which now haunts me in the same way a favourite melody will sometimes dwell upon the ear, and constantly repeat itself."

"A story and a pretty one too!" said the artist. "Then you must instantly let us have it as a matter of course. Have we not agreed to a community of goods of all kinds so long as the rain lasts, and would you keep a pretty story all to yourself? That *would* be a pretty story indeed!"

"Perhaps, however, it might not please you," replied Erminus, standing still beside her and twisting the long stalk of a water-lily into a loop. "I at least care so little for many stories that have a great run now-a-days, that I came long ago to the conclusion that mine was an old-fashioned taste, and that I did not advance with the age. But in my character of historian, I can console myself for this. We are not entirely dependent upon the latest novelty. And perhaps the sources I apply to for *history*, have spoiled my relish for stories as they are now-a-days written and admired. The difference between the wood-cut style of an old city-chronicle, and the photographic, stereoscopic, stippled minuteness and finish of a modern novel, is altogether too wide. In the one, all is raw material, blocks seldom sufficiently hewn, joints gaping, subjects so shaken together that only an expert or genuine amateur can pick out what answers his purpose. In our artificial modern days on the contrary, all is so smooth and polished, so conscious and premeditated, so reduced to mere form and style, that the subject often utterly vanishes, the *what* is forgotten in the *how*, and owing to the very psychological finesse of the narrator we come to be almost indifferent to the human beings on whom he practises. I for my part still occupy so obsolete a stand-point, that in every story the chief interest for me lies in the story itself. One man may tell it better than another, but for that I hardly care. If an incident that has really happened or been evoked by imagination makes an impression on me in the rough and incomplete version of an old chronicle, I would rather not have it tricked out with any gewgaws of style, but trust to my own fancy to supply omissions. But you moderns," and here he threw a sarcastic glance at the chess-player and the smoker, "you are never satisfied till you have bestowed all conceivable ornamentation and decoration on any and every story whatsoever, even though it should be most fair when naked as God made it."

"Each age has its own style of attire, and *nolens volens*, we have to conform to fashion," said the recumbent figure on the sofa without disturbing itself further.

"And each age acts and relates its own stories," interpolated the chess-player. "So long as the right of the strongest prevailed, stories were decidedly material in their interest, from Achilles down to the noble knight of La Mancha. Since life has become more spiritual, and its incidents more internal, they can no longer be outwardly expressed by a few coarse strokes, as was the case with a middle-aged dagger-and-sword-romance. Mere outline with some light and shade no longer suffices; we want the whole range of colour, the most delicate gradations of tint, and all the charms of chiaroscuro, and as we ourselves have become in a great measure men of sentiment, the sentiment an author manifests either for or against his characters is no longer indifferent to us."

"Oh I know," returned Erminus, "little flesh, much soul, that is the motto of the present day. But I happen to be just a man of the unsentimental middle ages, though not in the romantic sense, and therefore I had better keep my story to myself, for its structure is by no means adapted to the attire of the present day, and while the poets now present might turn up their nose at its very decidedly old-fashioned form, I should fear to shock the ladies by its incidents, though I for my part consider it perfectly moral."

"Since you yourself are quite sufficiently moral for us," said Frau Eugénie, "this assurance will induce us to listen to your story without a scruple."

"Especially since there is no un-confirmed young lady present," added Frau Helena.

"With the exception of the little innocent here in the cradle," observed Frau Anna, "but she apparently intends to shut her eyes to it."

"As to that point then I may feel safe in venturing,"

said Erminus. "But now a sudden fear comes over me that this favourite of mine that pleased me so much in private, may show itself awkward and unattractive if I introduce it into such a fastidious circle. And my old chronicler from whom I copied these few unpretending pages merely for my own pleasure, was, I own, no poet like Boccacio and his companions, though in this story he came pretty near them."

"Do not let us waste more time on the preface," said the professor. "The worst that can happen to your story, is a poet's looking on it as merely raw material, and, if it rains for another fortnight, making a tragedy or a comedy out of it which may remain as a blot on the stage."

"So be it, then!" sighed Erminus, thus fairly driven into a corner, and off he went to fetch his tale.

Before long he returned, a portfolio under his arm, from which he drew a manuscript volume.

"The manuscript is twenty years old," he said, taking his seat in the window, and spreading it out on his knee. "I chanced at that time to be gathering materials for a history of the Lombard towns, and had come to Treviso, where I hoped to find both in the Civic Records and in the cloister-library treasures, which, alas! did not fall to my share. It was only at the Dominicans at San Niccolo that I stumbled on a remarkable chronicle, dating about the end of the 14th century, which I would gladly have bought from the good fathers. But all that I could attain to, was leave to copy out in their cool refectory, under the eyes of a brother Antonio, whatever I thought useful for my purpose. These sheets bear traces of the fragrant ruby-coloured cloister wine with which I now and then washed down the dust of the chronicle, till after many and many dry records, I lit upon the history of the fair Giovanna, which like a spring of water in an arid steppe, suddenly refreshed me more than any wine could do.

"At this time," (the chronicle refers to the first quarter of the fourteenth century) "a bitter feud existed between the town of Treviso and the neighbouring one of Vicenza, originating apparently in trivial public matters, but fed by secret jealousy, even as the unseen wind fans a feeble spark into flame. The inhabitants of Vicenza called the Venetians to their aid, and were thus enabled by a rapid manœuvre to take possession, first of the castle of San Salvatore di Collatto, and next to conquer the very town of Treviso itself, and it was only after inflicting on it the utmost humiliation, and imposing a considerable tribute, that they consented to withdraw, encumbered with booty and hostages. As soon as these occurrences transpired—and the rumour spread as far as Milan—no one was more enraged than a noble youth belonging to our heavily-visited city, one Attilio Buonfigli by name, (son of the most distinguished of Treviso's citizens, and nephew to the Gonfaloniere Marco Buonfigli,) who had from early childhood been brought up as a page in the house of the noble Matteo Visconti, had at this time reached the age of twenty-five, and was thoroughly instructed and practised in all knightly arts. As soon as he learnt the misfortune that had befallen his beloved native town, he took an oath never to sleep except in his coat of mail, until he had revenged the insult; and accordingly he obtained leave of absence from his lord, and rode with some friends of his, all clad in armour, out of the gates of Milan. And since, young as he was, he had already made himself a proud name in the feuds of the Visconti, no sooner was his purpose known than adventurous youths from all sides flocked to swear fealty to him as to their Condottiere, against whatever foe he might choose to lead them.

"As soon, therefore, as he had secured a sufficiently large body of men to encounter the Venetians unaided, he sent secret messages to Treviso, to inform his father and uncle of his plans, and of the day when he purposed entering the gates of Vicenza to demand compensation for the wrongs endured. They were to hold themselves in readiness to support him, and with the help of God to place their feet on the necks of their enemies.

"And thus indeed it came to pass, and was all so judiciously and zealously carried out, that the men of Treviso succeeded in surprising the retreating troops on their homeward way to Venice and depriving them of their booty and hostages; while young Attilio, on the same day in a hot encounter on the small river Bacchiloni, proved himself victorious over the men of Vicenza. There was one thing only to trouble the joy of our good city. The youthful victor had received a deep wound in the throat from the sword of a Vicentine, and for some days his life hung on a slender thread. His own father, as well as his noble mother, nursed him in the conquered town's chief mansion, which belonged to its most leading citizen, Signor Tullio Scarpa, whose eldest son, named Lorenzaccio, had always been one of the bitterest foes of Treviso, so much so indeed, that while the wounded hero remained an inmate of the paternal abode, he never crossed its threshold. This only led to Attilio—although a foe to her city—being regarded with greater tenderness by the young Emilia, the only sister of Lorenzaccio; so that his father and mother became aware of her partiality, and began to found thereon a hope that through the union of the two leading families of both towns, the long-existing bad blood and mutual jealousy might be transformed into friendship and good will. And while his wound was healing, in a confidential hour Attilio was induced by his dear mother to entertain the idea, seeing that he had nothing to urge against it, as his own heart was perfectly free, and the young Vicentine a comely maiden. In secret, however, he felt a repugnance to take to wife a daughter of that city: even after their betrothal he held himself aloof from the girl, and would gladly have broken off altogether, but that he feared to sow the germs of fresh hate amidst the up-springing crop of peace. In this manner six or seven weeks passed by, and the leech declared that the wounded man would no longer be running any risk by mounting his horse and bearing shield and lance, even though he had better for a further season avoid the pressure of his steel haubergeon. Accordingly it was decided that he should set out for Treviso, whither, in the course of a few weeks, the bride with her parents was to follow, the rescued city being resolved to celebrate the marriage of their noble son and deliverer with all possible splendour. Meanwhile the good citizens had not lost the time spent by him on a sick bed, for they had prepared for their loved young hero, whose name was on every lip, an entry more triumphal than had ever yet been accorded to any prince.

"Amidst other offerings which the city meant to bestow upon him was a banner, which his own uncle was to make over to him in the name of the whole Council; a perfect marvel both as to material and skilful work. The pole of ten feet was of polished oak, ornamented by bosses of silver, the handle was set with rubies, and the point was gilt, so that when the sun shone it was dazzling to look upon. From this pole hung a heavy pennon of silver brocade, on which was represented a golden griffin—the crest of the Buonfigli crowned with the mural crown of Treviso—strangling a red serpent, whose coils were so natural, and covered with such fine gold scales, that you seemed to see a living snake writhing before your eyes. Above this was a Latin inscription in flaming letters, which ran 'Fear not, for I will deliver thee.'

"This wondrous achievement of a skilful needle had, during the six weeks that Attilio was laid low by his wound, proceeded from the hands of one maiden only, whose talent for executing such work in gold, silver, and silken thread, was renowned far and near. This maiden was named Gianna—that is, Giovanna— the Blonde, for her hair was exactly like bright spun gold, so that she had actually worked a church banner for the Blessed Virgin, in the chapel of San Sebastiano, with nothing but her own tresses. She had cut them off in her excessive grief when her betrothed, who was called Sebastian, a brave and handsome youth of the district, had died of small-pox a few weeks before their marriage. At that time she was eighteen years old, and the object of so many secret wishes and so much open wooing, that she had often to hear people prophecy that before her hair had grown again her bridegroom would have a successor—agreeably to the proverb, Long hair, short care. To speeches like these she would answer neither yea or nay, but calmly look down upon her work like a being whose ear and mind were closed against the idle sayings of this world. And in point of fact she falsified all these prophecies, for she continued to live as if by her votive offering of her hair to the Madonna she had vowed herself to perpetual maidenhood, and never meant that any man should uncoil the plaits which she again wound round her head, or twine their soft gold about his fingers. Many thought that she would go into a convent, because she preferred working church vestments and altar cloths, and kept aloof from all public amusements. But she even contradicted this opinion, and seemed to grow more cheerful as time went on, though still more ready to listen than to speak; and after the early death of her parents she removed to a small house in a turret on the city walls, which had a wide view over the peaceful meadows that are watered by the streams Piavesella and Rottiniga. There with an old deaf woman, her nurse, she lived above comment or censure, during a space of ten years, and no one entered her home except a neighbour now and then, or one of the noble ladies of the city who came to order some piece of work. Often, too, one of the spiritual fathers of the town might be seen to raise the knocker of her door. On these occasions she would call her nurse into the chamber while she received her visitors, and thus she contrived to keep malice at bay. Although it was only on Saints' Days that she allowed her needle to rest, and although she went but little out of doors, she kept her beauty so unimpaired, that if she ever took a Sunday walk in the cool of the evening on the walls, or in the neighbouring woods, accompanied by her old servant, everyone who saw her large black eyes look out calmly from between their fair lashes stood as it were transfixed, to gaze after her; and even strangers and distinguished noblemen who did not know her nature, and would not credit the reports concerning her, made her many overtures, hoping to lead her to renounce her single state. But she gave the same answer to each and all of them, namely, that the life she led was dear and familiar to her, and that she had no intention of changing it for any other.

"Thus she had already attained her thirty-second year when the feud between the two neighbouring towns broke out, and as she was a loyal daughter of Treviso, she so bitterly felt all the misery and humiliation that had befallen it, that its deliverance by the valiant arm of a young fellow-citizen on whom her eyes had never rested, impressed her as a supernatural portent, and the deliverer himself as an angel with a flaming sword. Never had she more gladly undertaken a task, or executed it with more skill and industry, than she did this banner which the city meant to offer its triumphant son on his entry; and when the festal day came, and everybody in Treviso who was not on a sick-bed, sought themselves out a spot on market-place or street, at gate or window, nay even on the very house-tops, from whence to shower down flowers and congratulations on Attilio Buonfigli, even the fair Gianna could no longer endure her narrow dwelling, though indeed she might from the turret window have seen the procession from Vicenza well enough. She procured herself a seat on a gaily decorated tribune near the town hall, that she might see the hero quite closely, and she dressed herself in her best attire, a bodice of silver tissue trimmed with blue velvet, and a skirt of fine light blue woollen material, her hair being according to the fashion of the time, richly intertwined with ribands, so that even an hour before the entry, there was a rush in the streets, and many exclamations of amazement when she, thus arrayed, was seen to take her place by the side of a female friend. But before long the eyes of the crowd were diverted from her, and fixed impatiently on the street up which the hero was to ride. Part of the town council had ridden at least a mile beyond the gates to meet and honourably welcome him and his parents. His uncle, the Gonfaloniere, remained standing with the rest on the steps of the town hall, which was covered with costly red cloth, from whence a broad stripe of the same led across the market-place to the door of the cathedral, a manner of preparing the way hitherto reserved for consecrated and anointed personages only.

"But who is able to describe the truly marvellous and unutterably solemn impression made on all, when at length Attilio, in advance of his escort, came riding up the street on his crimson-caparisoned bay charger, he himself in plain attire, a steel coat of mail thrown over a tabard; for the rest unarmed, with the exception of the sword that hung from his girdle, his head adorned merely by its dark brown curls. His chin and cheeks were shaded by a light beard, through which on the left side the broad red scar of his wound was visible. And although his management of his fiery charger proved his strength, a slight pallor still lingered on his cheeks, over which every now and then a modest blush flitted when he looked around him and saw on all sides white heads bend reverently before his triumphal youth, or mothers hold up their children the better to see the deliverer of their native city. But what crowned the whole was the shower of flowers falling so thickly from window and roof upon the hero, that his form was at times actually lost to view beneath a many-coloured veil; and his good horse, accustomed in battle to quite different missiles, pricked his ears, shook his mane, and mingled his shrill neighing with the shouts of triumph and the clamour of bells.

"As soon as the whole procession had gathered in front of the town hall, Attilio leapt from the saddle and hastened up the steps to kneel before his noble uncle, to receive from him the banner, and to kiss the hand that bestowed so high an honour. But as he rose from his knees and prepared to descend the steps and tread the way to the cathedral, he started as though from some sudden pain of body or mind, and required three minutes at least to regain consciousness of where he was, and of the many thousand eyes riveted upon him. The fact was he had seen on the tribune to his right, a face that, like a vision of paradise, seemed to ravish him away from earth; and when the large black eyes looked fixedly at him from under their blonde lashes with an indescribable expression, half sweet, half melancholy, the blood suddenly rushed to his heart, he grew pale as though an arrow had smitten him in the breast, and had he not been holding the banner, against the pole of which he was able to lean, he must a second time—but this time involuntarily—have fallen upon his knees. Those who stood nearest to him and noticed his faintness, attributed it to his wound, and to the fatigue of so long a ride upon a hot day, no one divining the real cause; and at last Attilio collected himself, and forcing his eyes away from the enchanting face before him, trod the path to the cathedral without once turning round his head to where the women sat.

"All the people now streamed after him, and the tribunes emptied themselves rapidly. The last who rose —and then only at the suggestion of her neighbour— was Gianna the Blonde, who as if lapped in dreams, or like one who gazes after the track of a falling star in the sky, followed the young man with her eyes, till the deep shadow of the cathedral portal swallowed up his lofty form. Her friend prepared to follow the rest and be present at the high mass, but Gianna pleaded indis-

position, said she had sat too long in the sun, and with
bent head took her solitary way to her own home. One
of the flowers with which the streets were strewn, she
picked up to carry back as a memorial; it was a red carnation trodden down by a horse's hoof. This flower she
placed in a glass of water, and secretly settled with herself
what it should be held to betoken if it were to revive.

"Her old nurse who had been gazing at the procession through one of the port-holes of the city-gates,
overflowed with praises and admiration of Attilio, of the
modest way in which he had looked about him, he, an
immortal hero at such an early age! dwelling on all the
honour and fame he was sure to win in the future,
making the name of his native town great amongst all
the cities of Italy, perhaps indeed · greater than even
Florence or Rome! Then she fell to speaking of his
betrothed, whom all ladies must needs envy, and to
wondering whether she was worthy of him, and not by
chance like her brother Signor Lorenzaccio, who stood
in the worst repute with the inhabitants of Treviso, the
women more especially. To all these remarks the fair
Gianna replied nothing, or at least very little, and much
to the old woman's surprise, sat herself down to her embroidery frame as though it were a common working-
day, only raising her eyes from time to time to look at
the flower in the glass. When afternoon came, and with
it the rest of the amusements, racing, dancing, and
beautiful fireworks, she still remained quietly seated,
while the servant went out to enjoy the general hilarity.
It was indeed only late in the evening that she returned,
tired to death and covered with dust, but still with
plenty to tell, and full of tender pity for her mistress, who
had lost so much by her sad headache. The fair Gianna
listened with a calm countenance, not joyous indeed,

yet not sad, as though she had no part in what was going on. Meanwhile she had added a large piece to the stole she was working, and apparently had never moved from her chair. But the carnation in the glass was now in full bloom.

"By this time night had come, and after the women had got through their silent supper, old Catalina, whose sexagenarian limbs had toiled hard during the day, betook herself to her bed in the kitchen. Her mistress remained up, looking at the rising of the moon above the broad plain, and the flow of the Rottiniga; and now instead of the festal sounds from the city, which had gradually died down, a nightingale who had her nest under the window, began to sing so sweet and amorous a strain, that tears came to the eyes of the solitary maiden as she listened. She felt her heart so heavy and oppressed that she rose, put out her light, and threw a dark cloak over her shoulders. Then she went down the steep and narrow stair, opened the house-door, and stepped into the empty street just to take a few steps in the cool night air, and quiet her beating pulses. But lost in her own thoughts as she was, she forgot to draw her hood about her head, so that although the moon did not shine into the street, she was easily to be recognized by any passer-by. And now, through a chance which, like all else that is earthly, obeyed a higher will, she encountered the very one her thoughts—like moths about a candle—had been fluttering round the whole day through.

"It was no other than Attilio, who had long ago been weary of all the honour done him, and who more exhausted by the revel and riot of the feast, than by the tumult of a battle-field, had made a pretext of his wound to slip away from the banquet, and alone and unrecognized, visit the old haunts where he had played as a boy. But still stronger was his impulse and longing to try whether he might not chance again to meet those eyes the glance of which was still glowing in his heart. He had by well-put questions elicited from a burgher that the blonde beauty was the clever artist who had worked the banner presented to him, and he had determined on the following day, under plea of thanking her, to pay a visit to her house. And now, just as he was sadly reflecting on all that had happened and was yet to happen, the half-veiled figure advanced as though she were awaiting him. Both were rendered speechless by this sudden meeting. But Attilio was the first to collect himself. 'I know you well, Madonna,' said he, with a chivalrous obeisance as he stepped nearer to her. 'You are Gianna the Fair.' 'And I know you too, Attilio,' replied the beauteous one. 'Who is there in Treviso that does *not* know you?' And thereupon both were silent, and both availed themselves of the shade of the gloomy street, to gaze at each other more closely than they had done yet, and to the young man it seemed that her beauty shone in the twilight a thousand times more gloriously than in the full day, and she for her part thought his eyes had quite another lustre while speaking to her now, than in the morning, when he only mutely contemplated her from afar. 'Forgive me, Madonna,' resumed the youth, 'for roaming through this street by night like a house-breaker. My purpose was to visit you in the morning to thank you for the great pains and the wondrous skill you have expended on the embroidery of my banner. If not disagreeable to you, suffer me, since you are alone, to reconduct you to your house. Truly I would that it were a greater service that I had occasion to render, that you

might see how devoted I am to you.' Whereupon the
blonde beauty, though generally well-skilled in the
choice of words, found nothing better to say than, 'My
home is only six paces off, and too humble for me to
invite you to enter it.' 'Say not so,' replied Attilio.
'Rather were you a princess, and I authorized to entreat
a favour, I should esteem it the very highest, if you
would allow me to enter your dwelling and rest there a
quarter of an hour, for indeed I am weary of wandering
about, and a draught of water would refresh me.' To
which the fair one replied, though not without hesitation
and blushes, 'Who is there in this town he rescued
who could refuse the hero of Bacchiloni the draught of
water he so courteously entreats. My poor house and
all it contains are at your service.' Then opening the
small door she bade him enter in, and after bolting it
again—for on festivals many loose characters prowled
about, bent on spoil—she courteously led her guest by
the hand up the perfectly dark winding stairs, so that
he was quite dazzled when she threw open the door of
her chamber into which the bright white moonshine
streamed. 'Be seated a moment,' said she, 'while I bring
you water; or would you put up with a glass of common wine such as we drink?' But he with quick-beating
heart that choked his utterance, merely shook his head,
and stepping to the window-seat on which her embroidery lay, fell to gazing on it, as though he wanted
to draw it from memory. So she left him and went
down into the kitchen where her nurse was fast asleep
on a rug which she had spread on the flags for the sake
of coolness. 'Oh nurse!' she whispered, 'if you only
knew who has entered in!' Then after filling a goblet
from a great stone pitcher that stood on the hearth, she
stood still a moment, pressed her two cold hands on her

burning cheeks, and said in a low tone, 'Holy Mother of our Lord, guard my heart from vain wishes.' Thereupon she grew stronger, and after placing a small loaf on a tin plate she carried both it and the glass of water up to Signor Attilio, who had meanwhile seated himself in the window, and was gazing out into the open country. 'I am ashamed,' said she, 'to bring you such prison fare as bread and water. But if you will only stretch your arm out of the window, an old fig-tree stands between the two walls and the moat, which, with its load of sweet fruit is easily reached from here.' 'Gianna,' said the young man, taking the glass from her hand, 'were I to remain here your prisoner for ever, I should never wish for any other drink.' And she endeavouring to smile, replied, 'You would grow weary of such imprisonment, whereas in the world without, by the side of your young spouse, a thousand pleasures, prosperities, and honours of all kind await you.' 'Why do you remind me of it?' cried he, his brow growing dark. 'Know that this betrothal which you hold out as a Heaven on earth, is to me a Hell itself. When I was still weak from the fever of my wound, and hardly indeed my own master, I allowed myself to be decoyed into this detested net, in which I now writhe like a captured fish on a burning strand! Alas for my youth! why have my eyes been opened now that it is too late? Why have I learnt to know my own heart just after, like a fool, pledging myself to an accursed duty!' And so saying, he sprang from his seat, and strode with echoing footsteps through the moonlit room, just like a young panther trapped in a pit, and confined in an iron cage. But the fair one, alarmed though she was at the vehemence of this strange confession, was far from imitating his demeanour, but gently said while stroking the carnation blossom with her white finger, 'You astonish me, Signor Attilio! Is not the bride young, fair, and virtuously nurtured, that you should consider it a punishment to become her husband?' 'Were she an angel from before the Throne of God,' cried he, suddenly standing still and facing her, 'that flower that your hand has touched would be a more precious gift to me, than her whole person with all her gifts and virtues! Oh, why have you done this to me, Gianna! He who has never seen the sun may live and even enjoy himself in twilight. But since my eyes met yours for the first time this morning, I have known that there is only one woman on earth for whose love and favour I would dare anything, and cast body and soul away, and that woman art thou, Gianna the Fair; and now I would rather that eternal night should swallow me up, than that I should have to creep back into the twilight yonder, frozen and wretched, to dream of my sun.'

"Thus saying he seized both her hands as though clinging to her to save him from falling into an abyss, but seeing that her face remained unmoved he let her go again, and returned to the open window. There he stood awhile quite still and silent, and only the nightingale in the bush below went on with her ceaseless trilling and warbling. Then as if seized by some sudden resolve the youth turned round and cried, 'But even though it should undo all that is done I will not consent, I will not endure these bonds and chains! Tomorrow with the dawn I send letters to Vicenza to take back my promise, and then I shall retire from both towns and challenge with sword and lance all who dare to deny that Gianna the Fair is the queen of womanhood.' 'This shalt thou not do, Attilio,' returned the beautiful being looking beyond him to the midnight sky with a calm and earnest gaze. 'That you should have been so suddenly attracted towards me, and should endow me so unqualifiedly with your affection, I acknowledge as an inexpressibly great gift, for which, although unworthy of you, I shall thank you as long as I live. But I cannot accept this gift without involving both in ruin. Reflect, my friend, how the scarcely smothered enmity between the two towns would burst forth again if you were thus to insult the house of Scarpa, and with it all the city, by despising your betrothed bride who has never offended against you by word or deed, merely because another face has pleased you better. And this very face, even granting that it does at this time deserve such excessive praise, and the passion it has excited in you, who can say that even in one year all its charms might not be faded, so that you would ask yourself wondering, how was it possible you could have been thus possessed by it? Do we not often see towards the close of summer, one single night of early frost avail to turn the trees that were green but yesterday, suddenly sere and yellow? I have overstept my one-and-thirtieth year; you my friend are in the fulness of your youth, you are still climbing the hill, the summit of which I have reached. Let me, therefore, being the elder, be the wiser as well, and show prudence enough for both. And to this end I declare to you my firm resolve, even were I to discover your love was more than a sudden caprice, and were all opposing circumstances miraculously to conform themselves to your wishes, I would *never* consent to be your wife, no, not though your parents came to me in person to lend their support to your suit!'

"It was only when she had ended this speech that she ventured to look towards him, and then seeing how pale he was, and how his fine eyes wandered round as in despair, she felt ready out of very love and pity to contradict all that she had forced herself to utter with incredible firmness.

"'Good-night, Madonna,' Attilio sorrowfully said, and seemed about to leave, but then stood still and looked on the ground. 'You are angry with me, Attilio,' said she. And he—'No, by God, Gianna, I am not; only give me leave to depart, for truly I have tarried but too long, and have spoken like a madman, without considering that what I offered you might prove so worthless in your sight, that you could not even stretch out your hand to take it, far less endure conflict and trouble for its sake. And thus I depart with well-merited humiliation, and it is no one's fault but my own that this my day of triumph, which began so gladly, should have so lamentable an end. Farewell, Gianna. The banner you worked, and which this morning seemed to me the most costly of possessions, I will now bestow upon a chapel, in order that the sight of it may not recall to me the hand which has so coldly rejected and repulsed me.'

"With that he bent low and was nearing the door, when once more he heard his name called. Gianna's heart, which had long been beating wildly, now burst its bounds, and made itself heard in speech. 'Attilio,' said the blushing fair, who had lost all self-control, 'I cannot let you go away thus, and continue to live. What I have said stands firm, nor will you ever change one iota of it, for it behoves your own good which is dearer to me than my own. But I have not yet told you all. Know then that since my betrothed died—it is now twelve years ago—I have never had the thought nor the wish of belonging to any man, and if I have kept the jewel of my honour thus pure, in good sooth it has cost me neither effort nor regret so to do. For I do not lightly esteem myself, not so much because of this poor and transient beauty, as because I know well that mine is a free and strong spirit, which I could never render subservient to the sway of one weaker or lower than myself, as in marriage a wife is often bound to do. And many as my wooers have been, I have never yet found one whom to serve would not have appeared to me a bondage and degradation. It was only to-day that I saw you ride into the town to which you have given back freedom and honour. When I saw how modestly you bent your head beneath so great a triumph, achieved in such early youth—showing neither vanity nor scorn, but receiving like a messenger from God, the gratitude of those whom you had delivered—I could not but say to myself, 'Why art thou no longer young to deserve the love of this youth?' And when I saw the crimson scar on your throat, I felt that I would go barefoot on a pilgrimage to the Holy Sepulchre, if mine might be the bliss of only once daring to press my lips to that sacred wound. And then when I came home, knowing well what had befallen me, I picked up a flower from the street—this one, see—just because it had been trodden under your horse's hoof; and I meant to have it laid under my pillow when I should be borne out hence to my last sleep. And now that I have told you this, Attilio, repeat, if you have the heart, that this hand has coldly drawn itself away from your grasp.'

"Then she held out her arms to her lover, who stood before her in speechless ecstasy, like one doomed to death who had been reprieved at the very edge of the scaffold. She drew down his head on her breast, and kissed the wound for which her lips had yearned. Then freeing herself once more from his embrace, she said,

‘What I do, my friend, is done with perfect deliberation and consciousness, and I shall never repent it, although many might censure and condemn my conduct if they knew of it. I give you the only jewel I possess, and which hitherto I have held dearer than my very life. For look you, on the very spot on which you stand, your future brother-in-law, Signor Lorenzaccio, stood and vehemently besought me to be his, and he would lead me to Vicenza as his wife. But what I denied to him, the enemy and oppressor of my city—and I was fain to threaten him with my dagger (the mark of which he bears on his right hand) before he desisted from his wild wooing—I give to you as the saviour of my city, give it in token of your triumph; and require from you in return no reward whatever, but that you forget me when you stand at the altar to plight your faith to another. And do not concern yourself as to what may betide me then. My lot will be blessed through all renunciation, and enviable in all sorrow, since I shall have endowed the noblest man on whom my eyes have ever rested with the free gift of my honour; and before the winter of years has covered this blond head with snows, I shall have enjoyed a late spring, beauteous beyond all I could have dreamed. These eyes and lips are thine, Attilio, and this un-touched form is thine, and thine is this heart which, when thou shalt part from me, will never more desire any of the sweetnesses of this world, but like the heart of a widow, will still feed upon its past joys till it beat no longer.’

“Thus saying she led him to the seat in the window, and knelt before him, and he took her head in his two hands, and was never satiated with gazing at her, and kissing her brow, cheeks, and mouth; and long after the moon had set they were still together and immeasurably blest. But when the first cock-crow was heard over the plains, Gianna herself constrained him to leave her arms, lest he should be missed in his parent's house. They agreed, however, that he should return the next night and all the following ones, and fixed on the signal at which she should open the door; and so he took his leave, as one intoxicated reels from a banquet: and in the arrogance of his bliss he scorned to descend the winding stairs, although the streets were empty, but swung himself out of the window, and profiting by the foot-hold afforded by the fig-tree, scrambled down to the walls below, often delaying to call out all manner of loving names and to throw the flowers growing on the edge of the moat up to the beloved one in the window, till she, fearing observation, withdrew from it. Then he tore himself away, and crept so carefully along the walls, that he reached the gate unnoticed by any. The sleepy watchman did not recognize him, and no one had missed him at home, so that he entered exultingly into his own room, and throwing himself on his couch, snatched a brief interval of needed sleep.

"With equal skill and secrecy, the lovers contrived their meetings for the nights following, so that no one in the whole town had the least idea of the relations between them; except the nurse Catalina, who was as silent about it as the fig-tree under the window. For the happiness and honour of her mistress were the first thought of her heart; and the sharpest tortures of the rack would never have extorted the youth's name from lips of hers. But one thing did grieve her much, and that was her dear lady's firm resolve that all must be over for ever, so soon as Attilio had exchanged rings with his bride Emilia Scarpa. 'What can you be thinking of?' said the old woman. 'Do you suppose you will be able quietly to endure that another should adorn herself with the flower that you have worn on your breast? As sure as I love you, lady, more than the fruit of my own body, you will die of it, your heart will break in twain like an apple when you run a knife into its midst.' 'Nurse,' said the Blonde, 'you may be right. But what of that? Better that I should be destroyed, than the one I love, and this dear city which is the mother of us both.' 'What folly you utter!' replied the old woman. 'If he love you as he says, and I believe, he will not be able to survive it; and so your obstinacy will bring about the death of two. And as for the city, now that it is defended by such a hero, it may safely challenge the enmity of three cities, each of them mightier than Vicenza.' Such arguments and others did Attilio too urge, and ever more and more pressingly as the time drew near when he must bid an eternal farewell to the eyes he adored.

"He still hoped, as he had hoped from the first day, to conquer her opposition, and was resolved to sacrifice everything for her. Gianna, on the other hand, to whom the bare idea of her lover's heart ever growing cold, and regretting that he had linked his young life with her faded one, was far more bitter than parting or death, tried, whenever he assailed her with fresh entreaties, to turn away his impetuosity by some jest about her age, and the inconstancy of men, and to make the Present so sweet to him, that in it he should forget the bitterness of the Future.

"Meanwhile in both houses, that of the Buonfigli as of the Scarpa, preparations for the marriage were eagerly carried on, and in nine weeks from the triumphal entry of the bridegroom, a no less brilliant reception was accorded by the inhabitants of Treviso to the bride. If, however, amongst the spectators there was even greater general joy than before, because of the now sealed and ratified treaty between the two cities, and also owing to the presence of the young and richly adorned bride with her escort of sixteen bridesmaids, all mounted on white jennĕts, and wearing costly apparel,—there were two in the festal procession who found it hard to conceal their anger and annoyance, one being the bridegroom himself, who would rather have touched a snake than his bride, and the other, Signor Lorenzaccio, his future brother-in-law, who secretly gnashed his teeth when he reflected that he had to play a quite secondary part to his young rival's, and would have gladly strangled, rather than embraced, him and his kindred. And yet a third heart there was, firmly closed against the rejoicings of the day, and that heart beat in the bosom of the fair Gianna, for she knew that the night that followed would be the last of her bliss. Accordingly she had not as on the former occasion exerted herself to procure a seat in the tribune in front of the town hall, but had kept at home while Attilio rode by the stranger's side through the streets, and a very rain of flowers rustled down about the pair. Even in the afternoon, while all the people were flocking out to the meadow before the town, where within splendidly decorated lists a tournament was to be held, she sat still at home lost in gloomy thoughts, and her tears falling so fast she saw nothing of the brightness of the day. 'O my poor heart!' she sighed, 'Now is the time to prove thyself strong enough to renounce thy own happiness; and thou art so weak, thou meltest away in tears. Thou hast undertaken more than thou art able to perform. True thou knewest not that love is a wine of which every draught but increases the thirst of those who drink. Now the cup of thy bliss is turned to poison that will slowly consume thee, and no leech on earth, nor help of all the Saints in heaven, will avail to heal thee!' At this moment in came Catalina, and persuaded her to go out with her, that at least if she really were resolved to part from her beloved, she might behold him once more in the full splendour of his knightly prowess and beauty, and as conqueror of all assembled. For the kind soul secretly hoped that a miracle would yet take place, and her mistress's mind change. Accordingly she dressed out the mourner (who was passive as a child) with the utmost care, and led her to the tilting-field, which was already swarming with people, and resonant with the neighing of horses and blare of trumpets. There then Gianna, standing amongst the crowd, saw the bride sitting on a raised daïs between the father and uncle of her bridegroom, and, heard what people thought of her, some admiring her to the utmost, and others finding this or that to censure as well as to praise. The fair Gianna spoke not a word, and what she thought was never known. Only on two occasions she blushed deeply, when of some young men who passed before her, one exclaimed loud enough to be heard, 'I would give ten Emilias for one Gianna the Fair!' and the other, 'Treviso carries away the palm in women as in arms!' and this led to many eyes being bent on the fair embroideress, whose colour suddenly changed into deadly pallor; for at that moment Signor Attilio rode into the lists armed cap-à-pie, except that his throat instead of being defended by a brass haubergeon, which the French call *barbier*, was only protected by a slight leathern curtain fastened to the helmet. His visor was up, so that all noticed how pale he was and what sad and searching glances he cast around, and many marvelled at his aspect, seeing that

he was such a triumphant young hero and a bridegroom
to boot. However he rode up to the daïs on which his
betrothed sat, bent before her, and allowed her to wind
about his helmet the scarf she had been wearing, in
token that he was her knight. Then the trumpeters blew,
and from the other side came Signor Lorenzaccio riding
into the lists, with visor closed, it is true, but all knew
him from his armour and device, and hoped with all
their hearts to see him stretched on the sand by the
strong arm of his future brother-in-law. It was, however,
otherwise decreed in the councils above. For scarcely
had the heralds given the signal with their staffs, and
the trumpets sounded, than both knights charged with
lances in rest, and their horses hoofs raised such a cloud
of dust, that for a moment after the shock, they were
lost to the view of the spectators, who only heard the
sound of lances on shield and coat of mail, followed by
sudden silence. But when the cloud dispersed they beheld with horror Attilio, his feet still in the stirrups,
thrown backwards on the saddle of his good steed (who
stood there motionless), a stream of blood flowing from
his throat, the undefended whiteness of which afforded a
welcome mark to the cruel weapon of his foe. The
conqueror faced him with his visor open, as though de-
sirous to ascertain that his revenge was thoroughly accomplished, and after casting one last look of devilish
hatred at his opponent, closed his helmet and rode, no
one applauding him, slowly away out of the lists and
through the petrified and horror-stricken crowds that
could scarcely believe their eyes.

Meanwhile Attilio's squire and the other attendants
hurried into the lists, lifted the groaning man out of the
saddle, and spreading a carpet on the sand laid him
thereon. And then a loud wailing arose, all order was

over, the people rushed wildly over the barriers; those who occupied the tribunes hurried from their seats; and scarcely could the heralds succeed by remonstrance and blows to clear so much space about the dying man, as that his parents, relations, and bride might be able to reach him.   He, however, lay still with eyes closed, and while some lamented, and others cursed the fiendish malice of Lorenzaccio, some called aloud for a leech, and others for a priest to afford the last consolations to the soul of the parting hero, no sound of pain came from his lips, nor of regret at having so early to join the heavenly hosts above.   Rather did this hard fate appear to him a rescue from hated bonds; and when he heard his name called and recognized the voice of his bride, he endeavoured to shake his head, as though to tell her that he would not breathe away his last breath in a falsehood.   Then all at once the crowd that pressed round this spectacle of woe parted asunder with a murmur of amazement, for they saw the fair Giovanna, pale as a spectre, yet crowned by the thorn-crown of woe, queen over all other women, advance and enter the circle: 'Go hence,' said she, stretching out her hand towards the bride, 'this dying man belongs to me, and as during life I was his, body and soul, so in death, too, I will be with him, and no stranger shall rob me of one sigh of his!'

"Then she knelt down by her beloved, and gently lifted his powerless head on to her knee, his blood streaming over her festal attire. 'Attilio,' said she, 'do you know me?' Instantly he opened his eyes and sighed, 'O my Gianna, it is over! Death has not willed that I should pledge to another the faith and truth that only belonged to thee. I die; my wife, kiss me with the last kiss and receive my soul in thy arms!'

"Then she bent down to his lips, and as her mouth rested on his, his eyes closed and his head sank back on her lap. And so mighty was the compassion felt by all for the noble pair, that no one, not even any of the Scarpas, ventured to trouble the parting of the lovers. Nay, when preparations began for carrying the lifeless form of the young hero back into the city, the people divided into two processions, one of which followed the dead, and the other the litter that bore his beloved to her house, for she had swooned away by the side of her lost friend. That same night the young Emilia returned with her mother to Vicenza. Her father, however, Signor Tullio Scarpa, remained in the house of the Buonfigli, in order to be present at Attilio's funeral, himself doubly a mourner, for his daughter's sorrow and his son's disgrace.

"But when on the third day the beloved dead was borne to his grave in the chapel of the Madonna degli Angeli, there was seen next to the bier, and taking precedence of all blood relations, the tall form of Giovanna, dressed in deepest black, and wearing a widow's veil. And when she threw back the veil to kiss the brow of the departed, all the people beheld with astonishment the marvel that had taken place, for the gold of her hair which used to shine out from afar, had in a few nights changed to dull silver, and her fair face was pale and faded like that of an aged woman.

"And, indeed, many thought she could not longer endure life, but would follow her beloved. Nevertheless she lived on for three years, during which she never laid aside her widow's garb, and was never seen in any public or festive place. In her retirement, however, she was industrious at her work, for she had vowed to the chapel of the Madonna degli Angeli, a large banner on which was represented the archangel Michael, clad in white armour, and slaying the dragon. And it was reported that the angel's coat of mail was worked with her own silver hair. And this banner was placed next to the first which hung in the chapel over Attilio's grave. This task completed, she held out no longer; they bore the embroideress too to her rest, and granted her her last petition, to be buried at the feet of him she loved. And that grave was long the resort of inhabitants and strangers, who went to admire the exquisite work of both banners, and to relate to each other the story of Gianna the Fair, who in life and death gave to her beloved all she possessed — even to her honour — though she might easily have preserved it unblemished had she held her peace."

When the reader had ended, there was an interval of silence in the saloon, and the rain, the pattering of which had formed a melancholy accompaniment to the whole of the narrative, was now the only sound heard.

At last the young doctor at the chess-table observed: "This story has somewhat of the gold tone of the Venetian school. And this the palettes of our moderns can no longer produce. Yet I own it seemed to me as if the copyist had introduced here and there some bold touches of his own."

"The copyist!" said he of the sofa, throwing away his cigar. "This shews you know little of Erminus. He has only been taking us in, in order to contrast a highly coloured picture with our faded hues. Who will bet that this chronicle of San Niccolo is not a much later production than the far-famed Ossian of Macpherson?"

Erminus seemed to turn a deaf ear to these remarks. "And how do you estimate the morality of the story?" asked he, addressing himself to Frau Eugénie.

The lady in question reflected for a moment, then said, "I do not know that one could discuss so singular a case in the light of precedent or example. Have not different times indeed different manners, and different modes of feeling? I confess that a passionate self-surrender which does not reckon upon eternal constancy, must always clash with my own sense of right; and that it is only the tragic end that reconciles me to the startling commencement. And yet, had the Fair Giovanna been my sister, I should not have scrupled to walk with her hand in hand in the funeral procession that followed Attilio's bier."

"A better testimony to the morality of the tale I could not desire," replied the narrator. "Allow me to kiss your hand in return."

END OF THE EMBROIDERESS OF TREVISO.

LOTTKA.

LOTTKA.

I was not quite seventeen years old, an over-grown
pale-faced young fellow, at that awkward and embarass-
ing age which, conscious of having out-grown boyish
ways, is yet very unsteady and insecure when seeking
to tread in the footsteps of men. With an audacious
fancy and a timid heart; oscillating between defiant self-
confidence and girlish sensitiveness; snatching inquisi-
tively at every veil that hides from mortal eyes the mys-
teries of human life; to-day knowing the last word of
the last question, to-morrow confessing the alphabet has
still to be learnt, and getting comfort after so restless
and contradictory a fashion that one would have been
intolerable to one's very self if not surrounded by fellows in misfortune—that is in years—who were faring
no better, and yet continued to endure their personality.

It was at this time that I became intimate with a
singular fellow who was some two years older than I,
but like myself doomed to spend nearly another year as
upper-class student. He did not attend the same gymnasium, nor were his relations, who lived out of Berlin,
at all known to mine. I am really puzzled how to explain the fact that in spite of these obstacles we two became so friendly, that scarcely a day passed without his
coming up the steep stairs that led to my rooms. In-

deed even then a third party seeing us together might have found it hard to say what made us so essential to each other. He was in the habit of entering with a mere nod, walking up and down the room, now and then opening a book, or looking at a picture on the walls, and finally throwing himself into my grandfather's arm-chair—my substitute for a sofa—where, legs crossed, he would sit for hours, speaking not a word, until I had finished my Latin essay. Often when I looked up from the book before me I met his quiet, dreamy, brown eyes resting on me with a gentle brotherly expression, which made me nod to him in return; and it was a pleasure to me just to feel him there. If he chanced to find me idle, or in a communicative mood, he would let me run on by the hour without interruption, and his silent attention seemed to encourage and comfort me. It was only when we got upon the subject of music that he ever grew excited, and then we both lost ourselves in passionate debate. He had a splendid deep bass voice, that harmonized well with his manly aspect, dark eyes, and brown satin-smooth skin. And as he was also zealously studying the theory of music, it was easy for him to get the better of my superficial lay-talk by weighty arguments; yet whenever he thus drove me into a corner he always seemed pained at my defeat. I remember him, on one occasion, ringing me out of bed, formally to apologise for having, in the ardour of controversy, spoken of Rossini's *Barbiere* which I had been strenuously upholding, as a wretched shaver whose melodies, compared with those of Mozart, were of little more account than the soap-bubbles in his barber's basin.

In addition too to the extreme placidity that characterized him, he was always ready to do me a number of small services, such as the younger student usually

renders to his senior, and there were two other things
that helped to rivet our friendship: he had initiated
me in the art of smoking, and set my first songs to
music. There was one, I remember, which appeared to
us at that time peculiarly felicitous both as to words and
melody, and we used to sing it as a duet in all our
walks together—

> "I think in the olden days
> That a maiden was loved by me;
> But my heart is sick and troubled,
> It is all a dream may-be.
>
> I think in the olden days,
> One was basking in sunny bliss;
> But whether I or another?
> I cannot be sure of this!
>
> I think in the olden days
> That I sang—but know not what;
> For I have forgotten all things
> Since I've been by her forgot."

Dear and ridiculous season of youth! A poet of
sixteen sings of the "old myth" of his lost love-sorrow,
and a musician of eighteen with all possible gravity, sets
the sobbing strophes to music with a piano-forte accompaniment that seems to foreshadow the outburst of the
world's denunciation on the head of the inconstant fair!
We were, however, as I have already said, so especially pleased with this melancholy progeny of our
united talents, that we were not long content to keep it
to ourselves; we burned with desire to send it forth to the
public. At that time the "Dresden Evening Times" under
the editorship of, as I believe the late Robert Schneider,
admitted poems over which my critical self-esteem could
not but shrug its shoulders. To him, therefore, we sent
our favourite—anonymously, of course—in the full persuasion that it would appear in the forthcoming number,
text and music both, with the request that the unknown

contributor would delight the Evening Times with other admirable fruits of genius. Full of a sweet shyness, spite of our incognito, we accordingly took to haunting the eating-houses where that journal was taken in, and blushingly looked out for our first-born. But week after week passed by without satisfying our expectations. I myself after twice writing and dignifiedly desiring the manuscript to be returned, gave up all hope, and was so wounded and humiliated by this failure, as first to throw down the gauntlet to an ungrateful contemporaneous world, and contribute to the pleasure of more enlightened posterity in the form of a longer poem; and then gradually to shun all mention of our unlucky venture, even requesting Bastel (my friend's name being Sebastian) to leave off humming the tune which too vividly recalled to me the mortifying history.

He humoured me on this point, but he could not refrain from privately carrying on his investigations in pastry-cooks' shops, the more that he was devotedly addicted to cakes and sweet things. It was then midsummer, and the small round cherry tarts were wonderfully refreshing to an upper class student's tongue, parched and dry with Latin and Greek. Bastel most seriously asserted that sweets agreed with his voice; he was only able to temper the harshness of his bass notes by plenty of sugar and fruit-juice. I on the contrary, despised such insipid dainties, and preferred to stick to wine, which at that time did very little indeed to clear up any mind I had. But in virtue of my calling I was bound to worship "wine, women, and song," and in the volume of poems at which I was working hard, there was, of course, to be no lack of drinking-songs.

We had now reached July, and the dog-days were beginning, when one afternoon Bastel made his appearance at the usual hour, but in very unusual mood. He lit his cigar indeed, but instead of sitting down to smoke it, he stood motionless at the window for a full quarter of an hour, drumming *"Non più andrai"* on the panes, and from time to time sighing as though a hundred-weight lay on his heart.

"Bastel," said I, "what's wrong?"

No answer.

"Are you ill?" I went on; "or have you had another row with the ordinary? or did the college yesterday give you a bad reception?" (He belonged to a certain secret society much frequented by students, and wore in his waistcoat pocket a tricoloured watch-ribbon which only ventured forth at their solemn meetings.)

Still the same silence on the part of the strange dreamer, and the drumming grew so vehement that the panes began to ring ominously.

It was only when I left off noticing him, that he incoherently began to talk to himself, "There are more things in heaven and earth—" but further he did not carry the quotation.

At last I jumped up, went to him, and caught hold of his hand. "Bastel!" I cried, "what does this fooling mean? Something or other is vexing you. Tell it out, and let us see what can be done, but at least spare my window-panes and behave rationally. Will you light another cigar?"

He shook his head. "If you have time," said he, "let's go out, I may be able to tell you in the open air. This room is so close."

We went down stairs and wandered arm-in-arm through quiet Behren Street, where my parents lived, into Frederick Street. When he got into the full tide of carriages and foot-passengers, he seemed to be in a measure relieved. He pressed my arm, stood still a moment, and broke out: "It is nothing very particular, Paul, but I believe that I am in love, and this time for life."

I was far from laughing at the declaration. At the age of sixteen one believes in the endless duration of every feeling. But I had read my Heine and considered it bad taste to become sentimental over a love-affair.

"Who is the fortunate fair?" I lightly enquired.

"You shall see her," he replied, his eyes wandering absently over the crowd flowing through the street. "I will take you there at once if you are inclined."

"Can one go thus unceremoniously without being better dressed? I have actually forgotten my gloves."

"She is no countess," said he, a slight blush shewing through his dark complexion. "Just think! yesterday when I wanted to look once more through the Evening Times—yes, I know we are not to speak of it, but it has to do with the whole thing—chance, or my good star led me to a quite out-of-the-way little cake-shop, and there—"

He stopped short.

"There you found her eating cherry-tarts, and that won your affection," laughed I. "Well, Bastel, I congratulate you. Sweets to the sweet. But have you already made such way as to be able to calculate upon finding her again at the very same place?"

He gave no further reply. My tone seemed to be discordant with his mood. So indeed it at once became with my own, but my principles did not allow me to express myself more feelingly. Minor chords remained the exclusive property of verse; conversation was to be carried on in a harsh and flippant key, the more cold-blooded and ironical the better.

We had walked, in silence for the most part, all the length of Frederick Street to the Halle Gate, I, for all my air of indifference, actually consumed with curiosity and sympathy, when my friend suddenly turned up one of the last side streets that debouch into the main artery of the great city. Here were found at the time I am speaking of, several small one-storied private houses of mean exterior, a few shops, little traffic, so that the rattling of cab wheels sufficed to bring the inhabitants to their windows; and numbers of children who played about freely in the street, not having to take flight before the approach of any heavily-laden omnibus. When almost at the end of this particular side-street we came to a halt before a small house painted green, and having above its glass-door a large and dusty black board with the word "Confectionery" in tarnished gilt letters. To the right and left of this door were windows, with old brown blinds closely drawn, although the house was not on the sunny side of the street. I can see the landscape on those blinds to this hour! A ruined temple near a pond, on which a man with effaced features sat in a boat angling, while a peacock spread his tail on the stump of a willow tree. The glass door in the middle looked as though it had not been cleaned for ten years, and its netted curtain, white once no doubt, was now by reason of age, dust, and flies, pretty much the colour of the blinds.

I was startled when Sebastian prepared to enter this un-inviting domicile: however I took care not to ruffle him again, and followed his lead in no small excitement.

We were greeted by a hot cloying smell, which under ordinary circumstances would instantly have driven me out again, a smell of old dough, and fer-

menting strawberries, mingled with a flavour of choco-
late and Vanilla, a smell that only an inveterate sweet-
tooth or a youth in love could by possibility have consented to inhale! Added to this, the room was not
much more than six feet high, and apparently never
ventilated, except by the chance opening of the door.
How my friend could ever have expected to find the
Dresden Evening Times in such an out-of-the-way shop
as this was a puzzle to me. Very soon, however, I discovered what it was that had lured him again—spite of
his disappointment—into this distressing atmosphere.
Behind the small counter on which was displayed a
limited selection of uninviting tarts and cakes, I could
see in the dusky window-seat behind the brown blind, a
young girl dressed in the simplest printed cotton gown
possible, her thick black hair just parted and cut short
behind, a piece of knitting in her hands, which she only
laid down when after some delay and uncertainty we
had determined upon the inevitable cherry-tarts. My
friend who hardly dared to look at her, still less to
speak, went into the narrow, dark, and most comfortless
little inner room, where the "Vossische Journal," and the
"Observer on the Spree" outspread on a round table
before the faded sofa, kept up a faint semblance of a
reading-room. A small fly-blinded mirror hung on the
wall between the two wooden-framed lithographs of
King Frederick William III. and Queen Louise, over
which was a bronzed bust of old Blücher squeezed in
between the top of the stove and the low ceiling and
looking gruffly down.

Sebastian had thrown himself in feverish haste into
one corner of the sofa, I into the other, when the young
girl came in with the small plates for the tarts. I was
now able to look at her leisurely, for she waited to light

a gas-burner, it being already too dark to read. She was rather short than tall, but her figure was so symmetrical, so round, yet slender, that the eye followed her every movement with rapture, spite of her unbecoming, and almost ugly dress. Her feet, which were made visible to us by her standing on tip-toe to reach the gas burner, were daintily small as those of a child of ten, her little deft snow-white fingers looked as if they had always rested on a silken lap. What white things she had on, a small upright collar, cuffs, and a waitress's apron, were so immaculately clean as to form a striking contrast with the stained carpet, dusty furniture, and traces of the flies of a hundred summers visible on all around.

I ought, I am aware, to attempt some sketch of her face, but I despair beforehand. Not that her features were so incomparably beautiful as to defy the skill of any and every artist. But what gave the peculiar charm to this face of hers, was a certain spirituality which I found it no easy matter to define to myself, a calm melancholy, a half-shy, half-threatening expression, a spring-tide bloom, which, having suddenly felt the touch of frost, no longer promised a joyous fruitful summer; in short, a face that would have puzzled and perplexed more mature decipherers of character, and which could not fail to make an irresistible impression upon a dreamer of sixteen.

"What is your name, Fräulein, if I may venture to ask?" said I, by way of opening the conversation, my friend seeming as though he had no more important object than the mere consuming of tartlets.

"Lottka," replied the girl without looking at me, and already preparing to leave the room.

"Lottka!" cried I. "How do you come to have this Polish name?"

"My father was a Pole."

And then she was back again in the shop.

"Would you have the kindness, Miss Lottka, to bring me a glass of *bishop*," I called after her.

"Directly," was her reply.

Sebastian was studying the advertisements in the "Vossische Journal" as though he expected to meet with the real finder of his lost heart there! I turned over the "Observer." Not one word did we exchange.

In three minutes in she came again, bringing a glass of dark red wine on a tray. I could not turn my eyes away from her white hands, and felt my heart beat while gathering courage to address her again.

"Will you not sit a little with us, Fräulein?" said I. "Do take my place on the sofa, and I will get a chair."

"Thank you, sir," she replied, without any primness, but at the same time with almost insulting indifference, "my place is in the shop. If there is anything I can do for you—"

"Do remain where you are," I insisted, venturing to catch hold of one of her hands which felt cool and smooth, and instantly slipped out of my grasp. "These newspapers are horribly dull. Allow us to introduce ourselves. My friend here, Mr.——"

At that moment the shop-door opened, a little girl pushed shyly in, with two copper coins in her small fist, for which she wanted some sweeties. Our beauty availed herself of this opportunity of declining our acquaintance, and after having served the child, sat down again in her window-corner and took up her knitting.

Our position grew more and more unbearable. As to the tarts they were eaten long ago, and I had, partly

out of embarrassment, and partly to give myself the air
of an experienced wine-bibber, tossed off my glass of
bishop at a draught, and now sat with burning brow
and wandering mind, looking at the flies crawling along
the glass's edge, and intoxicating themselves with the
crimson drops. Sebastian was as silent as an Indian
Fakir, and seemed to be listening intently to what was
going on in the shop, where indeed there was not a
sound to be heard, except now and then the click of the
knitting-needles against the counter.

"Come, you trappist," said I at length, "we will pay
our bill and get some fresh air. My lungs are as it
were candied. For any one but a fly this atmosphere is
insupportable."

"Good-bye, pretty child," said I at the counter with
all the importance of a roué of sixteen, who has a volume of lyrical poems at home written in the style of
Heine, and ready for the press. "I hope that we may
improve our acquaintance at some future time when you
are less absorbed. Au revoir!"

I should no doubt have indulged in greater ab-
surdities, but that she looked at me with so strangely
absent an expression that I suddenly felt ashamed of
my impertinence, made her a low bow, and hurried
out into the street. Sebastian followed me instantly; he
had hardly dared to look at her.

"Now then," he said, as we rushed along through the
silent street, "what do you say?"

"That the bishop is very fair, but the tarts execrable.
I cannot understand how you forced your portion down
as well as half of mine. I suspect that confectioner's
shop of only selling old cakes bought second-hand."

"What of that?" growled he. "I did not ask about
such things. I want to know what you think of *her*."

"My good friend," I returned in an authoritative and fatherly tone. "What can one say about a girl who is able to breathe in that atmosphere! Woman is ever an enigma as you well know."

(He nodded assent and sighed; I had contrived—God knows how—to pass with him as a great discerner of feminine spirits, and was fond of introducing into my generalisations the word "Woman," which has always a mystical charm for youths of our age.)

"This monosyllabic creature—that she is enchanting it is impossible to deny! But I warn you against her, Bastel. Believe me, she has no heart."

"You think so?" he interpolated in a horrified tone without looking at me.

"That is to say she has either never had one, or destiny has changed it into stone in her breast. Otherwise would she so coldly have turned away when I addressed her? She has a past I tell you, perhaps a present also, but no future."

This stupendous sentence of mine thrown off in mere thoughtlessness produced an unexpected effect upon my chum. He started as though a snake had bitten him, snatched his arm out of mine and said—

"You think then that she—that she no longer—in a word you doubt her virtue?"

I saw now the mischief I had done. "Be easy, child," said I, throwing my arm over his shoulder. "Come, we must not have a scene here. We have agreed woman is an enigma. But as to character I have no grounds for suspecting hers. I only meant to say, take care that you do not get involved in an unpromising affair. For she looks like one from whom a victim would not easily escape! If you like I will keep an

eye upon her, and I promise to render you every assistance that one friend can to another."

We had now reached a dark and deserted street-
corner. Suddenly he embraced me, squeezed my hand
as though bent on fusing it with his own, and instantly
vanished up the nearest side-street.

I for my part walked home very slowly in order to
grow cool and collected, but the singular form I had
seen never left me for a moment. I was so feverishly
abstracted at the home tea-table that my good mother
grew alarmed, and sent me early to bed. When I went
to my class the following morning, I found I had not
prepared my Plato, and was obliged to put up with
many mocking remarks from the lecturer on history in
consequence of my having pushed the date of the battle
of Cannæ a good century too far back. The day was
wet, and I lounged down the street full of depression
and *ennui*. Sebastian kept himself out of sight. I stood
an hour at the window on which he had drummed
"*Non più andrai*" the day before, and looked medita-
tively at the rain-pools in the street below, out of which
the sparrows were picking a few oat-husks. I heard the
horses stamping in the stable, and the stable-boy whistling Weber's "Jungfern Kranz" and found myself suddenly whistling it too, and stamping the while. I felt so
absurd and pitiable that tears nearly came. At length I
armed myself with an umbrella, and ran out into the
wet and windy street.

I had been invited to a party at a friend's house for
that evening, but I had an hour to spare. And this
hour, I thought, could not be better spent than in saun-
tering through the street where the confectioner's shop
stood, and patrolling a short time on the other side to
watch who went in. As it was already growing dusk I

felt pretty well concealed under my umbrella, but all the same I was conscious of a certain agreeable mysterious sensation as though playing an important part in some deed of honour. In point of fact, however, there was nothing remarkable to be seen. The shop seemed to be pretty well frequented, but only by a humble class of customers, children, schoolboys intent upon devouring their pocket money, coughing old women going in for a penny-worth of lozenges. Dangerous young men did not seem aware that behind those brown blinds lurked a dangerous young girl.

Much relieved by the result of my observation, I finally crossed the street just to find out whether there were any possibility of peeping in. The gas was lit in both rooms, but the shop-window was so well-protected that one could see nothing whatever from without. But on the other hand the blind of the reading-room had a crack just across the back of the angler. So I stood and looked in, a good deal ashamed of myself for spying. And there, on the very same corner of the sofa that he occupied yesterday, sat my poor friend Sebastian before an empty plate covered with flies, his eyes wandering beyond the newspaper into empty space. A singular thrill came over me, half jealousy, half satisfaction, at his having got on no further. Just as I was watching him, he made a movement as if to take up his cap and leave. I drew back from the window, and crept along the houses like a thief who has had the narrowest escape of capture. When I got to the house where I was expected, I had of course to collect my wits. I was more lively than usual, and paid my court to the daughters of the house with all the awkward nonchalance of a man of the world of sixteen, nay, I even allowed myself to be persuaded to read out my last poem, and drank several glasses of strong Hungarian wine, which made me neither wiser nor more modest. When ten o'clock struck, I suddenly took my departure under the pretext of an appointment with a friend. To keep late hours seemed to me congruous with the character of a youthful poet. Had people but known that the real engagement was the copying out fair a German essay, all the halo would have vanished!

And as it was that luckless essay fared badly enough. The night was wondrously beautiful. After long-continued rain, the air was as soft and exquisitely still as a human heart just reconciled to a long-estranged friend (I involuntarily fall back into the lyrical style of those early days!), and the sky sparkled and shone with thousands of newly-washed stars. In spite of the lateness of the hour, girls and women went chattering through the streets without hat or shawl, with merely a kerchief thrown over their heads, as though the lovely night had enticed them out just to inhale, before going to bed, one draught of fresh air after the discomfort of the day. Every window stood open, the roses gave out their fragrance; one heard Mendelssohn's "Songs without words" played on the piano, or some sweet female voice quietly singing to itself.

How it happened I did not know, but all of a sudden there I was again at the little shop, and had hold of the door handle before I could make out even to myself what it was that led me there.

As I entered, Lottka raised her head from the counter where it had been resting on her arm. Her eyes shewed that she had been asleep. The book, over which she had been tiring herself, fell from her lap as she rose.

"I have disturbed you, Miss Lottka," said I. "Forgive me, I will go away at once. I happened to be passing by—and as the night was so beautiful—as since yesterday you— Would you be so kind as to give me a glass of bishop, Miss Lottka?"

Strange that my usually reckless eloquence should so regularly fail me in the presence of this quiet creature!

"What have you been reading?" I began again after a pause, walking the while up and down the shop. "A book from the lending library? Such a torn shabby copy is not fit for your small white hands. Allow me —I have a quantity of charming books at home—romances too—"

"Pardon me," she quietly rejoined. "I have no time to read romances. This is a French Grammar."

"You are studying by yourself then?"

"I already speak it a little, I wish to understand it more thoroughly."

She relapsed into silence, and began to arrange the plates and spoons.

"Miss Lottka," said I after an interval, during which I had regained courage from a contemplation of the gruff old Blücher in the smaller room. "Are you happy in the position that you occupy at present?"

She looked at me out of her large weary eyes with the amazement of a child in a fairy-tale when suddenly addressed by a bird.

"How come you to put such a question?" she enquired.

"Pray do not attribute it to heartless curiosity," I went on, in my excitement upsetting a small pyramid of biscuits. "Believe that I feel a genuinely warm interest in you— If you need a friend—if anything has happened to you—you understand me— Life is so sad, Miss Lottka—and just in our youth—"

I was floundering deeper and deeper, and the drops stood on my brow. I would have given a good deal if that old Blücher had not encouraged me to make this speech.

However I was spared further humiliation. The door leading from the interior of the house opened, and the person to whom the shop belonged made her appearance. She seemed a good-natured square woman, with a thick cap-border, who explained to me as civilly as she could, that I had already remained a quarter of an hour beyond the usual time of shutting up, for that she was in the habit of putting out the gas at half-past ten. Accordingly I paid in all haste for my half-emptied glass, threw an expressive and half-reproachful glance at the silent girl, and went my way.

That night my couch was not one of roses. I made a serious attempt to finish my German essay:—"Comparison between the Antigone of Sophocles and the Iphigenia of Goethe," but what were either of these Hecubas to me? I began to scribble verses on the margin of the book, and their melody had so lulling an effect that not long after midnight I fell asleep in my chair, and in spite of the uncomfortable position never woke till morning, though in my verses I had confessed myself once more in love; and what of all the untoward circumstances of the case was the darkest, in love with the heart's choice of my best friend!

This too was my first waking thought on the following morning. I remember distinctly, however, that the misfortune which I clearly saw to be ours, did not after all make me actually miserable, nay that it rather exalted my self-complacency and rendered me very interesting in my own eyes, as I had now a chance of personally experiencing all that I had hitherto merely read of. I was never tired of conjuring up the disastrous and heart-rending scenes to which this complication must necessarily lead, and an indefinably pleasurable kind of pity for myself, for Sebastian, and for the innocent source of our woes suffused all my thoughts.

Instead of going to the gymnasium, where I should have had to appear without the German essay, I preferred to visit the "hedge-school" as the French say, that is to lounge about the park, and there on a lonely bench in the most out-of-the-way corner, commit my youthful sorrows to paper. Heine and Eichendorff were at that time contending for my immortal soul. On that particular morning I was not yet ripe for the irony of the "Buch der Lieder," and the tree-tops rustled too romantically above my head for the utterance of any tones but such as suited a youthful scapegrace. About noon I saw with melancholy satisfaction that the poem entitled "New Love," begun that morning, would form a very considerable addition to my volume, if it went on long at this rate.

In the afternoon when I sat, thinking no evil, in my room, and attempting to draw the profile of my secretly beloved one from memory, I heard Sebastian's step on the stair. I hastily hid away the sheet of paper, and dipped my pen in the ink-stand to seem as though I were interrupted at my work. When he entered I had not the heart to look up at him.

He too gave me a very cursory greeting, stretched himself out as usual in my arm chair, and began to smoke a short-pipe.

In about half-an-hour he asked,

"Have you been there again?"

"Yes," I replied, and seemed to be very busy looking out a word in my lexicon.

"And what do you think of her now?"

"What I think? I have not yet found out the riddle. So much, however, I know, that she is not a flesh and blood girl, but a water-nixie, a Melusina, 'cold even to her heart,' and who knows whether her very figure does not end like a mermaid's '*desinit in piscem?*'"

He sprang up. "I must beg you not to speak in such a tone!"

"Patience, old boy," said I. "Do not go and suppose that I think lightly of her. A past history she has that is quite clear. But why need there be any harm in it? Suppose there were only some misfortune, a great grief, or a great love?"

"You think so?" and he looked at me anxiously and sadly.

"I should not be at all surprised," I continued, "if she, with those precocious eyes and that wonderful composure, had already traversed the agonies of hopeless love. Do not forget her Polish father. Polish girls begin early both to excite and to feel passion. How the poor child ever got into that fly-trap, God knows. But you and I together should find it difficult to deliver her out of it."

After that followed a silent quarter of an hour, during which he turned over my MS. poems.

"I should like to copy out this song," he suddenly said, reaching out a page to me.

"What for?" asked I. "Bastel, I half suspect you want to pass it off as your own."

"Shame upon you!" returned he with a deep flush, "*I* give myself out for a poet! But I have a tune running in my head; it is long since I have composed anything."

"Look out something better and more cheerful.

What could you make of that feeble-minded whimper? That song is half a year old" (dated from that 'olden time' that I could not myself distinctly remember!)

He had taken back the sheet, and was now bending over it, being somewhat short-sighted, and singing in a low voice the following verses to a simple pathetic melody:

> "How could I e'er deserve thee,
> By serving long years through;
> Though thou wert fain to own me,
> Most stedfast and most true.
> Or what though high exalted,
> Though glory were my meed:
> Love is a free gift from above,
> Desert it will not heed.
>
> Thou tree with head low bending,
> Thy blossoms may prove vain;
> Who knows if God will send thee
> The blessing of his rain?
> Thou heart by joy and anguish
> Proved and refined indeed:
> Love is a free gift from above,
> Desert it will not heed."

He sprang up, just gave me an absent nod, and rushed out of the room.

Not long after I went out myself. I had no particular object, except to quiet the tumult in my veins by bodily fatigue.

After walking with great rapidity about the town for an hour or so, I found myself unintentionally in the neighbourhood of the mysterious street. It attracted and repelled me both. I had a dim consciousness of not having played a very creditable part the night before. I was pretty sure that the young stranger who had so zealously offered himself as her knight, would be greeted by a satirical smile by Lottka. But that was reason the more, I argued, for seeking to give her a better impression of me. And therefore I plucked up courage, and rapidly turned the corner.

At the same moment I was aware of my friend and rival, his cap pressed down on his brow, advancing with great strides towards the small green house, from a contrary direction. He too was aware of me, and we each of us came to a halt and then turned sharp round the following moment as though we had mistaken our way.

My heart beat wildly. "Shame upon our ridiculous reserve and suspicion of each other!" I inwardly cried, feeling that if this went on I should soon hate my best friend with my whole heart.

I was in the angriest of moods while retracing my steps, and reflected whether the wisest and most manly course would not be to turn round again and take my chance even if a whole legion of old friends stood in my way. Had I not as much right as another to make a fool of myself about the girl? Was I timidly to draw back now after speaking out so boldly yesterday and offering myself as champion to the mysterious enchantress? Never! I'd go to her at once though the world fell to pieces!

I turned in haste—there stood Sebastian. In my excitement I had not even heard his quick steps following me.

"You here!" I cried in counterfeit amazement.

"Paul," he replied, and his melodious voice slightly trembled. "We will not act a part. *We*—we have been fond of each other, you and I. But believe me if this were to go on I could not stand it. I know where you are going: I was bound the same way myself. You love her—do not attempt to deny it. I found it out at once."

"And what if I do love her?" cried I, half-defiant and half-ashamed. "I confess that the impression she has made on me—"

"Come here under the gateway," said he. "We are blocking up the way, and you speak so loud you will attract attention. You see I was right; indeed I should have been surprised if it had not turned out thus. But you will agree that it is impossible to go on. One or other must retire."

"Very well," returned I, endeavouring to assume an inimical and dogged expression. "One of us must retire. Only I do not see why it should be I. Just because I am the younger by two stupid years, though as advanced a student as yourself."

I had hardly spoken the hasty heartless words before I regretted them. At that moment they sounded like a humiliating boast.

"Besides," I hastily added, "it does not signify so much which of us takes precedence, as who it is she cares for. At present you and I seem to have equally poor prospects."

"That is true," he said. "But none the less I cannot find it in my heart to enter into a contest with you; and then you are the bolder, the more fluent, I should give up the game beforehand if we were both to declare our feelings for her: you know what I mean."

"If this be so," I rejoined, looking with artificial indifference through the dark gateway into a garden where a lonely rose-tree blossomed; "if you have not more confidence in yourself than this, you cannot after all be so much in love as you suppose, and as I can fairly say I am. I have spent a sleepless night" (I did not reckon those seven hours snatched in a chair) "and a wasted day. And so I thought—"

I could not end my sentence. The pallor of his good, true-hearted face shewed me how much more deeply he was affected by this conversation than I, for whom indeed it had a certain romantic charm. I felt fond of him again.

"Listen," said I, "we shall never get on this way. I see that neither of us will retire of his own free will. Fate must decide."

"Fate?"

"Or chance if you prefer it. I will throw down this piece of money. If the royal arms are uppermost, you have won; if the inscription—"

"Do so," he whispered. "Although it would be fairer—"

"Will you cry done?"

"Done!"

The coin fell to the ground. I stooped down in the dim light we were standing in to make sure of the fact.

"Which is uppermost?" I could hear him murmur, while he leaned against the door-post. He himself did not venture to look. "Bastel," said I, "it cannot be helped. The inscription is uppermost. You understand that having once appealed to the decision of Providence—"

He did not move, and not a sound escaped his lips. When I drew myself up and looked at him, I saw that his eyes were closed, and that he stood as if in a trance.

"Don't take it so to heart," said I. "Who knows but that in two or three days I may come and tell you that she does not suit me, that the field is open for you, and that—"

"Good night," he suddenly whispered, and rushed away at full speed.

I only remained behind for a moment. At this abrupt departure the scales fell from my eyes. I was conscious that my feelings for the mysterious being

were not to be compared with his, and that I should be
a villain if I were to take advantage of this foolish appeal to chance.

In twenty yards I had caught him up, and had to
employ all my strength to keep hold of him, for he was
bent on getting away.

"Hear me," I said. "I have changed my mind. Nay,
you *must* hear me, or I shall believe you were never in
earnest in your friendship for me. I solemnly swear,
Bastel, that I make way for you. I resign utterly and
for ever, every wish and every hope. I see it all clearly.
You could not recover it if she were to prefer me. I—
why I should make up my mind! You know one does not
die of it even if all one's dream-blossoms do not come
to fruit. Give me your hand, Bastel, and not another
word about it."

He threw himself on my breast. I meanwhile feeling
very noble and magnanimous, as though I had renounced a kingdom to which I was heir, in favour of
some cousin belonging to a collateral line. Any one
who had seen us walking on for an hour hand in hand,
and been aware that we were disposing of a fair creature who had probably never given either of us a
thought, could hardly have refrained from laughing at
so shadowy an act of generosity. I insisted upon
accompanying him at once to the shop. I was bent
upon proving that my sacrifice did not exceed my
strength. "Success to you!" I cried, as he turned the
handle of the door, and I shewed him a cheerful face.
And then I went away wrapped in my virtue, whose
heroic folds were full compensation for all that I had
resigned.

I slept so soundly that night, that I felt ashamed of
myself the next morning for not having dreamed of *her*.

Could it be that the flame of this "new love" had gone out thus suddenly, not leaving so much as a spark behind? I would not allow it to myself, and thereby diminish the importance of so tragic a collision. As it was Sunday I had plenty of time to give myself up undisturbed to my happy-unhappy sensations. A few verses written down that morning still linger in my memory:

> "Sad and consumed by envious desire,
> A Cinderella sits beside the fire:
> The hearth grows cold, the ashes fly about,
> There is no sunshine in the air without.
>
> Oh strange that friendship should so cruel prove
> As to inflict a pang on yearning *Love:*
> Pale and half-blind she weeps the long hours thro',
> Yet are they children of one mother too!
>
> Love decks herself and proudly lifts her head:
> More and more glows her cheek's soft rosy red:
> The pale one bears the weight of household care,
> In games and dances never claims a share.
>
> Yet when her sister comes home late at night,
> Poor Cinderella laughs and points with spite:
> ' Blood's on your shoe for all you're gaily drest,'
> And thus she robs the proud one of her rest!"

And yet people persist in calling youth the time of unclouded bliss—youth, which through mere mental confusions and self-invented tortures lets itself be cheated out of heaven's best gifts; counterfeits feelings in order to achieve unhappiness, and passionately presses the unattainable to its heart!

About a fortnight may have sped away without my ever seeing my fortunate rival except by accidental glimpses. From some delicate scruple, for which I gave him full credit, he left off climbing the stair to my study as heretofore, and if we met in the streets we soon parted with a commonplace word or two, and a pretty cool shake of the hand.

However, by the time we reached the third week, this estrangement became intolerable to me. It was holiday time; the days were too hot for work or exercise, and I even found the Castalian fount run dry. I became aware that the silent presence of my friend had grown to be a positive want. I longed even to hear his deep voice sing once more, "I think in the olden days," and was as uncomfortable in my isolation as Peter Schlemihl when he had lost his shadow.

At last I determined to seek him out. He lived the other side of the Spree in an upper room of a house belonging to a tailor's wife, by whom his cooking was done, and his few wants attended to. I must just mention here that he received a very small allowance from his family, and made up the deficit by giving music-lessons, for which indeed he was but poorly paid.

When I entered his little room he was sitting at an old, hired piano, and writing down some notes in a music-book on his knee. He jumped up with an exclamation of pleasure, let the book fall, and caught hold of my hand in both his. He made me sit down on the hard sofa and light a cigar, and spite of all I could say, would have me drink a glass of beer which the tailor's wife fetched from the nearest tavern. At first we said but little, as was our wont, but often looked at each other, smiled, and were heartily glad to be together again.

"Bastel," said I at length, shrouding myself as completely as I possibly could in tobacco-smoke, "I have a confession to make. You need no longer keep up any reserve with me about—you know what. The wound inflicted by a certain pair of eyes" (again the old lyrical style, this time with a touch of Spanish colour), "either was not so deep as I at first believed it, or else absence has done wonders. Suffice it that I am perfectly recovered, and if you have turned these last weeks to good account and been made happy, I shall rejoice with you unqualifiedly."

He looked at me with beaming eyes. "Is it really so?" he said. "Well, then, I can tell you, you remove a great weight from my heart. I have reproached myself a hundred times for accepting your sacrifice, and my best hours with her have been embittered by the thought of having done you wrong. I did not indeed feel sure that you would have been satisfied with what made me so happy. And besides I felt that it would have been wholly impossible for me to have renounced her. But now— now all is right."

And. again he pressed my hand, his joy so genuine and touching that I felt myself and my artificially excited feelings, very small indeed in comparison.

He then went on to tell me how far matters had advanced. It certainly did require a modest nature, and a very sincere affection, not to be rather disheartened than encouraged by the amount of progress made in the course of three entire weeks. He had gone evening after evening, to spend an hour in that small reading-room. It was plain that his silent reverential homage had touched her, and the last few evenings she had permitted herself to sit with him, and keep up an innocent chat. Once even, when he was two hours later than usual, she received him with evident agitation, and confessed that his delay had made her anxious. She had become, she said, so accustomed to their daily talk, and as there was no one else who took the least interest in her; and then she stopped—perhaps because he too vehemently expressed his delight at this her first kind word. He, for his part, had told her all about his relations, and everything connected with himself that could in any way interest her. But she had not confided to him the very slightest particulars about her family or her past history, had only said how she was pining in this dark shop-corner, and longed to go far away into foreign lands. She had been putting by, she told him, for a year past to meet travelling expenses; and privately teaching herself both French and English in order to go into the wide-world at the first opportunity. "If you had only seen her, Paul," said he at the end of his narrative, "and only heard her voice, how sadly and resignedly she told me all this, you would have pledged your life that no evil thought had ever stirred her heart, that she was as pure and innocent as saints and angels are said to be, and you would understand my resolve to leave nothing undone in order to make her happy."

"You really then mean to marry her?"

"Can you doubt it? That is if she will accept me. She must have plainly seen that my intentions were honourable, although, as to any formal declaration, you know that my heart overflows least when it is fullest. And besides there is no hurry. She cannot be thinking of leaving for some time to come, and as for me—if I make great efforts in four or five years—"

"Four or five years? Why, you will scarcely have passed your legal examination."

"True," he rejoined. "But I have given up the idea of it. I shall not seat myself on the long bench of law students, which is but a rickety one after all. I think I can in a shorter time make something of music, and at the worst if we are not able to get on here—and indeed my parents would hardly be pleased at the marriage—we can seek our fortune in America."

I looked at him sideways with pride and amazement.

He seemed to me to have suddenly grown ten years older, and I confessed to myself that all the lyrical enthusiasm of my views of life, would not have rendered me capable of so bold a plan.

"And she," I asked; "will she consent to this?"

"I do not know," he replied, looking straight before him. "As I told you before, I have never asked her point-blank. Our talk once turned on marriage. She said most positively she should never marry. 'Not if the right man appeared?' I ventured to put in. 'Then least of all,' said she suppressing a sigh. So one of us is wise it seems."

"Nonsense," said I. "All girls say the same to begin with. Afterwards they think better of it."

"It seems, too, that she is a year older than we thought—only a month younger than I am. Apropos, I have a request to make to you; that is, if you are able—"

"Come, no preamble. You know that I am never shy of asking you to do me a favour."

"To-morrow is her birthday. I had just contrived to find out the date, when she said that she already felt herself very old, and was weary of life. That if she knew she were to die on the morrow it would give her no regret. I was busy just when you came in, writing out the air of one of your songs: you know the one beginning, 'How could I e'er deserve thee?' and I meant to give her a nosegay with it. But it does grieve me to think that I have nothing better to offer her. She has her dress fastened with an old black pin, and its glass head is cracked. A little brooch would be sure to please her—only unluckily my piano and singing lessons are over just now, most of my pupils are away, and so I cannot get at some fees that are owing; and to sell any of my effects is impossible, since all the superfluities I had—"

He looked with sad irony around his bare apartment.

"We must contrive something," I said. "It stands to reason that the birthday must be duly honoured. Certainly I am no Crœsus at this moment,"—and therewith I drew out a very small purse from my pocket, in which rattled only a few insignificant coins—"but at all events I have some superfluities. It now occurs to me that I have not used the great *Passow* for some months, never indeed, since I accidentally discovered little *Rost* at my father's, in which one can hunt out words so much more conveniently. Come! The old folios will help us out of a difficulty."

After a few weak endeavours to prevent my laying this offering upon the altar of friendship, he accompanied me to my room, and then we each loaded ourselves with a volume of the thick lexicon. And an hour later, richer by five dollars, we betook ourselves to the shop of a small working-goldsmith, as we had not courage to make our intended purchase at one of the great jewellers of *Unter den Linden*.

It is probable that our man taxed us no less heavily. But, however, he treated us like two young princes, who in Haroun-al-Raschid mood had chosen to knock at a lowly door. For a gold snake which after a few coils took its tail into its mouth, and glared at us with two square ruby eyes, he asked ten dollars, but let himself be beat down to seven, the pin being probably worth about half that sum. It was I who had to carry on the whole transaction. Sebastian was so embarrassed, and absorbed himself so persistently in the contemplation of the other ornaments on the counter, that the shopkeeper evidently grew suspicious, and kept a sharp look out after him, as though he might be having to do with pickpockets.

"Here is the trinket," said I, when we got into the street, "and now good night, and I say—you may just congratulate her from me too to-morrow. But indeed I ought to hope that she has forgotten all about me. I certainly did not display my best side to her. Let me see you again soon, and come and tell me what effect the snake has produced in thy Paradise, happy Adam that thou art."

And so I left him, conscious of a faint glimmer of envy. But I manfully trod out the first sparks, and as I walked along the park in the cool of the evening, sang aloud the following song, which apart from the anachronism of budding roses in the dog-days, gave a pretty faithful description of the mood I was then in:

> "'The roses are almost full-blown,
> Love flings out his delicate net:
> 'Thou butterfly fickle and frail
> Away thou shalt never more get.'
>
> 'Ah me! were I prisoner here,
> With roses all budding around,
> Though satisfied Love wove the bands,
> My Youth would repine to be bound.
>
> No musing and longing for me—
> I stray thro' the woods as I will.
> My heart on its pinions of joy
> Soars beyond and above them still!'"

The following evening I was sitting innocently and unsuspiciously with my parents at the tea-table, when I was called out of the room: a friend it seemed wished to speak to me. It was about ten o'clock, and I wondered who could be paying me so late a visit.

When I entered my room I found Sebastian as usual

in the grand-paternal arm-chair, but I started when, turning the light on his face, I noticed his pallor and look of despair.

"Is it you?" cried I. "And in such agitation? Has the birthday celebration come to a tragic end?"

"Paul," said he, still motionless, as though some heavy blow had stretched him out there. "All is over! I am a lost man!"

"You will find yourself again, my good fellow," I replied. "Come, let me help to look for you. Tell me all about it to begin with."

"No jesting if you would not drive me out of the room. I tell you it is all too true. I have only now fully discovered what an angel she is, and I have seen her for the last time."

"Is she gone away—gone to a distance?"

He shook his head gloomily. Only by very slow degrees could I extort from him the cause of his despair. Briefly it was as follows: He had found himself in the presence of his beloved at the usual hour, and after eating an extra tart and drinking a glass of bishop in honour of the day, he had brought out the gifts with which he meant to surprise her in a sequence which seemed well advised. First he had freed the bouquet from its paper coverings, and she had thanked him with a kindly glance, and put it at once in a glass of water. Then he gave her the song, and sang it for her under his voice, she sitting opposite with downcast eyes, and giving not the slightest sign by which to judge whether she saw its application or not. Only when he had ended she held out her hand—a favour of which she was chary—and said in a cordial tone: "It is very kind of you to have thought of my birthday, and to have brought me such beautiful flowers and such a charming song. There is nothing I love so much as flowers and music, and I very seldom come in for either. I shall soon know the tune; indeed I half know it now." He could not part with the hand given him, and as her graciousness had inspired him with courage, he now brought out the serpent-pin, and placed it in her hand. "Here is something else," he said; "it is but a humble offering, but I should be very happy if you would not disdain to wear it."

She looked full at him, opened the little case slowly and with evident reluctance, and as soon as she saw the shining of the gold, dropped it on the table as though the metal had been red-hot. "Why have you done this?" she said, hastily rising. "I have not deserved it from you— at least I do not think I have behaved in such a way as to authorise you to make me a present like this. I see I have been mistaken in you. You, too, think meanly of me because I am poor and dependent. I cannot conceal that this pains me, from you of all people," and her eyes grew moist. "Now I can only request that you will instantly leave me, and never return," and with that she laid the flowers and song down before him on the table, and spite of his distracted assurances and entreaties, with burning face and tearful eyes she contrived to elude him, and not only left the little inner room, but the shop as well.

It was in vain that he awaited her return; in her stead the square-built woman entered, but apparently without the least idea of what it was that had scared the young girl away. A full half-hour he continued in a most miserable state of mind to occupy his accustomed seat on the sofa. But as she remained invisible, he at length took his departure, and once in the street, plucked the nosegay to pieces, and tore up the song into shreds, and—"There," he cried, "is that wretched pin that has made all the mischief, you may take it, and give it to whom you will! I could hardly resist the temptation as I came along to open a vein with it."

"And is that all?" enquired I coolly, when he had come to an end of his shrift.

He sprang up as if to rush away. "I see I might have spared myself this visit!" he cried. "You are in so philosophical a mood that a friend expiring at your side would seem nothing to wonder at. Good-night."

"Stay," I remonstrated. "You ought to be very glad that one of us at least has the use of his five senses. The story of the pin is a mere trifle. Who knows whether she did not reject it after all from the superstitious fancy that pins pierce friendship. Or even if there were more in it, if she actually felt a suspicion that you meant it as a bribe, that is still no cause for desperation; on the contrary she has proved that she is a good girl, and respects herself; and if you go to her in the morning as though nothing had happened, and in your own true-hearted way explain—"

"You forget she has forbidden me to return."

"Nonsense! I would bet anything that she is already very sorry she did so. Such a faithful Fridolin is not to be met with every day, and whatever she may think she feels for you—whether much or little—she would be conscious of missing something if you left off eating your two cherry tarts daily, and she no longer had to strew the sugar over them with her little white hand. Teach me to understand women indeed!"

He gazed for a long time at the lamp. "You would do me a kindness by going there with me and explaining matters for me. She would at least allow you to speak; and if you were to bear witness for me—"

"Willingly. I shall say things to her that would melt a heart of stone. Trust me, this serpent will not long exclude thee from thy Paradise, or Miss Lottka is not that daughter of Eve, which hitherto much to her honour I have held her to be."

He pressed my hand as if somewhat relieved, but was still gloomy, and I soon lighted him down the stairs.

——— ———

I had a very beautiful and touching address all ready composed when we set out the next evening on our common mission, and my poor friend gave me plenty of time to rehearse it, for he never said a word. When we approached the shop he drew his arm out of mine, I was not to find out that he was beginning to tremble!

I myself was not thoroughly at ease. To see her again after so long an interval, and now to address her on behalf of another—I was fully conscious of the difficulty of the position, but my honour was pledged to play my part well, and to guard against any selfish relapse into my old folly.

When we entered she was not alone. For the first time we found a fashionable-looking man in the shop, sitting on a stool close to the counter, and while drinking a glass of lemonade, trying apparently to make himself agreeable to the young attendant. Sebastian's melancholy visage darkened still more at this spectacle, although the calm manner and monosyllabic replies of the girl might have convinced him that the conversation of this coxcomb was as displeasing to her as to us.

"We shall soon drive him away," whispered I, and

ordering wine and cakes with the air of an habitual customer, I together with my mute companion took possession as usual of the familiar inner-room.

I had, however, reckoned without my host. The stranger, who now carried on his conversation in a lower tone, appeared to have no idea of vacating his place in our favour. I was able to contemplate him at leisure in the small mirror that hung between the royal pair. His hair cut short round a head already bald at the top, his light whiskers, and the gold spectacles on his pinched nose, were all highly objectionable to me; and I wondered too at the insolent familiarity of his manner, and the careless way in which he crumbled a heart-shaped cake in his white effeminate hands, as if to typify his facility in breaking hearts. I took him for a young nobleman or landed proprietor, and little as I feared his making an impression upon the girl, yet it was annoying to me to see her exposed in her position to the attentions of such a man. I was even concocting some bold plan of getting rid of this incumbrance, when I felt Sebastian convulsively clutch my arm.

"What is the matter?" I said. "Are you going mad?" Instead of answering, he pointed to the mirror, in which he too could see a portion of the shop reflected. "Impudent fellow!" he muttered between his teeth, "he shall not do that a second time."

I had just time to see that the stranger was bending over the counter, and trying to take the girl—who had retreated as far as ever she could—under the chin, when my friend, having noisily pushed away the table before us, confronted him with flushed cheeks and flashing eyes.

"What do you mean, sir!" he began, and his deep voice put out all its strength. "Who are you that you dare to take a liberty with a blameless girl—a girl who—"

His rage actually choked him. He stood with hand raised, as if determined to punish any fresh act of audacity on the spot, while the stranger, who had drawn back a step, measured this unexpected champion from top to toe with a look, half amazement, and half compassion.

"The bishop is too strong for your head, young friend," said he in a sharp tone, while he twirled his smart cane between finger and thumb. "Go home before you talk further nonsense, and be more careful another time, for you may not always meet with persons who can take your greenness into proper account. What I was saying to you, Lottka—"

And therewith he turned as if his opponent had already vanished out of sight and mind, and addressed the girl, who, pale as death and with eyes closed, was leaning back in the furthest corner between the window and the wall.

I had followed Sebastian, and whispered to him to take care what he was about, but he never heard me.

"I only wanted to ask you, Fräulein," he said in a hollow voice, "whether it is with your consent that this gentleman allows himself to take such liberties with you as are not generally permitted by respectable young ladies; whether you know him sufficiently well to justify him in using your Christian name, and whether it is agreeable to you that he should remain talking to you so long?"

She did not answer. She only raised her large eyes entreatingly to the angry lover who did not understand their glance.

"Who is this amiable youth, who plays the part of

8*

your knight, Lottka?" now asked the stranger in his turn. "I begin to suspect that I have interfered with some tender relations between you. I am sincerely sorry for it, but still, my child, without venturing to impugn your taste, I would advise you in future to pay more attention to solid advantages in the choice of your adorers. The declamations of schoolboys are no doubt pretty to listen to, but they may lead as you see to awkward consequences. What do I owe?"

He threw a dollar on the table.

"You can give me the change another time. I will not disturb you further just now."

He took his hat and was about to leave when Sebastian barred the way.

"You shall not go," said he in a constrained voice, "before you have in my presence apologised to this young lady, and given your word of honour never again to forget the respect due to her. I hope you understand me."

"Perfectly, my young friend," replied the other, his voice now trembling with excitement. "I understand that you are a crazy enthusiast, and take the world for a raree-show. I do not grudge you your childish amusement, and esteem you accordingly; but I have no wish further to prosecute your acquaintance, lest a joke should turn to earnest, and I should be forced—spite of the lady's presence—to treat you like a young whipper-snapper who—"

Here he made a pretty unequivocal movement with his cane. I had just time and sense enough to interfere.

"Sir," said I, "I have to request your card; we can best settle this matter in another place."

He laughed loud, drew out his pocket-book with an

ironical bow, and reached me a visiting-card. Then he nodded familiarly to the girl, shrugged his shoulders, and pressing his hat low down on his brow, left the shop.

We three remained for several moments in the same position as if we had been touched by a magic wand.

I as the least deeply implicated was the first to recover myself.

"For God's sake, Fräulein," said I to the pale statue in the window, "tell us who this man is. How comes he to behave so to you? Since when have you known him?" Then in a lower tone. "I pray you by all that is good, speak, if but one word. You see the state my friend is in; this concerns him more deeply than you are aware. You do not perhaps know that there is nothing more sacred to him than yourself; you owe it to him—"

He seemed to have heard what I said. With a sudden gesture as though shaking off some heavy weight, he tottered to the counter, behind which she stood entrenched and unapproachable.

"Only one word, Lottka," he murmured. "Do you know that insolent man? Have you ever given him cause so to think of and speak to you? Yes or No, Lottka?"

She was silent, and her hands hung down helplessly by her side. I could plainly see two great tears forcing their way between her lashes.

"Yes or No, Lottka," he repeated more urgently, and his breast heaved fast. "I wish to know nothing further. Do not imagine that the first rude fellow I come across, has any power to shake my holiest convictions. But how was it you had not a word to crush him with? Why are you silent now?"

A convulsive shiver passed over the young girl's frame. With eyes still closed she felt for her chair in the window, but did not seat herself—sank down on her knees beside it, and hid her face against it. "I beseech you," she murmured in an almost inaudible voice, "do not ask anything about me—go away—never come here again. If it can in any way comfort you, I am innocent so surely as God lives; but so unfortunate that it is almost worse than if I were a sinner too. Go away. I thank you for all you have done, but go, and forget that I am in the world. I would I were in another!"

"Lottka!" cried Sebastian wildly, about to rush in and raise her up, but that she put out her hands to ward him off with such a lamentable gesture that I held him back; and after a struggle, during which I represented to him that they were both too excited at present to understand each other, I persuaded him to leave the poor child to herself, and we went off, promising to return on the morrow.

We walked in silence through the streets. It was impossible to tell him that the scene we had witnessed had considerably shaken my faith in his beloved. For the rest I was perfectly satisfied with the part he had played, and owned to myself that I should have done just the same in his place.

It was only when we reached the door of my house that he broke silence. "You must do me the favour," he said, "to go to that man very early in the morning" (we had read his name and address on his card; he was an assessor at the Town Court). "I leave all details to you."

"Of course," I returned, "it stands to reason that I should do all I can for you; but in this matter—I have never delivered a challenge, and have only twice seen a duel of any kind; and in this case, as I believe, we must employ pistols. If you knew any one more conversant with such matters?—one would like to do things in the regular way with a fellow like this, who treats us both like schoolboys."

"You are probably right," said he. "But there is no help for it. I can have no third party admitted into this affair. It is possible that he may make some disclosures to you—invent more calumnies—how should I know? So everything must be kept to ourselves. I shall be at home all the morning, and as soon as you have done with him you will come straight to me, will you not."

That I promised, and we parted. What my parents must have thought of me that evening, when I gave crooked answers to every question put, Heaven only knows.

That night in good truth I really slept very little. I kept thinking of all that might ensue, hearing pistol-shots fired, and seeing my poor friend fall. But I was also much engaged in puzzling over Lottka's conduct, and came more and more strongly to the belief that she was not worth an honest true-hearted youth throwing down the gauntlet in her cause, and answering for her virtue with his life.

The day had scarcely dawned before I was up, but on this occasion I had no idea of verse-making. I dressed myself at first entirely in black like an undertaker's assistant; then it occurred to me it might be better to be less carefully got up, and rather to treat the matter with indifference, as though such things daily occurred to me. So I merely put on a comfortable summer attire, just substituting a black hat for the cap I usually wore, and drawing on a pair of perfectly new gloves. When I looked in the glass, I viewed myself as decidedly grown up, and also decidedly easy-going and dignified. But for all that I could make nothing of my breakfast. I had a bitter taste on my tongue.

About nine o'clock I set out. The house in which our enemy lived stood in the best part of the town, and the porter told me he did not think it would be easy to get an interview with the assessor. Nevertheless a footman, although certainly treating me rather *de haut en bas*, ushered me into a small room, and signified that his master would soon appear.

I had plenty of time to look about me, and firmly resolved as I was not to be cowed by outward circumstances, I could not help feeling, while silently comparing this elegant bachelor's snuggery with the four bare walls of my friend's room, that the game was very unequal. Two raw half-fledged novices pitted against a thorough man of the world, and not even perfectly certain that we had the right on our side. I owned to myself that we were in a fair way to act a ridiculous part, and all my lyrical idealism was powerless against the awkwardness of prosaic facts.

The longer I waited, the more I made up my mind to see our enemy enter with a mocking smile, and asked myself how to meet it with becoming dignity. But to my surprise there was nothing of the kind.

In about ten minutes the door opened, and the assessor just put in his head, saying in the most urbane tone possible, that he was very sorry to be obliged to keep me waiting, not being quite dressed, but that he begged me in the meantime to use his cigars and make myself at home.

Another five minutes, and in he came, shook my hand like an old acquaintance, and begged me to be seated on his silk-covered divan. I had to light a cigarette, but declined to share his breakfast which the footman brought in on a silver tray, and I was looking out for the pleasantest introduction possible to our affair, when he anticipated me, and while pouring out his tea began in quite a friendly tone—

"I am very glad you have come. I can easily imagine what brings you, and I may frankly tell you that yesterday's scene to which I owe your acquaintance, made upon me a most painful impression. You will easily understand that it is by no means pleasant to have a youth—an utter stranger—fall upon one out of a clear sky with a perfect torrent of invective. But on the other hand, I am sufficiently versed in human nature to be able to explain the very peculiar conduct of your Hotspur of a friend. He is in love with the little girl, and in that shows very fair taste. He has diligently read romances and old legends, and thinks he has gained from them a knowledge of the world. This sweet illusion will vanish all too soon, but while it lasts it makes so happy, that it is positive cruelty to blow away its soap-bubbles prematurely. I at least would never deprive any one of his innocent enjoyment. And so I am sincerely sorry to have disturbed any tender tie. I hope your friend will be content with this explanation, and for my part I wish him pleasant dreams, and when the time comes as gentle a waking as possible. The cigar does not seem to draw well? Try another. What are you studying if I may ask? You are still a student, are you not?"

I felt myself blush crimson. For a moment I doubted whether I would not deny my position. However I stuck to the truth. "We shall pass our final examination at Easter," I said.

He was magnanimous enough not to misuse his superiority.

"So young," he said, with a good-natured shake of the head, "and already such Don Juans! You seem entitled to fair hopes, my young friend, and if you would only accustom yourself to more self-restraint—"

"Forgive me," said I, "but I must return to the matter in hand. My friend, as you rightly perceive, has a serious affection for this girl, and feels himself deeply aggrieved by the disrespectful manner in which you behaved to her. I believe he might be satisfied by a few lines in your handwriting, expressing your regret for your conduct to Fräulein Lottka. If not—"

He looked askance at me with such amazement, that I felt suddenly paralysed.

"Are you really in earnest?" he said. "You look too intelligent for me to believe that you can approve of this commission you have undertaken for your friend. My conduct to Fräulein Lottka! That is going a little too far! No, my good friend, let us make ourselves as little absurd as we can. Have you considered what you are proposing to me? With all the respect to the honourable feelings and true-heartedness of a student of the upper class, can he seriously imagine that I owe him reparation, because in a public shop I chanced to stroke a girl under the chin." He burst out laughing, and threw the end of his cigarette out of the window.

I rose. "I doubt," I said, "that this will satisfy my friend. If you would at least declare that you know nothing of Fräulein Lottka, which casts a shadow on her reputation."

"Just sit down, and hear me out," he broke in.

"Now that I see you are really in earnest, it is my duty to tell you the truth in the interests of your friend who takes up the case so tragically, that he is sure to commit himself to some folly. About ten years ago I was acquainted with a lady of a certain character here in Berlin. She was a German, but bore a Polish name, that of her first lover, a Polish nobleman, who had left her, *plantée là*, with one child. As she was beautiful and not inconsolable, she found plenty of adorers, and lived in wealth, keeping a small gambling-house too; and I can well remember the strange impression it made on me when first I entered it, to see a child of eight years old sitting at the faro table, looking at the gold heaps with her great sleepy eyes, and then at her mother and her friends, till the Champagne, of which she seemed to like a sip, took effect, and she fell asleep on a sofa amidst laughter, the rattling of money, and very free talk indeed. I was sorry for the pretty child, and it crossed my mind that she could have little respect for her mother, who exercised no sort of self-control even in her presence. After a few years I broke off the connection, which proved a very expensive one, but I heard in a roundabout way that the Polish Countess—as we used to call her—went on still in her old course, except that she relied less on her own attractions, and called in younger faces to her aid. I enquired casually after her daughter, but the conversation had turned, and I received no answer.

"Well—yesterday as I chanced to be passing by that miserable cake-shop, thinking of anything else than of this old story, I saw an old lady getting into a cab at the door, while the shop-girl put in the various parcels of purchases. When she turned round to re-enter the shop, I recognized the child with the weary eyes, now grown up into a beauty, who might, if she chose, enter into formidable competition with her mother. As I had nothing particular to do, I followed her into the shop, reminded her of our old acquaintance, and was not a little surprised to find her just as rigid and unapproachable as her lady-mamma was the reverse. With all my long practice in cross-examination, I was only able to get out from her that she had parted from her mother three years ago, but as to what she had been doing since, or through how many hands she had passed, or whether her icy manners were artificial or natural, that I had not been able to unravel, when our Orlando Furioso, your excellent friend, suddenly burst in upon us. And now, after I have given you this explanation, you may yourself judge, whether the idea of my coming forward to vouch for the poor child's character or having to fight with an enthusiastic boy about her virtue is not quite too absurd!

"No, no," he continued, "if you have any influence over your friend, my dear fellow, do warn him not to go too far. For even if the daughter were as yet perfectly pure, what good could come of it with such antecedents, and such a mother? Your friend is the son of respectable people, tell him that he must not compromise his parents and himself—a mere passing liason, *à la bonne heure!* but to stake his very heart's blood, and to interfere with fire and sword, *allons donc!*—I do hope you may be able to bring him to reason; and now you must excuse me, I have a case coming on."

He had risen, while I still sat petrified by such a revelation; then he called his servant, and after reciprocal assurances of high esteem, had me shewn out. I tottered down the steps like a drunkard.

____

It was not for an hour afterwards—I needed a long circumbendibus before I could take heart to bring this melancholy business to an end—that I found myself knocking at Sebastian's door. A faint voice bade me come in, and then I found the unhappy fellow lying dressed upon his bed, and one glance at his disordered hair and attire shewed that he had spent the night in that fashion. Before I could say a word, he held out a letter that was open beside him on the pillow. A boy had brought it very early in the morning, but had not waited for an answer.

Of course I do not pretend to give the exact words in which it was couched, but their purport was as follows:

"You had scarcely left me when the idea struck me that the dispute of which I was the miserable cause, might have fearful consequences. I write to you to entreat and beseech you, if there were any earnestness in the feelings you professed for me, to let the matter drop, and to believe that in reality *I am not worthy*" (these words were doubly scored) "that you should sacrifice yourself for me. Promise me that you will try to forget me utterly. I am a poor lost creature, and only death can deliver me. But I shall not die yet, so have no anxiety on that head. I will try whether it be possible for me to live without my misfortune dogging every step I take. I thank you for all your love and kindness, and I never shall forget you. But do not attempt to find me out. I am firmly resolved never to see you again, and you will only increase my misery if you do not obey my wishes, but attempt to force a meeting."

The letter had neither address nor signature, it was firmly written, and there was not a mistake throughout.

I silently returned him the letter, not liking at that moment to tell him that under the circumstances nothing could be more propitious than such a decided step on her part. But I gradually discovered that nothing in the letter impressed him so much as the pretty clear confession of her own liking for him. This it was he dwelt on; their separation seemed to him comparatively unimportant, probably not seriously resolved upon, and practically impossible.

I therefore felt myself bound no longer to keep back my information, and gave him an exact account of my interview with his enemy. To my surprise it did not seem to produce on him the overwhelming effect I had dreaded. He told me he had himself conjectured something of the kind, and much as he regretted it, it could in no way change his feelings, rather it could only increase his love to positive worship to find that she had worked herself free from such degrading relations, and was high-hearted enough to wish to bear alone a sorrow she had never deserved. He knew indeed, that he should have some obstacles to confront, as regarded his parents, friends, home, &c. But since she had plainly told him that he was dear to her, no cowardly scruples would prevent his making up to her for the sufferings brought on her by a cruel fate. If the world bespattered her pure life, he would wash it all away in his heart's blood.

He ran on in this half-feverish way, and his high-wrought enthusiasm, his innocent brave spirit so carried me along, that not only did I keep all objections to myself, but actually became of opinion that this was all exactly as it should be, and the one important matter now was to find out the young girl, and induce her to change her mind. I threw myself into a cab, and drove to the shop, hoping to get upon her track there. Sebastian remained at home; he did not venture contrary to her expressed command, to take any part in the search. We had settled to meet again at noon. Alas! I came back as ignorant as I went. The mistress of the confectionery business had only been apprised of the departure of her young shopwoman early that morning by an open note found on her table. None of the neighbours had seen her go away. Most of her effects were left behind, she had only taken with her some linen and a travelling-bag which the good woman knew her to possess, and could not now find. She had instantly given information to the police. But all in vain as yet —the poor child had utterly disappeared.

It was now that grief and the after effects of the excitement of weeks, began to tell severely upon my poor friend. He was in such utter despair that I at first feared for his reason; not because of his frantic outbursts, or delirious grief, but from a certain suppressed wildness that tried to smile while the teeth chattered, a quite aimless way now of walking, now standing still; speaking to himself and laughing loud, while the tears, of which he seemed unconscious, rolled down his cheeks. It was the first time that I had ever seen the elemental throes of a true and deep passion, and I was so shocked that I forgot all besides, and at all events never presumed to attempt consoling the poor fellow by commonplaces.

I remained with him the whole day and a good part of the night. It was only about midnight, when I saw that he was quite exhausted (he had not closed his eyes the previous night), that I yielded to his entreaties, and consented to leave him alone, after exacting a solemn promise from his landlady to listen how he went on, for that he was very ill. I knew he had no weapons of any kind, and I hoped that sleep would do him some good.

The next morning, however, I could not rest, reproached myself for having left him, and anxiously hurried to his lodgings. But there he was no longer to be found. His landlady gave me a note of two lines, in which he bade me farewell for the present. He could not rest till he had found her, but he would do nothing rash, for he was not unmindful of his other duties, and so I might confidently expect his return.

He had packed his knapsack, and taken his walking-stick with him. And the landlady told me he seemed to have had two or three hours sleep, for that his eyes looked clearer.

This was but meagre information, but I had to content myself with it. And moreover I was about to accompany my parents on a tour which kept me absent for several weeks. To the letters I wrote—for I was always thinking of him—no answers ever came, so on my return when my first walk led me to his lodgings, I was fully prepared to find an empty nest. I was the more rejoiced, therefore, when he himself opened the door, and I met a sad face, it is true, but free from the morbidly strained expression which had so much pained me.

That he had failed to meet with any traces of the lost one I guessed rather than actually heard from him. A melancholy indifference seemed to pervade him; he set about whatever was proposed, as one who took no part in it, whether for or against,—and what to me was most striking of all, his passion for music seemed completely over. He never sang a single note, never alluded to any composition, and would willingly have given up

his music-lessons, had he been able to live without
them. The mainspring of his nature seemed hopelessly
broken, something had got wrong which there was no
repairing.

In the following spring, when we both went to the
University, I used to see him almost daily. He regularly
attended law lectures, and had become member of a
society in which his admirable fencing and his now pro-
verbial taciturnity rendered him prominent, and I was
hoping that the incident which had so deeply affected
him would after all leave no bad results in his healthy
nature, when something occurred that tore open every
wound anew.

I will for the sake of brevity relate the sad tale con-
secutively, and not as I learned it from him, bit by bit,
and at long intervals.

It was the Christmas of 1847. He had resolved
upon spending the holidays—not as usual, in paying a
visit to his parents, but in the strenuous study of his
law-books, a long indisposition having thrown him back
considerably. I had in vain attempted to coax him to
come to us for this Christmas Eve. Indeed as a rule he
avoided parties, and if he ever did appear at a social
gathering, he usually made an unfavourable impression,
especially on ladies, because of his silence and his obstinate refusal to sing.

On this particular 24th of December, he spent
the whole day hard at work in his own room, got
his landlady to give him something to eat, and only
went out at five o'clock when it had grown too dark to
write, leaving instructions to keep up his fire, as he
should only spend an hour or so looking at the Christ-

mas market, and then return, and go on writing late into the night. When he got into the street, he felt the winter breeze refresh him. The intense cold of the last few days had somewhat abated, snow was falling lightly in large flakes, which he did not shake off, but liked to feel melting on his flushed face. His beard, which had grown into a very handsome one during the last year, and much improved his looks, was white with them.

Slowly he went through Königsstrasse to the Elector's Bridge. There were crowds of well-wrapped figures flitting about, who having made their purchases at the last moment, were now hurrying home fast, for already the windows were beginning to shine with Christmas candles. The solitary student worked his way through the throng, without that melancholy yearning for home which would, on this particular evening, have oppressed most youths, if compelled to spend it away from their own people. He had sent off presents to his parents and sisters two days ago, and this very evening expected a Christmas box from them, which, however, he felt no impatience about. No one could care less for any addition to his possessions than he did; indeed, since he had lost the one thing to which he had passionately clung, he had grown indifferent to all besides.

He stood for a while before the equestrian statue of the great elector, who in his snow mantle looked even more majestic and spectral than usual against the pale winter sky. Below, the stream, hemmed in by ice on either side, flowed darkly and silently on, and in one of the barges the bargeman had already lighted up a small Christmas tree, which sent out a radiance through the open door. A couple of red-cheeked children were standing by the lowly table, one blowing a penny trumpet, the other eating an apple, and the solitary observer on the bridge might have stood there long in contemplation of this humble idyll but that the human stream swept him along with it, and landed him in the very centre of the busy noisy Christmas market going on in the Schlossplatz.

He walked awhile up and down the chief passages between the booths, looking at the cheerful traffic of buyers and sellers, listening to the chattering of the monkeys, and the shrill screams of boys advertising their various wares; and silently he sighed, reflecting that he had positively no connection with the world in which the festival was so joyously kept, that it would be all one to him if he were suddenly transported to Sirius, amongst whose inhabitants he could not feel more alone than here. Then he suddenly resolved to cheer up, and actually hummed the tune "I think in the olden days." A garrulous saleswoman in a booth of fancy-goods now interrupted him, entreating him to look out some pretty trifle for his "lady-wife." At that he hurriedly turned off, and made for one of the less frequented alleys where small dealers were offering their penny-worths as bargains.

He had not proceeded far when a singular spectacle caught his eye. Before a booth of cheap toys stood a lady in an elegant fur-trimmed polonaise, such as were then worn, a square Polish hat on her head, and a thick veil drawn over her face to protect her from the snow, so that there was no seeing her features. She had put down her large muff on the counter before her, and with tiny hands in daintiest gloves was busy picking out various toys, and dividing them amongst a number of street-children who crowded closely about her, and struggled for these unexpected gifts in a very tumult of delight. A few expressive words on the part of the seller in the booth reduced them to something like order, and at length they all dispersed, their treasures tightly clutched in their little fists, but it was only a minority that said "thank you" to the giver.

"And now what have I to pay you for them all?" said the lady.

Her voice ran like an electric shock through the youth, who had approached unobserved.

"Lottka," he said in a whisper.

The lady turned round quickly, and her first impulse was to draw her veil closer about her face. Then, however, by the light of the booth lamps and the glare from the snow, she was able to recognize the figure that only stood two paces off. She hurriedly paid the sum required, turned to Sebastian, and held out her hand.

"It is you," she said, without showing any special excitement. "I had not expected ever to see you again. But I am only the more glad of it. Have you any engagement? Are you expected anywhere this evening? No? Then give me your arm. I too am free—quite free," she added with a singular expression. "It is so pleasant to walk about in the snow, and see so many happy faces. It seems to me sometimes as though it could not be necessary to take any great pains to be happy since so many are so, and so cheaply too. Do you not agree with me?"

He did not reply. The utterly unexpected meeting had positively stupefied him, and the quick way in which she spoke and moved was perplexing. She had at once hung upon his arm, whereas formerly she carefully avoided every touch, and now she walked on beside him, daintily putting down her little feet in the snow, her head bent, with a bright thoughtful expression, as though planning some mysterious surprise. He only dared to steal glances at her now and then. She had evidently grown, her features were rather more marked, but that added to her beauty, and her fur cap was wonderfully becoming.

"Fräulein Lottka," said he at length, "that I should find you here! You do not know—you would not believe how I have sought for you—how ever since—"

"Why should I not believe it?" she hastily replied. "Do you suppose I have not known that you were the only human being in the world who ever really loved me? That was the very reason why I was obliged to part from you. Your love and goodness deserved something better than to be made unhappy for my sake. It is enough that one wretched life should be destroyed, and even that is not very intelligible when one thinks that there is a Providence—but why should we talk of such melancholy subjects? Tell me what you have been doing all this while. Do you know that you are much better looking than you were? Your beard becomes you so well, and with it you have the same innocent eyes that would better suit a girl's face, and yet they can look brave and resolute enough too when they flash out at a villain.

"Forgive me," she went on, "for being so talkative, but you cannot guess how long I have been silent— almost *always*, since we parted. I had too much to think about. But now I have arranged it all, and since then I am quite happy. It is not very long ago that I have done so. Last night even I had quite too horrible thoughts; they actually pierced my brain like needles of ice. So I said to myself, 'there must be an end to this.' Neither man nor God can require any one to live on with thoughts like these. And after becoming quite clear about that, my spirits returned, and even my tongue is loosed again. But you are all the more silent. What is the matter with you? Are not you a little tiny bit glad that we can wander about together so confidentially, and feel the snow on our faces, and see so many poor men enjoying their Christmas Eve? I too wanted to make a festival for myself, and so I spent my last two dollars in an improvised Christmas gift. But it did not answer so very well either: unless one loves the person one gives to, there is not much pleasure in giving. Now I am sorry that I have no more money. You and I might so well have made presents to each other."

"O Lottka," said he, "now that I have found you again—that you are so kind to me—that you know how I love you—"

"Hush!" interposed she, "this may be felt, but not spoken of. For to-day everything is as sad as it ever was, and as utterly hopeless."

He stopped suddenly and looked full at her. "Hopeless," he groaned. "But are you aware that I know everything, and no more heed it than if it were some story going on in the moon. That I have no one in the world to consult but myself, and if my own father and my own mother—"

"For God's sake do not go on," she cried, with a look of distress, and placing her hand on his lips. "You do not know what you are saying, how horrible it is, and how you would one day repent it. You have a mother whom you can love and revere, and who loves nothing on earth better than you, and who is proud of you, and you would bring sorrow and shame on her? If you had rightly considered what that means—but we will say no more about it. Come—I will confess to you that I am hungry; since yesterday evening I have eaten nothing out of sheer disgust. I thought, indeed, I should never have a pure taste in my mouth any more, but since I have chatted so pleasantly with you, I feel much better. Take me where there is something to eat. And then we can still go on chatting away for a couple of hours, and you really must treat me, for as I said I have spent the last money I had in those toys."

At once he turned off into a side street, and rapidly led her to a small eating-house that he knew, which was generally empty at this hour. They were both lost in thought, and he was wondering, half in terror, half in rapture, at the way things had come about, and asking himself what turn they would take now. For although her dark allusions made him very anxious, yet on the other hand he found comfort in her free and frank manner towards him, and her clear recognition of his feelings for her.

"Here," said he, throwing open a small door over which a blue lamp was burning.

They entered a bright comfortable dining-room in which was only an elderly waiter with a green apron of the good old fashion, sitting half-asleep in a corner. He looked at the pair with some surprise, and then hastened off to bring what Sebastian had ordered.

"He takes us for brother and sister," whispered the young girl.

"Or for a newly-married pair on their travels. Ah, Lottka!" and he seized one of her little hands which she had just ungloved.

She heartily but without any embarrassment returned his passionate pressure. "It is charming here," said she, beginning to free herself from her warm wraps. "I do so rejoice to be for once with you thus before I—" She stopped short.

"What are you thinking of?" he enquired in great agitation. "This is not *really* to be the last time—"

"Do not ask me," said she. "I am provided for, you need have no anxiety for me. When I wrote you that little note I really did not know what would become of me. It was only at first that I was safe. While you and perhaps others were looking everywhere for me, I sat up in the attic of an old friend not far from that shop—the only friend I had, an asthmatic sempstress who used often to buy cough-lozenges from me, and got fond of me because I would put in a stitch for her now and then. The poor thing when at her worst was unable for weeks together to earn anything. It was at her door that I knocked in the night, and actually I remained a couple of months hidden there, for no one concerned himself about her, and I used to help her with her sewing, and to cook our frugal meals; but at last I could no longer endure life in such a cage. I had saved a little money, and meant to cross over into France, where no one would have known me. But I was stopped on the way, there was something wrong in my passport, and so I was of course transported back like a vagrant; and here in Berlin—but we will say nothing about it. I already feel that nausea coming back, and here is our supper, and I must not let that be spoiled."

He poured out for her a glass of the wine the waiter had brought, and pledged her. "Thou and I," he whispered gently.

"No, thou alone," she replied, and sipped at the glass.

"Is the Rhine wine too strong for thee?" asked he. "Shall I order Champagne?"

She shook her head vehemently. "I could not touch a drop of it. I drank it too early, and in too bad company. But you must eat with me if I am to enjoy my supper."

He put something on his plate, though he could not get a morsel down, and kept watching her while she did full justice to their simple meal. Her hair was cut as short as ever, her dress was quite as plain, her form so full and so supple that each movement she made was enchanting to contemplate. Every now and then she apologized for her appetite.

"It is only," she said, "because I am for once happy, and everything is so good, and we are so delightfully alone—you and I. There"—and she put a bit of game from her plate on to his—"you must positively eat that, or I shall believe you have a horror of eating from the same dish even as I. If things had been different, and we could really have travelled off together through the world—that would have been beautiful! But it cannot be, and some day you will be happy with some one else, and she with you; lots are very unequally divided, and one must put up with one's own till it gets too bad. But do pour me out some wine—I drank that last glass off unconsciously. Thanks—and now—to thy mother's health! And that shall be the last."

She emptied the glass, and as she put it down again, he noticed that she shuddered as if some ice-cold hand had suddenly grasped hold of her.

"Let us go," she said.

He paid the bill and again offered her his arm. When they got out they found that the large soft flakes had changed into a driving snow-storm, that met them full in the face.

"Where shall we go now?" asked he.

"It is all the same to me. I have no longer any home. I thought indeed—but it is quite too boisterous and wretched to take leave of each other in the open air. Are we far from your lodgings?"

"I am in the old quarters still. Over the bridge, and then only a hundred yards. Come."

"That is—" said she, holding him back as if considering. "What will the people you lodge with think if you suddenly bring a girl back with you?"

"Have you not your veil on?"

"I? I do not care about myself. To-morrow I shall be—who knows how far away, where I can . defy all comments. But it might get told to your mother, and give you trouble hereafter."

"Have no fear," he said, pressing the hand that rested on his arm. "My room has a private entrance, and the people of the house burn no light on the stairs. We shall not meet any one."

With rapidly beating heart, he led her along the now deserted streets, and often they were obliged to stand still and lean against each other, while the icy blast swept by. Once when he turned his back to the storm and drew her closer to his breast, he bent down and hurriedly kissed her through her veil. She made no resistance—only said, "I think the worst is now over, we may go on." After that they did not speak another word till they reached the house.

The steep staircase was—as he had said it would be—quite dark, and as they went up it, on tip-toe, he first, holding her hand so that she might not miss a step, no one came across them. Only they heard children's voices through the door, and saw a light shine through the key-hole of the room in the upper story, telling of a Christmas tree there.

He carefully closed his door, and let her precede him into the small dark room, which was only lit by the glow in the stove, and the reflection of the snow. He then bolted both doors. "The kitchen is next to us," he said, "but there is no one there now. We need not talk in a whisper. But the landlady may just come back once to enquire whether I want anything."

She answered nothing; she had placed herself on a chair in the window, and was looking out at the whirls of snow.

When he had lit his small student's lamp with its green shade he noticed a box on the table. "Look," said he, "that is my Christmas box from home, we can put that in a corner for the present. Will you not take off some of your wraps, and seat yourself here on the sofa? You must be too warm in your furs."

"I shall soon be going," said she. "But thou art right, the stove does burn well." And she began to draw off her polonaise, and put away her fur cap and gloves —he helping her.

"But now shall we not begin to unpack?" said she, shaking back her hair. "I should much like to know what is in the box."

"I am in no hurry," he laughingly replied. "I have just been unpacking something far more precious to me."

"You ought to be ashamed of yourself," returned she, suddenly assuming a colder tone (she had been saying *thou*). "You do not deserve that people should be planning how to give you pleasure. I—if a mother had sent *me* such a Christmas box from a distance—give it me—I will undo the string."

She hastily began cutting open the cover with a little knife of hers, and he gazed in carefully suppressed emotion at every movement of her exquisite hands.

"Lottka," said he; "if you and I were both together in America, and this box had come over the sea—"

She shook her head. "No box would have come then."

"And why not, Lottka? If my mother knew thee as I know thee, dost thou suppose she would hold thee guilty for circumstances over which thou art powerless. Naturally she has her prejudices—like all good mothers. But I know that she loves me more than any of her prejudices."

The girl left off her unpacking, and with her little knife cut all sorts of patterns on the lid of the box.

"Do you call that a prejudice?" said she, without looking at him. "Could you eat an apple that you had found lying in the dirt of the streets? You might wash it ten times over, the repugnance would be all the same. And who knows what foot might have trodden on it, who knows that some slime might not have penetrated the rind, even though it should still be sound at the core? No, no, no! It is so once for all, bad enough that so it should be—but it must not be made even worse."

He wound his arm about her, but rather like a brother than one passionately in love. "Lottka," he said, "it is impossible that this can go on. You cannot waste your life in unavailing regrets." He stopped short —he could not find words that expressed his meaning without fearing to pain her.

"In regrets," she repeated, looking at him firmly and sorrowfully. "Oh no! Who is thinking of it? I have already told you that you may be quite easy about my future. I am provided for. I am not so forsaken as I appear, provided my courage does not desert me—my courage and my disgust. And why must every one be married? If I chose I might be so, and very well too. All possible pains have been taken to make me fall in love, and I have had a choice of very desirable wooers, rich, young, and handsome, and some were really willing regularly to marry me in a regular church, with a regular clergyman in gown and bands. There was only one hitch."

"What was that?" he eagerly asked.

"It is unnecessary to mention it. But no—I will tell it to you straight out, that you may never judge me wrongly. Do you know what has given me a horror of all men except perhaps yourself? I will whisper it in your ear. It is because I did not know whether the proposed bridegroom might not have stood too high in the mother's favour before he concerned himself about the daughter."

She turned away and went hastily to the window.

After a time she again felt his arm around her. "What you must have had to endure, dear heart!" he faintly whispered.

She nodded slowly and significantly. "More than you would suppose so young a creature could have survived. About seven years ago, when I first understood it all, I still thought I could change my lot. I would not remain another day in the house. I went out to service. I cut off all my beautiful long hair to prevent any one admiring me, and the ugliest clothes were good enough for me so only they would restore my respectability. How little it has availed me thou knowest. Later, when I was taken up as a vagrant, I was brought back to the house, to *her* who naturally had a legal right over me. I had to bear it. I was powerless against the law.

But I at once declared that I would destroy myself if I were not left in peace. And so I have sat nearly a year in my own room, and as soon as any one came near it I bolted the door. But still as I was obliged sometimes to breathe the air, people saw me, and she herself—though I never would speak a word to her—pretended that she loved me very much, and only yesterday—it was to be a Christmas treat—she sent me in a letter; guess from whom?"

"How can I guess?"

"You are right. No mortal ever could suppose it. But you remember the creature with whom you quarrelled on my behalf?"

"Lottka!" he cried beside himself. "Is it possible—"

She nodded. "It was a very affectionate letter, the most beautiful things were promised me in it—the paper smelt of Patchouli: since then I have had that nausea, that loathing which only passed off when you and I met again. But I have but to think of it, and—fie!—there it comes again!"

She wiped her lips, and the same strange shudder passed over her. He seized her hands—they were stiff and damp.

Suddenly she shook her head as if to get rid of some importunate thought. "But we were going to unpack," said she. "Pretty subjects these for Christmas Eve! Come to our box—*ours* I say. You have bewitched me with your dream about America."

"We will make it come true," he impetuously cried. "I shall remind you on some future day of our first Christmas Eve, and then you will be obliged to confess that I have more courage, and am a better prophet than you."

She made no reply, but cut the last string and opened the box. All sorts of small presents came to view; a pair of woollen gloves that his eldest sister had knitted for him, a watch-chain woven of the fair hair of the younger, with a pretty little gold key hanging to it, home-made gingerbread, and finally a large sealed bottle.

"Have you vineyards?" asked she playfully.

He laughed in spite of all his sadness. "It is elder wine, and the grapes grow in our little garden. As a child I thought it the best of all things, and ever since my good mother believes she cannot please me better than by sending me on every Christmas Eve, and every birthday, a sample at least of her last year's making."

"I hope it tastes better to you than the most costly Rhine wine," said she earnestly, "or you would not deserve it. Look—there are letters."

"Will you look them over? I am too much distracted. I should not know what they were about if I read them."

She had seated herself on the sofa, and taken the letters on her knee; one after the other she read them with most devout attention, as though their contents were wonderful and sublime, yet they were only made up of sisters' chat; little jests, apologies for the insignificance of their offerings; and in the lines written by the mother, there was traceable, together with her pride in having so good a son, her sorrow at being unable to embrace him at such a time, and her anxious fear that it was not so much work that kept him away, but rather the melancholy unsocial mood which even made his letters short.

"Are you still reading them?" he at length asked. "They are simple people, and when they write, the best that is in them does not always get put on paper. Good God! thou art weeping, Lottka!"

She laid the letters on the box, rose hurriedly, and pressed back the tears that still welled from between her long eye-lashes. "I will go now," she faintly said. "I shall be better out of doors."

"Go? now? and where? The storm would blow you down. Remain here for to-night, and if you like—the kitchen is close by—two chairs will do for me—and besides I have not a thought of sleeping."

She shook her head, and looked down. Then she suddenly raised her eyes, and looked full at his with an expression that made his heart beat wildly.

"Not so," she said. "But it is true that the storm without would blow me down, and where too could I go? Is this not Christmas Eve, and the last that we shall ever spend together. And I must give thee something, my presents to the children gave me no real pleasure, and why should I not on this day at least think of *myself* as well? Am I not right, Sebastian?"

She had never before called him by his name.

"Thou wilt give me something?" enquired he, amazed and uncertain.

"The only thing I still possess—myself," she gasped, and wound her arms about his neck.

When he woke in the dark on the morrow, and half raised himself from bed, still uncertain whether it had been real or only the most wondrous of dreams, the chamber was empty, not a trace remained of the last night's visitor. He felt all round his little sitting-room, called her gently by name, thinking she had perhaps stolen into the kitchen just for a freak, and would soon return. But all was silent. The intense cold overcame him, and with teeth chattering he slipped back into bed, and there, propped by pillows, tried to collect his thoughts.

Before long a horrible fear sprung up within him. With burning brow, despite the icy air, he hastily drew on his clothes, and kindled a light. The Christmas gifts of his family were still on the table, and he suddenly discovered a sheet written over in pencil pushed between the letters from his mother and sisters. The characters were uncertain and tremulous, as though written in the dark. The words ran as follows:—"Farewell, my beloved friend, my *only* friend! It grieves me much that I must grieve you so, must leave you so! But there is no other way. You would never let me go there where I needs must go, unless both are to be made unhappy. I thank thee for thy true love. But all the sweetness in thy soul can never wash away the bitterness from mine. Sleep well—farewell! I kiss thee once more in sleep. I know not whether thou wilt be able to read this. Do not grieve; believe that all is well with me now. Thy own loving one even in death."

The maid who was in the habit of coming about this time to light the kitchen-fire, heard a hollow cry in the next room, and opened the door in her terror. She there saw the young student lying on the sofa as though prostrated by some heavy blow. When she called him by name, he only shook his head as if to say she need not concern herself about him, and then stooped to pick up the paper that had fallen out of his hand.

"What o'clock?" he enquired.

"It has just struck six."

"Give me my cloak and stick. I will—"

He tottered to the door.

"You are going out bare-headed in all this cold? All the shops are closed, there is not a creature in the streets: you know this is a holiday?"

"A holiday," he said, repeating the syllables one by one as though trying to make out their meaning. "Give me—"

"Your cap? Here it is. Will you not first of all have a cup of coffee? The water will soon boil."

He made no further reply, but went out with heavy steps, and stumbled down the dark staircase. The snow crunched under his feet, and thick icicles hung in his beard. Far and near there was not a living creature to be seen in the dim streets; the sentinels in the sentry-boxes looked like stiff snow men. As he passed the bridge he saw that the river had frozen over during the night. He followed its course a long way, his eyes riveted on the ice as though looking for something there. Then he plunged into the neighbouring streets, quite aimlessly, like one walking in his sleep. For he could not expect to find what he was searching for by any pondering or thinking of his own. But the fever of an immeasurable agony drove him restlessly on, until he was utterly exhausted.

He might have been wandering a couple of hours or more, for the streets were beginning to look alive, when he reached the Potsdam Gate. He there saw a cab stopping in front of the small toll-house, coming as it seemed from the park. The toll-keeper came out in his furs, and as he reached out his snuff-box to a policeman who sat by the driver, asked laughingly—

"Anything that pays duty?" pointing to the closed cab windows.

"Not anything that pays duty here," was the reply. "I must give up my contraband to the proper authorities. She has smuggled herself—not into, but out of the world, but she is a rare piece of goods all the same. I was making my first round this morning yonder there by Louise-island, when I saw a well-dressed lady sitting on a bench, her head drooping as though she were asleep. 'My pretty child,' said I, 'look out some warmer place than this to sleep in, in such bitter cold as this.' But there was no waking her. Her hand still held a small bottle—it smelt like laurel leaves. She must have drunk it off, and then *tout doucement* have fallen to sleep! Good morning. I must make haste to deliver her up!"

The driver cracked his whip. At that very moment they again heard the toll-keeper's voice.

"Stop!" (he called out). "You can take another passenger. A gentleman looked into the cab window—and bang!—there he lies in the snow. Do get down, comrade, he is quite a young man; he must have weak nerves indeed to be knocked down in a second at the sight of a dead woman! How if you put him in beside her? They seem much of a muchness."

"No," returned the policeman, "that is contrary to regulations. Dead and living are not to be shut in together. Wait, we will carry him into the toll-house. If you rub his head with snow, and give him something strong to smell at, he'll come round in five minutes. I am up to these cases."

They bore the unconscious figure into the house: then the cab set out on its way again. But the policeman's prognostics were not fulfilled. Sebastian's consciousness did not return for five weeks instead of five minutes. It was only when the last snow had melted away that the miserable man began to creep about a

little with the aid of his stick. Then he went off to his
parents, who never knew what a strange fate had deso-
lated his youth, and cast a shadow over his manhood,
that was never entirely dispelled. When he died at the
age of five-and-thirty he left behind him neither wife
nor child.

END OF LOTTKA.

THE LOST SON.

THE LOST SON.

ABOUT the middle of the seventeenth century there lived in the town of Berne a worthy matron named Helena Amthor, the widow of a very rich and respected burgher and town councillor, who after twelve years of happy married life, left her with two children while she was still in the prime of her age and beauty. Nevertheless she declined all the advantageous and honourable offers of second marriage made to her, declaring on every such occasion that she had now only one thing to do on earth, and that was to bring up her children to be good and worthy members of society. But as it often happens that too great anxiety defeats itself and achieves the very reverse of what it aimed at, so it proved here. The eldest child, a boy, who was eleven when his father died—an intelligent but very self-willed fellow—rather required the discipline of a man's strong hand than the tender but too indulgent care of a mother who positively idolised him as the image of the husband she had prematurely lost, and who never knew how to oppose any of his impetuous wishes. The consequence was that the older the young Andreas grew, the worse he behaved, and rewarded his mother's unwise love by almost breaking her heart. When she first came to some recognition of his faults it was already too late. The remonstrances and admonitions of his uncles were all in vain, and even the grave censure and heavy fines he incurred from the town authorities, owing to his irregular conduct, tamed his rude nature as little as did his mother's tears. At length Frau Helena made up her mind to the greatest pang she had known since her husband's death—to a parting with her son, whom a cousin in Lausanne, a wealthy merchant, now offered to take into his house, in the hope that change of scene and regular work might exercise a healthy influence on the reckless youth. Andreas, who was twenty years old at the time, consented willingly enough to leave the old-fashioned "bear-garden," as he called his native town, for a strange place, where he promised himself, spite of his cousin's *surveillance*, a far freer and more amusing life. Neither did he show the least tender feeling on parting from his mother and his little sister of twelve, Lisabethli, but kept his large stock of travelling-money far more carefully in his belt than his mother's counsels in his heart. No wonder, therefore, before six months were over, news came from Lausanne that Andreas had secretly quitted the town, leaving behind him disgraceful debts at gambling-houses and taverns, and making off with money entrusted to him for the business, in lieu of which a heavy bill drawn on his mother was found in a corner of his desk.

That bill and all other debts Helena Amthor paid without delay; she said not a word about them to anybody, and always gave one answer to whatever enquiries might be made about her son, that he was well and upon his travels, and that he wrote to her from time to time. Nor was this statement untrue, for as soon as his money ran short—which often happened—he turned to his mother, who at that time never refused him. But as to what there was in his or her letters no mortal creature ever knew. She left off speaking of him, never introduced his name, so that at length people grew shy of touching on the sorrow of her life, and Andreas was virtually dead as far as the whole town of Berne was concerned, He himself seemed quite content to be so, nor ever expressed any wish to see his home again. When he came of age and had to settle matters with his guardian, he curtly sent the latter word what day and hour he was to meet him at the "Vine-tree," in Strasburg, there to make over the fortune inherited from his father. But his guardian, a man already in years, neither could nor would travel so far on his ward's account. Therefore Frau Helena resolved upon undertaking the sorrowful journey herself, probably with a last unspoken hope that this meeting might have some softening effect upon his estranged affections. When, however, she returned after a ten days' absence, the traces of confirmed sadness on her fine face were more marked than before, and from that time forth no one could say that they ever saw her laugh.

And yet fate that had laid this heavy burden on her, had also granted her consolation in another direction, that might well have gladdened a less deeply-wounded heart. Her other child Lisabethli, who was about eight years younger than the lost son, was as admirably endowed, as obedient and loving, and as completely the delight of every one who saw her, as her brother was the reverse. And these sweet and lovely characteristics, though originally a matter of temperament no doubt, were in no small measure owing to her own self-training and self-culture; for her mother—more particularly during the years when Andreas was at home—had erred quite

as much on the side of severity towards her youngest
child as on that of indulgence towards her favourite.
Even when Lisabethli was quite a small thing in the
school-room, she had shed many hidden tears over the
reproofs and constant putting-down she received; and
pitied herself for her inability by all her love and duty
to win from her mother one of the fond words or
caresses which the else stern lady lavished upon her unruly boy. All her anxiety on his account seemed but
to estrange her from her sweet girl, about whom, by the
way, her brother no more concerned himself than though
she had not been in existence. And yet the child continued to be gentleness and brightness itself, and was
soon wise enough to estimate the misery that disturbed
the balance of her mother's mind, and to resolve to treat
all injustice towards herself as she would the mood or
caprice of a suffering invalid.

Later—after the flight of Andreas from Lausanne,
and while the rumour of it was spreading more and
more amongst the inhabitants of Berne—the relations between mother and daughter improved. Indeed the former
had never been blind to the pure beauty of her child's
nature, though, like one under an evil spell, she wrought
out her own wretchedness by her partiality. Her mortally wounded maternal pride still forbade her to betray
to her daughter, even by a sigh, the pangs her son inflicted on her. But in all other respects she now seemed
to give the young girl the next place in her affections,
and was even anxious to make up for all that in her
earlier days she had inflicted or withheld. Still she was
sparing of her caresses. If she but passed her delicate
white hand over the girl's brown head when wishing her
good night, still more if she kissed her eyes and said,
"my good child," Lisabethli would blush crimson for

joy, and the happy beating of her heart would keep her awake a whole hour.

At the same time, Frau Amthor endeavoured so far as was compatible with her stern character, to procure for her daughter all the pleasures and amusements of her age, and was in the habit of inviting her friends on Sundays to the quiet home, behind which lay a beautiful terraced garden, and during the summer time the young people used to enjoy little excursions, and out-door parties; but she forbade them most strictly to go to any dances however respectably carried on, or in accordance with long established custom, they might be. It seemed that some innermost feeling of her nature shrank from the idea of the sister dancing while the brother, homeless and friendless, might at that very moment be driven by despair to end his life. For that it would come to this at last, was the one spectral thought that cast its shadow over the mother's soul both in her waking and sleeping hours.

The house that had belonged to the Amthors for many generations, was a narrow three-storied antique building, with wainscoted walls and ceilings, and handsomely furnished with old silk tapestry and heavy hangings. On the ground-floor were the offices and the room in which dwelt the old man-servant and the faithful maid by whom the work of the house was done. Above were the rooms inhabited by the mother and daughter, which opened at the back upon the garden; and in the third story were what had been the late councillor's library and study, and of later years rooms entirely devoted to Andreas. The chamber where his bed stood had not since his departure been entered by any one but the old maid-servant. His mother never set her foot in it, and if his sister crept by it to take a book from the library, she held her breath as she passed the door as though it were haunted.

Our story begins on a September evening—on the very day that Lisabethli had completed her nineteenth year. In honour of the anniversary, her mother had invited some half-dozen of the girl's favourite companions and what with singing and other amusements, which the grave matron left the young people to carry on alone, the hour of ten had struck unobserved. Indeed the girls, who after a very sultry day were still pacing the garden walks arm in arm, deep in important confidential talk, might easily have forgot time till midnight, if a storm that had gathered on the other side of the river had not scared them in. And once in, they found that their respective attendants had come for them with lanterns, and so kisses and good-byes were heartily exchanged, and in the great room looking out on the terrace the usual stillness prevailed, when the first roll of thunder resounded through the darkness.

Frau Helena had joined her daughter, who stood in the open doorway looking down, beyond the dark steps leading into the garden, to the river Aar, lost in vague, dream-like thoughts, such as are wont to succeed a festive day when the soul is once more free to retire into itself. She gently laid her hand on her daughter's hair, and the sweet child silently leaned her head down on the mother's shoulder, as though to seek shelter from the vivid flash of lightning that suddenly rent the black cloud above them. "Come in, child," said the mother, "we shall soon have rain."

The daughter shook her head without saying a word. She was now gazing steadily on the clear space of sky at the horizon, where the snow peaks of the Oberland far away from the range of the thunder-cloud, rose glittering in the moonlight, a wondrous spectacle indeed. "Dear little mother," at length she said, "how vast the earth is! Yonder they neither see nor hear anything of the storm that rages here. And yet still further off, in that star just above the Rothhorn, they would know nothing of it if our earth were to be shivered to atoms!"

Her mother made no reply. Her thoughts were—she herself did not know where, but well she knew with whom—with the one they had always flown to at the approach of bad weather for many years past; because, while the sky was growing dark, she could not tell whether her boy had a roof over his head or not.

"How the river feels and answers to the storm!" resumed the girl. "One might really fancy one saw the surface shudder with terror as the lightnings flash down. And yet they can go on dancing and fiddling in the tavern on the little island yonder. They must be a godless set."

"They will soon leave off," said the mother, "it will be too bad even for them. No human being is so hardened but what the hour comes when he hearkens if God warns him. But let us come in. The drops that fall are large as hazel-nuts."

"Look, mother," said the daughter holding her back, "there is something not right going on there. The door of the tavern is suddenly thrown open—people are rushing out—there is a girl in their midst—something flashes like a sword-blade—listen! they are quarrelling—oh, what wild unruly creatures!"

The thunder now paused, and a sound of angry voices as well as of breaking glass was plainly audible, while a single clarionet, undisturbed by all the noise and confusion, went shrilly on playing gay dancing tunes.

"I would give a hundred crowns," said Frau Helena with brows knit, "if that sink of iniquity yonder were removed from the town. I really might be driven to think of changing my house in my old days, merely to escape hearing and seeing such things as these."

"And just at this sweetest of all hours," interposed the girl, "when everything else is so peaceful, and one might for once dream and think at will. Just look, they are all crossing the bridge now. For God's sake—why they are actually fighting—one is being pushed against the railings—the woman throws herself between them—his arms are free again—if they should push him into the river—"

"Come, that is enough," said the mother authoritatively, "now let us go in. It is no sight for Christians to gaze at when men attack each other more cruelly than wild beasts would do. Just read me the evening lesson and then we will go to bed."

A brilliant flash now suddenly lit up the houses by the side of the Aar, the tavern on the island, and the high sweltering current of the river.

For a moment the dark group massed on the narrow bridge was distinctly seen: a tall youth with a red feather in his cap in their midst, struggling against them, with only a woman with white head-gear on his side. The clash of swords was heard, and a shrill female cry for help, and then with a terrific thunder-clap like the fall of some mighty tower, the clouds sent down sheets of rain, darkness swallowed up the wild doings on the bridge, and nothing remained visible but the red light in the window of the island tavern.

The two women had retreated into the house horrified, and while the mother slowly walked up and down the carpeted floor, Lisabethli sat at the table, her hands folded on the open book before her, and her eyes fixed upon a large nosegay which stood in a beautiful Venetian glass, a present from her godfather on this her birthday. As to reading, that was not to be thought of, the thunder would have drowned her voice; still less was sleep possible, for the scene of violence was too vividly present to her mind. ·She kept listening intently for what might be going on without. "Oh God!" she almost unconsciously prayed, "have pity upon them all, and let no harm be done!" Just then another flash shone through the window and the door which had been left ajar that the fresh night-air might enter the room, and she fancied that she saw a shadow on the upper terrace show through the pane for one moment, and then vanish. "Mother," she faintly called out, "let us lock the door, someone has climbed over the wall, and—"

She could not end her sentence, for the door was pushed open and a man rushed into the room. "For the sake of God's mercy," cried he, sinking half from exhaustion, half in the attitude of entreaty at the knees of Frau Helena. "Whoever you be, noble lady, save an innocent man! They are on my track. Where—where—" and he looked around, and with blood-stained hands pushed his dripping hair from his eyes. "Where can I hide myself? What can I say to move your heart to pity? If you knew how it had all come about, how entirely without fault of mine I have fallen into this horrible strait—am hunted down as a murderer—oh noble maiden—" and he turned to the pale girl who gazed with a shudder at the red feather in the stranger's cap; "if you have a brother who is dear to you—who may perhaps at this moment be asking hospitality in some strange land—implore your lady-mother not to thrust me out into the night where Heaven knows what disgrace may overtake me. By the head of your own son, noble lady——"

"Silence!" interrupted Frau Amthor in a hollow trembling tone, more awful in the ears of the suppliant than the roar of the thunder. Meanwhile she looked at him with such an absent far-away expression that her daughter flew to support her in case she should swoon. But it passed over.

"Close the terrace-door," she hastily said, leaning back in her chair, "then call Valentin. But make haste! I seem to hear voices in the garden below."

The young girl bolted the heavy door in the twinkling of an eye, and hurried off. The stranger remained a moment or two alone with the mother.

"You are saving my honour and liberty!" he stammered out, "perhaps my life. But believe, noble lady, that what you do is not done for one unworthy or reprobate, and my own mother, who would ransom the life of her son with all she has, were he to fall among bandits, will in return for your noble-hearted deed——"

"Not another word," broke in the matron, "what I do is not done for your sake. But you are bleeding," she suddenly said, and paused—her glance falling upon a spot on his shoulder where great drops were oozing through his black silk doublet.

"It is nothing," returned he, hastily pressing his glove on the place. "I hardly feel it. Would to God that the blow I dealt in return may not be more dangerous! But I fear——"

Lisabethli now returned with the old servant. "Valentin," said the lady, "take this stranger gentleman to the upper story, and then see him to bed—in the room —you know which. No one is to know that he is in the house. I will give my own instructions to Donate. You understand how to foment. Look to the gentleman's wounds; there is linen in the cupboard; there are shirts in the press—he is to be treated *as though he were my own son*. Go—I hear footsteps."

They all listened with beating hearts. In spite of the noise of the rain, voices were audible in the garden. The next moment the old servant had pushed the stranger out of the room, and mother and daughter were alone.

"My child," said the mother, "go for a time downstairs to Donate. I shall have to lie, and I would not that your ears should hear me."

"Mother," returned the girl, "I pray you to let me remain with you. I should die of terror down there. Never believe that anything you do can seem wrong in my eyes; and you are doing it to save a human life."

Meanwhile there were three knocks at the bolted door. "In the name of the law, open," a deep voice called out.

"Who knocks at this late hour?" returned Frau Amthor, and her voice sounded as unconstrained as though nothing had happened.

"The sergeant, with the train band," was the reply. "Open, or we burst the door."

"Go, Lisabethli," said the lady in so loud a tone that every word was audible without. "I must say that customs are changing in our old town of Berne: the idea of the watch breaking into a peaceable private dwelling in the dark night-time! I hope you have some satisfactory explanation to give of this visit of yours, sergeant," this in a majestic tone to the intruder, "you know who I am, and that my house is not likely to contain any disreputable character whom the bailiffs are after."

The sergeant who had cast a hasty glance all round the room, now stood confounded opposite the lofty figure of the matron, and his eyes fell before the steady gaze of hers. "Forgive me, Frau Amthor," he mumbled, while he beckoned to his followers to stay where they were, and kept awkwardly turning the handle of his dagger round and round. "We are on the track of a dangerous fellow who has taken part in riotous, murderous doings on the island yonder. When I and my men were approaching the tavern the people in it saw him flying in this direction, leaping over hedges and walls, and we traced his foot-marks to your garden, and even found one of his gloves below the window. Therefore I held it to be my duty—"

"To break into my house as though it were a likely refuge for murderers," interposed the matron, looking at him with so undaunted a gaze that the bearded man stared down at the carpet much embarrassed by the wet foot-prints he had left on its pattern. "Go your way," she continued, "and be more careful another time at what door you knock. To-morrow I shall go to the Town Council and lay a complaint before them about their endurance of the disorder and riot that goes on on the island, exposing even the quietest householder in the neighbourhood to an invasion of the watch by night on a charge of unlawful concealment!"

The sergeant would fain have broken out into further apologies, but an imperative gesture of the lady, in the direction of the door, prevented his uttering a word. He retired with head sunk low, and had scarcely crossed the threshold, when Lisabethli shot the bolts after him, and then sunk down on a seat, with a deep-drawn sigh, so much had the short scene affected her.

"Remain here," said the mother after a pause. "Light a taper for me. I will go upstairs."

"Dearest mother," pleaded the girl timidly, "would you not rather— Indeed you are too pale—it will distress you too much."

Frau Helena made no reply, but taking the light out of her hand, left the room with face rigidly set, as though no worse thing could happen to her. She was a sternly virtuous woman, a proud woman, who had always felt too much self-respect to condescend to a lie. Now she had degraded herself in her own estimation and in the presence of her child, and this for the sake of a stranger who had no other claim to such a sacrifice than that of having adjured her by her deepest grief.

The door through which she had passed remained half open, and Lisabethli could hear with what slow and heavy steps she went up the stairs, and how often she rested on the way, as though needing to gather breath and courage for the painful entrance into her lost son's room, which she had not visited for years.

"He is in a swoon," said old Valentin, meeting her on the threshold. "I have bound up his wounds, but as I was putting a clean shirt on him he fell lifeless from under my hands. I will fetch some cold water: there is no danger—it is only faintness from loss of blood."

He hurried down stairs, and the lady entered the room.

There lay the stranger on the bed, his eyes closed, his mouth half open from pain, and showing his white teeth. His light hair still dripping with blood and rain, was pushed back from his pale brow. His cap and silken doublet lay on the ground, as well as the blood-soaked shirt which the old servant had replaced by a clean one. Frau Helena trembled all over when she saw this stranger clothed in the fine linen she herself had spun for her son, and marked with his initials. That she might avoid seeing anything else in the room, she fixed her eyes on the young face that in spite of its deadly pallor had a boyish, harmless, good-natured expression. She saw at once from his clothing that he was the son of respectable parents, and the tone in which he had implored her to save him, still rung pathetically in her ears. A motherly feeling overcame her, and great tears rolled down her faded face.

Then the old servant returned with a pitcher of cold water, and prepared to wash the temples of the unconscious youth. "Leave that to me," said his mistress, taking the sponge out of his hand. "Bring the best vinegar out of the side-board, and a flask of our old wine. When he comes to himself he will need a cordial." Then she washed the blood out of his hair, and held the ice-cold sponge to his lips. This brought him round: he opened his eyes, and on seeing the noble lady who had saved him bending over his couch, he tried to sit up and speak to her. But she gently constrained him to lie down again, and to let her go on with her ministrations. "I am better already," he gasped out, while he took hold of her hand to carry it to his lips. "O how much you are doing for me! And you do not know me, and must think ill of me. Let me just tell you how it all came about."

"Not another word to-night," interposed the lady, gently laying her hand on his lips. "You have lost too much blood to exert yourself safely. I leave you in the care of my old servant who will sit up with you. I hope

that you will get some sleep, and to-morrow be on the
way to recovery. Good night."

She left the room without casting a look around at
any of the things that evoked such bitter memories. But
as soon as she found herself in the dark lobby, she leant
her head against the wall, and sobbed in secret. This
burst of grief lasted but a few minutes, then she raised
her head again, and with her usual lofty bearing went
down to her daughter. "Valentin thinks that there is no
danger," she said. "Let us go to our rest."

"Mother," asked the girl, "do you believe that he is
a murderer? There is something about him that seems as
if he would not hurt the meanest thing that lives, let
alone a fellow creature."

"Yet on the other hand how did he get to that
tavern on the island?" said the mother, as if speaking to
herself.

"Because he was a stranger," hastily broke in the
daughter. "He does not speak the German of Switzerland. Did you not notice that, mother dear?"

"It is useless to theorise about it," abruptly replied
Frau Amtlior. "Come to bed, child, the storm has passed
over."

And so after the daughter had read the evening
prayers, they went to their rest. But it was long after
midnight before either of them closed an eye. Lisabethli
kept constantly seeing before her the true-hearted terror-
stricken gaze of the stranger, when he appealed to her
to help to soften her mother's heart, the blood on his
forehead, the red feather in his cap, while the scream of
the woman who threw herself between the combatants
on the bridge, still sounded in her ears. Frau Helena
for her part was listening anxiously to what went on
overhead. For the room where the wounded man lay

was immediately above her chamber, and she thought of all the nights she had lain awake till morning expecting the return of Andreas from his orgies, and how when at length she heard his unsteady step, she used to turn on her pillow, not to sleep, but to shed bitter tears. Now everything was silent enough, only from time to time Valentin gave a short cough. The poor lady sat up in bed, and tried to pray; "Oh Lord God," so ran her prayer; "let him in foreign lands meet a mother to stand by him in all time of need; and if no one will have pity on him, let him find his way back to his own mother, that I may not die before I have once more held his hand in mine."

The morning was just breaking pale and cloudy through the small round panes, when Frau Helena left her room, and hastily dressed herself. "Sleep another hour," said she to Lisabethli, who at once bestirred herself too. "I will just go upstairs, and see how our guest is faring."

The girl, however, had no wish for further rest. Very quietly she too rose and dressed, and crept on tip-toe after her mother. On the stair she met Donate carrying a small tray. "He has not made much of his breakfast," said the faithful old servant. "Fearfully weak he still is, and his hand shakes so if he tries to hold the spoon. But for the rest a very fine handsome creature, and I would rather bite my tongue out than betray him."

The young girl made no reply, but went on to the top of the staircase. Once there, as the door had been left ajar, she could see the stranger lying in bed, but raising his head a little to greet Frau Helena, who was bending over him and enquiring how he had slept.

"I really hardly know, noble lady," answered the youth. "My faithful watcher there will be better able to tell you whether I was quiet or talked nonsense and threw my hands and feet about. But I dreamed a great deal, and such lovely dreams—nothing in them of blood or wounds. And this morning when I came to myself it gave me a sudden stab in the heart to think how I must have alarmed you last night, and that you do not even know to whom you have been so unspeakably kind. Nay," continued he, seizing hold of her hand on seeing that she was again going to impose silence, "I will not let you go, even though it should be better for me to remain four-and-twenty hours without speaking. It makes me wild to lie here and let that good Samaritan, and yourself above all, feel that you are wasting your time and trouble upon a fellow who better deserves to lie on the straw of a hospital amongst brawlers and swash-bucklers whom the beadle picks up half-dead on the streets. I owe my present plight to my greenness and presumption, having always held that with a good conscience and good courage, nobody need fear to face the devil. My father has often enough shaken his head at me warningly and said, 'Touch not pitch if thou wilt keep clean hands; and don't mix with wolves if thou dost not mean to howl with them.' And when I left Augsburg how my mother charged me only to enter respectable houses and keep good company! The egg, however, thought itself wiser than the hen. For you see, noble lady, I am naturally a restless sort of a fellow, and beautiful as my native town is, and cheerful too at times, I found it too confined, and wanted to see the world, Switzerland more especially, because I had heard so much of it from my father. He served his apprentice-ship here in Berne in the house of the rich master-clothier,

Aufdembühel, whom you doubtless know. Afterwards he settled in Augsburg, and married my mother and set up a great fabric of his own; and yet he has always thought fondly of Berne, so that when I told him my wish to visit it he made no objection. I almost think he had some idea of a daughter-in-law from that house, which suited my notions too, for I have grown to the age of five-and-twenty in Augsburg, and all the blue and brown eyes there have left me scathless. And so for about a fortnight I rode southward in highest spirits, and crossed the beautiful Lake of Constance in a boat, and last evening when it was getting rather late I came through the gates by the bear-pits, thinking no evil; but I did not like to come down at once upon Herr Aufdembühel, bag and baggage as they say, so put up my horse at the "Stork," and then set out strolling about the town to take a general survey of it, as I always do on first getting to any new place. Yesterday, however, it was unfortunate that I did not first of all have a meal at the inn. For owing to the long ride and great sultriness while the storm was gathering, I suddenly became intolerably thirsty, and felt that I should turn to tinder unless I could get a draught of wine. I was looking about me, therefore, for a tavern, just as I passed the one on the island where I heard music and dancing going on, and I asked a well-dressed burgher whether one could get tolerable wine there. 'The wine was good enough,' he said, 'much better than the company. If he were to judge me by my dress he should say I should not find people of my own class there.' 'I would go into a stable full of cows and goats,' I laughingly replied, 'if I could find red wine in one of the milk-pails.' And there I left my worthy, standing, looking rather anxiously after me, and crossed the bridge to the tavern.

"When I opened the door, however, I saw that my friend had not cautioned me for nothing, and that in a stable with brute beasts I should have found better manners and customs than there. Whether it be a haunt of thieves I cannot say, but most of the people looked to me as if they had narrowly escaped the gallows, or were on the high way thither, men and women both, and when I entered they nudged each other with surprise. But I who did not like to show the white feather, and held that a stranger might safely do what an inhabitant of the place could not, boldly seated myself in a corner, and ordered a measure of wine. And as I kept quiet, they seemed to be getting used to me, at least most of them had either drunk themselves stupid, or else were taken up with their female companions. Amongst the last class, was one better dressed, and with hair neater than the others, but a bold hussy like the rest. She neither danced nor sang, nor seemed to care for drink. She sat on the knee of a tall strong man, whose clothes looked as if they had originally been good, but were now stained with rain and wine. His face too might once have been handsome, before he got the red scar across his forehead, or his red eyelids and straggling beard. I could not help watching the pair— he throwing down the dice disdainfully, as though good or bad luck were all the same to him, and when he won giving a push to the girl to collect the money, whereupon she would take a long dagger that lay on the table, and with the bare blade just sweep the coins to one side as if they were so much dirt. Neither of them spoke a word, while their partners—rough young churls with red faces and glassy eyes—cursed freely in Spanish and French, and struck the table with their clenched fists. The girl seemed at length to tire of the game, and looking round her with a yawn, chanced to spy me out for the first time, for when I entered she was dozing on the man's shoulder. I suppose my dress took her fancy, or the ring on my finger; suffice it to say that she began to cast meaning glances at me, and to make signs with her hand behind her lover's back, which I neither understood nor attended to, but gulped down my wine the more quickly that I might slip away, when all of a sudden she sprang from the knee of the gloomy gambler, and seated herself on the bench beside me as if intending to sleep, but in reality she kept ogling me all the time. The man with the scar seemed aware of something wrong, for he loudly called to her in French to come back at once, but she pretended to be asleep, and not to hear him. At that he started up in a rage and bade me go my ways at once—said he had seen me making signals to the girl, and luring her from his lap. I who was inwardly furious at his brutality, put on a careless semblance, and said that no one had a right to bid me leave, that I was interfering with nobody, and paying for my wine like the rest. At that he grew frantic, dragged the girl from the bench, and called out to the host to know why he did not keep his house clear of suspicious characters who only came to spy, called me all sorts of opprobrious names, and when the girl took my part, seized hold of my doublet, and tore my collar. I saw now pretty plainly what I had brought upon myself, for all the rest of the gamblers joined in the outcry, and the landlord, who got his livelihood through men of that class, and did not want decent customers, rudely told me that I was out of place in a house like his where people knew their manners. 'Very good,' I said, 'I will no longer disturb you.' I threw my money on the table and moved away. But as

I was opening the door, the girl suddenly clung to me
and begged me to take her with me for a walk, as she
was sick of the company. '*Allez-vous-en*,' cried I. '*Je
ne veux pas de vous*,' and what else of bad French I
could muster. Just then the storm began, and the uproar within got worse and worse, for the lover wanted
to tear her away, and the others screamed and stormed,
and she clung to me like a wild cat to a tree, and I
could not help thinking in my anger and vexation,
'What if thy good mother saw thee?' Then came so
dazzling a flash, that even those rude beings were
quieted for a moment, the music stopped, and the landlady put up a sort of prayer. I took advantage of this
interval to shake off my troublesome fair one, and slip
out of the house. But while I was on the bridge, thanking God for having got off with only a black eye, the
whole of them rushed out upon me with drawn blades,
and had they not been half-drunk, my last hour would
inevitably have struck! The French girl too came to
my aid, and when she saw her lover—the man with the
scar—drive his dagger into my shoulder, she yelled like
a maniac, pushed me against the railing, and covered
me with her own body. Meanwhile, seeing my life was
at stake, I drew out my short sword, and laid about me
so lustily, that all fell back with the exception of my
chief foe who was maddened with jealousy and wine.
He actually ran in upon my sword, gave a roar like a
bull, and then fell speechless on his face. Instantly all
was so still one only heard the thunder and the rush of
the river. But then came two flashes and showed us
the train-band marching towards the island. 'Get him
into the boat,' said one of the fellows to another. 'He
is already in,' was the reply; 'the best way were to
throw him into the river.' Meanwhile they had caught

hold of the whimpering girl, and were pushing her off
by the shoulders. '*Allons, depêchez-vous,*' she cried.
'*Voilà les gendarmes! On nous attrapera tous.*' And
then there was such a rush along the narrow bridge that
no one took any notice of me, and under cover of the
darkness and pelting rain I made my escape. The rest,
you know, noble lady. And now just picture to yourself my fate if Heaven had not touched your heart, if
you had refused me your protection. Indelible disgrace
must have attached to me as a brawler, if not as a murderer; found in a disreputable house; no worthy man to
bear witness to my innocence, and Herr Aufdembühel,
instead of writing word to my father that he rejoiced to
renew their old friendship by welcoming his son, would
but have come to see me in prison, and have shaken
his head incredulously over my self-justification, whereas
I read in your eyes that you do not hold me an empty
liar, but feel compassion for my reckless youth, and will
not withdraw your hand from me."

After this impetuous narrative, which evidently excited him much, the youth sank back on his pillows
with a deep sigh, and closed his eyelids. "Be of good
cheer," said Frau Helena, her black eyes moist with
tears. "You shall want for nothing under my roof, and
since I have had you laid in this bed, I should look
upon you as my son, even if everything about you did
not assure me that I might give credence to your words.
Valentin thinks that in about a week you may be able
to rise. Till then I shall only ask one thing from you,
to be a tractable patient, and not through impatience or
anxiety to retard your recovery. If you wish, as you
cannot move your arm, I will write word to your
mother how you are, and that she need fear no danger
for you."

"Oh, my gracious hostess," cried the youth, catching hold of the sleeve of her dress and pressing it to his lips; "you are indeed like a mother to me, for you offer of your own accord what I scarcely dared ask. And yet I know what a favour you will be conferring upon my dear mother. For indeed both parents are now sitting anxiously together like two birds in a nest whose young one has just taken his first flight, and I had promised to send them tidings as soon as I reached my journey's end. But now, if you are good enough to write to Frau Martina Brucker, Augsburg, will you make light of my hurt and keep back from her the way I got it, until I can send her a circumstantial account. For she is very easily frightened, and as I am her only child, she has always taken as much care of me as though I were a girl, and hitherto I have tried to give her as little uneasiness as possible. If she were to know what a scrape her Kurt got into on the very first night of his arrival at Berne, she would not have an hour's peace until she could get him out of this dangerous atmosphere. But you will see at once what to do. You will know perfectly what to say to a mother so as to comfort even more than alarm her."

He grew so pale while uttering these last words, that Valentin hurried to the bed-side with a cordial, and gave his mistress plainly to understand that her interview had been too long. So after a few further directions, she crept softly out on tip-toe, and in the lobby came upon Lisabethli.

"You have been listening?" said she sternly.

"Dearest mother, forgive me," returned her child. "I could not help it. I needs must know how it all happened. God be praised and thanked—I was right—he is innocent."

“Come down, child, you have nothing to do up here. Should any one call I am engaged. I must sit down at once and write to his mother.”

But nevertheless a visitor came whom neither Donate could send away, nor Lisabethli receive alone. It was no other than the chief sergeant, the greatest man in the town next to the mayor, and distantly related to Frau Helena. He came on the part of the Town Council to apologise for the intrusion of the previous night, and also to say that the disorders on the island should now be effectually put a stop to by the closing of the tavern, which had long been a thorn in the side of the civic authorities. As to the savage doings of yesterday evening, a mystery lay over them which up to the present hour no one had been able to penetrate. Both combatants had disappeared as completely as though the earth had swallowed them up, their bloody traces had been washed away by the heavy rain, and nothing was known of their names or their antecedents. Only a boat usually fastened to the bridge had been found two or three miles from the town keel uppermost, and the landlord of the Stork stated that a horse had been left in his stable last evening, whose rider had never made his appearance since.

During this communication Frau Helena had often changed colour, but did not utter a syllable which could have betrayed her secret knowledge, nay, she was even careful not to speak a word of any kind, as it must needs have been at least indirectly untrue. As soon as she was alone again, she wrote to Frau Martina Brucker in Augsburg, judiciously keeping back all that might have made her uneasy as to her son’s conduct, and con-

cluding by a cordially expressed promise to nurse him
as a real mother might, since she—this she added with
silent tears—was not so favoured by Heaven as to have
her own son under her roof.

This letter she herself took in the afternoon to the
post, accompanied by her daughter, without whom, indeed, she seldom left the house. Neither of them said
a word about their hidden guest, and yet neither thought
of anything else. So it was in the evening too when
they silently sat at their spinning wheels. It was only
when Donate came in at a late hour to announce that
the fever was higher, the patient unable to sleep, and
delirious, calling constantly for his mother, and wanting
to get up and ride off homewards, that they held a council as to whether it was any longer possible or justifiable
not to call in a chirurgeon, but trust to the skill and
experience of old Valentin, who had served half his
time as apprentice to a leech before Herr Amthor took
him into his service. At last Frau Helena went up herself to inspect the wound. There was nothing in its
aspect to alarm, and the old man assured her that the
rambling, Donate had been frightened by, merely re-
sulted from the full-bloodedness of youth, and that in
four-and-twenty hours all danger would be perfectly
over. Frau Helena knew that her faithful servant was
accustomed to weigh his words before he spoke positively. She stood for a while by the side of the feverish
sufferer, who did not know her, but when he felt the
touch of her hand called her "mother," and then with a
sudden brightness in his face began to talk to her in a
tone of affectionate confidence, telling her she was not
to suppose he had set his heart on Herr Aufdembühel's
daughter—that she knew he would never marry unless
he found some one like her. Then he would break out

into French, as if violently remonstrating with the bold girl of the tavern, telling her not to hang about his neck, since though she might stain his doublet with wine, she could not ogle the ring off his finger—and all sorts of delirious fancies. To all which the judicious matron listened attentively, for she well knew men, and was silently touched by the evidence thus afforded of a good and innocent nature. She felt her motherly partiality for the young stranger grow hour by hour, till she was almost angry that this youth should assert a claim to a place in her heart, long entirely filled by sorrow for her lost one.

The night was again restless, and so was the day. But just as Valentin had foretold, on the third night came a refreshing sleep, and when Frau Helena paid her morning visit to her guest, he looked at her with clear intelligent eyes, and even tried to move his wounded arm, which was still helpless, but going on as well as possible. The lady shook her head lovingly at him, and bade him not play any pranks, or fancy himself well before the time, and the youth, although in the highest spirits, gravely assured her that he would be passive as an unweaned child. But that very evening, as mother and daughter were sitting in their saloon by candlelight, and Lisabethli practising some foreign tune upon the spinett, there came a knock at the door, and in answer to a somewhat nervous "Come in,"—for the ladies were not accustomed to such late visitors—their young guest appeared leaning on the arm of Valentin, who by silent shrugs, gave them to understand that this was no doing of his, and that he washed his hands of the consequences of such imprudence. Kurt, however, over whose pale cheeks a flush of pleasure passed at this escape from the sick room, gaily and gracefully bent his knee before the grave matron, and prayed her forgiveness for having ventured once more to stand on his own feet contrary to her command. He only wanted to wish his benefactress good-night, and to thank the young lady too, whom he had not seen since that terrible evening, for the trouble she had taken in making lint and sewing bandages together. It was impossible to resist his lively cordial manner: and even Lisabethli, who had been more startled by his unexpected appearance on this occasion than on the first, soon regained her natural ease and replied playfully and intelligently to his friendly talk. At a signal from her mother she brought in a tray of fruit and pastry, and their guest who had fasted for some days (first, however, asking and obtaining leave from Valentin), was soon biting with his white teeth into the juicy early pears.

"Noble lady," he said, "I cannot describe to you how pleasant it is to me to find myself at this table. When I first saw your lights shine from the terrace below, and directed my fugitive steps hither, how little I dreamed that I should ever sit here safely and happily, and that you would be so very kind to me! You must know that I am a thoroughly spoilt child, and on my journey here, much as I enjoyed the freedom and novelty of it, yet in the wretched hostelries, spite of good food and fiery wine, I used to long for the clean tablecloth laid by our maid at home for our simple fare. I never ventured to sleep in any of their beds without spreading my cloak over the sheets. Now here I find everything just as it is at my own mother's—only better appointed—and that there I have to be son and daughter in one, while here I sit merely on sufferance, because, as my old friend tells me, your son is on his travels, while a daughter is left to you such as my mother has long vainly wished for."

At these words the old servant slipped away, for this reference to the absent son distressed him, but Lisabethli came to her mother's rescue. "Often," she playfully observed, "did people wish themselves a cross, and if her mother would be candid, she would admit that she not seldom found herself desiring better companionship than that of a silly little daughter, her head full of freaks and fancies, who strummed on the spinet half the day through, roasted the meat too brown, and made the soup too light, and cost more than she was worth in ribands and tuckers." At this the mother with a faint smile, observed that the picture was certainly like, though somewhat darkly shaded; but that even were it a correct one, each must accept the punishment Heaven adjudged him. And so saying her face grew very sad, for she thought that in her case this was but too true. The young people, however, paid no attention, but went on chatting in the liveliest manner, and becoming so thoroughly at home with each other that they felt like old acquaintances; and when Lisabethli had risen from her instrument after playing three or four national airs to their guest, the minster tower struck twelve before any of them knew that they had been more than an hour together.

There is little to record about the following days and evenings, except that both the young people, and even the mother, daily thought the time longer until —the house-door being barred and bolted—they were able to receive their guest in safety, and chat half the night away in the cheerful, well-lit sitting-room. They seemed to fall into this state of things as if it always had been and must always continue, and the very fact of having a secret to keep and a peril to avert, gave to these innocent meetings an excitement and a charm against which even Frau Helena herself was not quite proof. She was wise enough, however, to foresee that there was another danger besides that of the discovery of her hidden guest and of her own untruth. Lisabethli, who until the present time had very seldom, and only for short periods, been in the company of young men, had already spent eleven days under the same roof with this stranger; and if, since she had fathomed his candid and upright nature, the mother had learnt to love him, was it not expecting too much to suppose the daughter blind to all his gifts and virtues? He, indeed, confidential and friendly as he was, appeared to have taken good care of his own heart, and in all the unchecked playfulness of their talk throughout the long evenings, not a word escaped his lips that sounded other than brotherly in its tone. But if it were really so, if this bird of passage had no thought of nest-building, it would be all the worse for the child, and a mother's duty was to put an end to it at once. She blamed her own weakness and inability to remind her guest (who was really now quite able to travel) of the journey he no longer seemed anxious to take. She felt how much she should miss him, when she had him no longer to expend her motherly care upon, and no more heard his frank loving voice call her "lady-mother," or even vie with her little daughter in devising pet names for her. Then, too, she had a sense of the ungraciousness and unfitness of hastening a guest's departure. And so she was glad and sorry both, when a letter arrived from Augsburg, written by his parents, who at its close enjoined their son not to trespass too long upon the hospitality of the noble lady to whom he owed his life, but to set out as soon as ever his wound was healed and journey homewards; as so only could his anxious mother be fully convinced that he was really out of danger, and that the punishment of his recklessness had been on this occasion a lenient one.

When young Kurt had read out this letter to his two friends, not a word was spoken by any of the three for a long time, and afterwards the talk turned only on grave or indifferent subjects. For the sense of this being their last evening was heavy upon the hearts of all, though none chose to confess it. After midnight—when he had left them—mother and daughter went on sitting up, pretending to have something to do, for neither felt able to sleep. Then Lisabethli left the room to give some last directions to Donate. On her return she held a sheet of paper in her hand, and her face was as white as the paper.

"Dear mother," she stammered out, "Donate has just given me this. It is from *him*. Will you read it."

"Read it yourself," said her mother, "there can be no harm in it."

"Oh mother," whispered the girl, "I cannot see to read it. There is a cloud before my eyes—I know that it is a farewell!"

"Give it me," said Frau Helena. "He asks you," she said, after a pause, "whether you have any objection to his applying to me for my consent to give you to him. He does this in writing because if you do not love him, which he fears is but too likely, as you have always seemed so cheerful and unconcerned—he would prefer not to see you again, but to set out without any leave-taking, and take his unhappy heart as far as possible from hence."

The girl did not answer, and her mother too was

silent. Suddenly Frau Helena felt her child's arms around her neck, her tears on her cheek, while her soft little mouth whispered in her ear. "I should have died, dearest mother, if he had not loved me." Then her mother took her upon her knee as she had not done since she was a child, pressed her closely to her heart, and said with trembling voice, "God bless you, my good children: you have to make up to me for much."

That night no one closed an eye till morning, when they snatched an hour or two, and the daughter, who woke first, glad as she was that her mother should have more rest, could yet hardly wait patiently until she rose and went to return an answer to the young lover's letter.

When Frau Helena went upstairs, she found her guest—who had like herself only closed his eyes a short time before—fast asleep, and so she sat by his bedside contemplating the good innocent countenance that beamed with hope and happiness even in its sleep. But as still he did not wake, she called him by his name. At that he started, and in his confusion could find no words, especially as he did not know what she would say to his letter. But though her face remained grave, her words at once gave him comfort and confidence. "Dear son," said she, "you must not remain here any longer. After what you have written to my child, it would not be fitting that I should persuade you to go on accepting our well-meant though poor hospitality. As soon as you are ready to set out we must part, and Valentin will let you out at the garden door, from whence you must make your way to the "Stork," and there get your horse, explaining your long absence in the most credible way you can. And further I must insist that you do not before your departure say a word to my

daughter that might not be spoken to a stranger. She loves
you dearly, and I may truly say that I could wish nothing
more than to have so worthy a son, since my own son,"
and here she sighed from the depths of her heart, "is
alas! lost to me, as I shall tell you later. But I do not
choose your parents to think that after nursing you here
we have taken advantage of your gratitude to procure a
husband for my daughter; and you yourself, when you
go off and mix with the world again, may wonder at the
especial charm you found in my simple child, when she
was your only companion. Therefore you must part
without one binding word on either side, and thus my
child, too, will have time to examine her young heart,
and to find out whether compassion and the interest of
an adventure may not have produced an illusory belief
that you are her Heaven-appointed bridegroom. If when
you have spoken to your parents and obtained their
consent you are still of the same mind as now, you can
let us know by letter or in person, and God will then
give his blessing if this marriage be really made in
Heaven. And now, dear son, I leave you, and shall
expect you at breakfast, for you shall not leave my
house fasting and unrefreshed, although I must still impose abstinence upon your yearning heart."

She rose and pressed a mother's kiss on the brow
of the youth, who had listened in speechless rapture.
But if he drew from this token of affection any hope
that she would not be so stern as to prevent him pressing his loved maiden to his heart once at least before
they parted, he did not know the strong character of
this mother, in whose nature severity and tenderness
were strangely blended. The farewell had to take place
exactly in the manner prescribed, and if Lisabethli had
not in reaching out her hand given him a look that was

one long confession of the deepest love and fidelity, he might have gone away, not in joyous hope, but in uncertainty as to whether or not he had found a heart that was his for life and death. He left a ring on the table of his room, wrapped in paper, with just one line to the mother. "Will you keep this token for me till you allow me to offer it to your child." As to Valentin and Donate, he rewarded their care so liberally that in their amazement they came to tell Frau Helena that Herr Kurt must surely have made some mistake. But when they saw the traces of tears in Lisabethli's eyes, they silently went their way, and began to put many things together.

This was about noon, when most persons were at home, and Kurt could go through Frau Amthor's garden-gate with least risk of being observed. Some hours passed by without the mother and daughter opening their lips even to speak on indifferent subjects. They were more occupied with each other than ever, and showed it in a hundred little loving ways, only they hardly dared to allow their eyes to meet, for each had a secret to keep. When the day got cooler, the mother was just going to invite her child, who was walking alone in the garden, to put on her hat and take a turn with her through the town, when Valentin suddenly appeared with an anxious visage, and hastily announced that the chief sergeant, who had paid his mistress a visit twelve days before, now requested to know whether she was at home. He had something, he said, of importance and urgency to communicate. Frau Helena —whose first idea was some fresh imprudence on the part of Kurt—had just time to make a sign to Valentin, enjoining silence towards Lisabethli, when in came the stately dignitary, looking far more solemn and mysterious than he had done on the former occasion, and requesting a private interview. After she had led him into a small study, where he took his seat facing her, coughed several times, and re-arranging the tags on his dress, he began in evident embarrassment to address her as follows:—

"I need not to premise, worthy Frau Amthor, how not only your family and house, but also your own character are held in honour by every person, public or private, in our good town, and your virtues, as well as the name and memory of your departed husband, looked up to as a Christian example. It is, therefore, the universal wish to keep sorrow far from you, and to offer you whatever consolation lies within human power for such trial as Heaven has appointed. It will not have escaped you that all as by common consent have long avoided touching the wound that your son's conduct has inflicted, and I indeed as your friend and relative, should have been especially bound never to name your lost Andreas in your presence, if my official duty had not required me so to do. Will you, therefore, not render my painful duty still harder to me by suppression or evasion, but openly tell me what accounts of your son you have lately had, and where you have reason to believe him now to be?"

"If you ask me thus earnestly," replied the mother, without betraying either in look or tone how fast her heart was beating; "I must, alas! return you for answer, that it will be four years next All Saints' since I saw my unhappy son for the last time, and that since then I have had no manner of communication from him. But now let me enquire what leads you and the rest of the Town-Council to make such enquiries about the absent one who—whatever his offences may be—has at least not given his native town any cause for complaint for a space of nine years?"

The sergeant coughed again, and resumed after a pause, during which he was evidently in search of the most appropriate words possible. "Hear me out patiently, my worthy friend and relative, and do not be startled if my communication should sound strange and alarming. Up to the present time it is only a surmise which may—God grant it!—prove to be entirely unfounded. You remember the night on which the trainband intruded upon you, and the disorderly conduct on the island, respecting which I waited upon you the following day, bearing the apologies of the Council. The tavern which caused you so much annoyance, was closed at once, and the scene of much nightly misdemeanour removed. Neither since that night had any trace of the chief offenders been found, so that I began to suspect the watchmen must have been bewildered with new wine, and seen phantoms. But last evening, just as we were breaking up, a young female was brought before us, who had gone to the sexton of St. Ursula to request him to give private burial to a corpse then in her room, since she feared—the fatal wound having been received in a brawl—that she might else as a stranger in the place be held in some way amenable to the law. The little money the girl possessed—she seemed to be no better than a French courtesan, and could scarcely put ten German words together—she had offered the sexton as a bribe for secrecy, but when he, as his duty was, gave information of the death, and took her with him to the Court, she seemed inspired with sudden courage, and being thoroughly cross-examined by us, was yet able to establish her innocence in this tragic matter. The dead man, who had been her lover and brought her with him from Lyons, had on the night of the storm picked a quarrel on the island with an unknown youth, and had been stabbed by the latter during a struggle on the bridge. When the train-band was seen approaching, she had just had time with the help of two of their travelling companions, to get the unconscious man into a boat, and to bring him to the obscure inn where they had arrived on the previous day. The two other men seeing that there was nothing more to be made, got themselves out of the scrape, but she had faithfully tended the wounded man by night and day, and persuaded the host that he was getting better, and would if secrecy were maintained reward him liberally by-and-by. It was only when he had drawn his last breath that she thought of herself with any anxiety, for during his illness she had been obliged to spend all the money he had won at play, and the few ornaments she had, she had sold to a Jew in hopes of getting him quietly buried. As to her future maintenance, however, she continued with brazen assurance, she should have no fear, as she was young and—thank God! —not ugly, if only she were acquitted by us, and could get to a country where people understood her. The dead man had, indeed, treated her liberally as regarded dress, food, and presents, but she had not had much pleasure with him, for he was of a sulky temper, and not a thorough Frenchman, spite of his name. She rather thought he must have been an Alsatian. He called himself Laporte, had travelled through many lands, had served in the Dutch army, and was not fond of speaking about his past. The idea of travelling in Switzerland occurred to him when he had exhausted all his means. She had never found out whether he had a treasure buried in this country, or friends who were in

any way bound to him, and at whose door he had only
to knock in order to be set on his legs again. This was
the simple truth, and more she did not herself know,
and therefore could not tell us, even if she were put to
the torture.

"After this declaration of Fleurette,—which was the
female's name—the mayor ordered that the body should
be moved from the inn (where as yet the death had not
transpired) to the hospital, and last night it was borne
upon a bier into the dead house, and a protocol was
made previous to the interment of the stranger—as such
—close to the churchyard wall. The foreign hussy was
meanwhile confined for a season in the tower of the
hospital. When we betook ourselves this morning to the
dead house, and the inspector had given us his report,
namely, that the wound had been dealt by a German
sword between the fourth and fifth ribs, and that it was
a marvel such a wound had been so long survived—
there came a judicial investigation of the clothes and
few effects found, the result of which in no way contradicted, but rather confirmed, the young woman's statement. We found that in his commission as officer in
the Dutch army, he was entered as a Monsieur Laporte
or De la Porte; there were no other papers. The clerk
had indeed already finished the protocol, when the surgeon called our attention to a seal-ring on the dead
man's clenched left hand. It was a thick gold ring of
curious make, with a blood-red cornelian, and it was
impossible to get it off. But as I chanced—being fond
of antiques—to bend down closer with a candle in
order to examine the style of it, I saw to my surprise
and horror, that it was exactly—but you must not be
alarmed, it may as I said be merely accidental—*exactly*
I repeat, like the family arms of the Amthors, two beams

supporting a cornice with an open door in the middle and a star above. The candle shook in my hand, all the more that at the same moment I saw in the pale bearded face, which had at first seemed to me that of a perfect stranger, an expression—I pray you, my good cousin, to forgive me if I pain you—an expression such as I had seen on the dead face of my excellent and honoured friend, your late husband, when on the day of his burial I stood for the last time beside his open coffin."

The worthy man, having got so far in his narrative, made a pause, during which he did not venture to look at the matron opposite him, though indeed he could but poorly estimate the amount of the woe that hung over her. He had no idea that the fate of both children might depend on whether the stranger proved to be her own son or not.

"Be comforted, my beloved friend," he at length resumed, wiping away the cold drops from his brow. "I have taken upon myself not to say a word of this discovery to any one but the mayor, whom you know to be an honourable man heartily devoted to your family. I asked him whether this melancholy supposition had not better be buried in our hearts. It is not probable, but yet it is possible, that a branch of the Amthors may have migrated to foreign lands, there changed their name to Laporte or De la Porte for the sake of convenience, retaining, however, the family arms. As to that look in the dead face, which is a good deal disfigured by a deep scar, I said nothing about it to him, as he had declared he saw no likeness whatever to Andreas, whom he remembered to have often met nine or ten years ago. Nevertheless he was of opinion that so singular a coincidence ought not to remain a secret to you. If indeed, contrary to all probability, it should prove to be your poor son who has met with so tragical an end, no one would deny a mother the bitter consolation of blessing to its eternal rest, the head she had carried beneath her heart. Again, as regards official formalities, it is unfitting that we should satisfy ourselves with the declaration of a vagabond female, when we have the most convincing witness at hand; for it may prove desirable hereafter, with regard to future demises, inheritances, and the like, to have some certain knowledge to go upon. Therefore I determined to come to you, to lay the whole case before you, and persuade you, if I can, to pay a visit to the hospital—as secretly as you will— in order to prevent all useless suspense or suspicion."

So saying he rose and went to the window to give Frau Helena time to collect herself and come to a decision. A quarter of an hour passed away, during which nothing was audible in the small room but the ticking of the great clock—a wedding present from Lisabethli's grandfather to his daughter-in-law, bearing on its metal face the family arms of the Amthors. Out of doors, too, all was still—nothing to be heard but the cawing of a flight of rooks wending their way over the terrace, or the muffled thud of an over-ripe apple on the grass.

At length the lady rose and approached her old and tried friend, who met her rigid gaze with an expression of sorrowful sympathy. "I thank you," she said, "for having come to me, and performed this painful duty with so much consideration. Say to the highly respected mayor that I shall find myself at about nine o'clock at the side-door of the hospital, and should wish to be met there by some trustworthy person, and this painful step concealed from all who might be likely to talk of it. The rest I leave in God's hand—He will order it aright."

"I shall be there myself to meet you," replied the sergeant. "May our Lord God strengthen your heart, and your frame, and grant us the fulfilment of our hope that this may prove merely an accidental coincidence!"

"Amen!" said Frau Helena in a hollow voice, in which was no hope whatever.

Thereupon her visitor left her. As soon as she was alone she sank down on her knees in the place where she had been standing, and waves of anguish closed over her mother's heart.

———

It was already getting dusk, when her daughter's voice speaking in the garden to old Donate, roused the mourner from her trance. Soon after Lisabethli entered, and found her mother sitting at her desk, as though evening had overtaken her at her accounts and letters.

"Dearest mother," said the girl, "he has sent me another letter—a boy brought it to Donate; he wrote it as soon as he had got beyond the gates, because you said he might write when far away. Will you read it? He says that I am to be as sure of his truth as of your love, and that nothing can ever part us but death."

She held the letter out to her mother, but the latter did not take it. "Leave me alone, awhile, child," she replied. "I have got something to think over."

The girl went away, happy to keep her treasure all to herself. The mother remained an hour longer in the darkening room, absorbed in darkest thoughts, through which pierced not one heavenly ray. She never for a moment doubted that the ring on the finger of the dead man, was the same that she had placed on the finger of her Andreas the first time that he went to Holy Communion. As to any accident which had transferred this ring to the hand of some one else, she never entertained the idea. He who lay in the dead house of the hospital with that sword-thrust in his breast was none other than her much-loved, much-wept son. And he who had killed this son—in self-defence it is true—was one to whom she had promised her daughter, who would probably return in a few weeks as a happy bride-groom to the desolate house, and with laughing face carry off her daughter, so that through him she should be bereaved of both her children. She hated him at that moment, she cursed the hour in which he entered her house, cursed her own tongue that had promised him protection and ratified that promise with a falsehood, when saving him from his pursuers. And yet the next moment her heart recalled that curse, for in her mind's eye she saw again the candid face of the innocent fugi-tive, heard his clear tones, remembered her own words when she vowed to be a mother to him, and her daugh-ter's voice when she came to her on the previous even-ing with her letter, and said, "I should have died, dearest mother, had he not loved me." She knew her child, and that these words were not lightly spoken. She felt, moreover, what she owed to this child, who had been for years defrauded of her due share of maternal love. Would she not have cause of bitter complaint against a brother who, after years of long wild wander-ing, had only returned to his country to bring fresh misery on his mother's head, and to destroy the whole happiness of his sister's life? "No," said the strong-hearted woman, "it must not be. No one is guilty here but I. I am the real cause of his miserable end, I with my foolish indulgence and subservience from excess of love! No one shall suffer—ought to suffer, but I. I shall not have any joy in the son whom God seemed to

have given me to replace my lost one; my other child
will go away, and I shall be left solitary, with only my
own misery—misery purchased by a double falsehood!"

She sank again into gloomy brooding, till the minster
clock struck nine. Then she started, and gathering together all the strength of a desolate soul, she called to
Lisabethli to bring her her coif, as she had a necessary
errand that took her out. The girl wondered at her
going so late, but did not like to ask any questions,
having indeed in her early days too many experiences
of unusual proceedings on her mother's part to dwell
much upon this wonder, especially now she had such
happy thoughts of her own. But old Valentin could not
refrain from enquiring whether he might not light the
lantern and accompany his mistress. She shook her head
in silence, doubled her veil over her face, and left the house.

It was no great distance to the hospital, but she
often felt as though she should never be able to reach
it. "O Lord God!" she inwardly prayed, "take me
away from earth! It is too much—Thou visitest Thy
servant too severely!" And yet something too seemed
to draw her onwards to the place where she should behold for the last time the long yearned after face of her
lost son!

When she reached the site of the old pest-house,
with its handsome chapel, a man dressed in black drew
near and whispered her name. It was, she knew, her
friend the chief sergeant, but they did not exchange
words, and he led her through the side-door, which he
unlocked, into the interior of the building. They entered a dimly-lighted hall, where the hospital attendant
on duty had fallen asleep on a bench. Their footsteps
wakened him, but at a signal from the sergeant he remained where he was, while the former lighted another

taper, and preceded the lady. They went up some
steps, and through a long passage to a kind of cellar-
door which stood half open. "If you prefer to go in
alone," said he, "take the taper. I will wait for you in
the passage."

She bowed assent in silence, took the tin sconce
into her hand, and entered the chamber of the dead.

It was a low stone-roofed room, with bare walls
blackened by smoke and time, and entirely devoid of
furniture. In its midst stood the coffin, roughly made,
and stuffed with nothing but half mouldy straw. In it
rested the corpse, beneath a grey pall, scarcely long
enough to cover the tall frame of the dead, who had
been laid down in the clothes he wore in life. At the
lady's entrance two rats who had been gnawing at his
boots, jumped out of the straw into their holes. She did
not notice them. Her eyes were fixed upon the head of
the coffin, where the pall just showed a high white forehead with a deep scar down to the very eyebrows. She
placed the taper in a niche of the wall, and with her
remnant of strength approached to raise the pall. *One*
glance at the rigid face furrowed by the conflict of life
and of death—and she sank down beside the coffin.

Yet it was no swoon that mercifully shrouded her
senses. It was only that her legs would no longer support her; her mind was fully awake, and her heart felt
all its old wounds open, and begin to bleed and burn
afresh. She had fallen on her knees, her hands folded,
her eyes fixed on the pale face of her dead son, averted
as it seemed from her in indifference, in almost anger,
and upturned to the black arch of the roof. Oh! she
would have given her life, the last poor remnant of her
days on earth, if those eyes could but have opened once

more for one farewell look, if those discoloured lips could once—only once—have called her "mother!"

The sergeant who was waiting in the passage, was under the impression that he heard a groan proceed from the chamber of the dead. What it meant he did not know. If indeed it were her son he would not disturb the mortal anguish of the mother. Suddenly he heard her steps approach the door, and saw her coming out, the light in her hand, her head erect as if no shock had bowed her down, her eyes strained and strange, but meeting his.

"I have kept you waiting," she said, "which was unnecessary. One glance is sufficient to reveal the truth to a mother: but it has shaken me. I had to rest a little."

"So it is not he!" cried her faithful friend. "God be praised!"

"To all Eternity!" said she. "Let us go. The place is ghastly."

She went on hastily with the taper, and steadily descended the steps. In the hall where the watcher sat, she put down the taper on the table, and her hand no longer trembled.

"You will see," said the sergeant to the sleepy official, "that to-morrow, not later than five, the sexton comes and bears the body to its rest."

"The grave is already dug, sir," was the reply, "near the place where a year ago Hans Frisdolin, the parricide was laid."

"Not so," returned the sergeant, "he shall have no dishonourable burial, only as a stranger he must lie next to the wall. His French girl has offered to pay the sexton. You can remind her, Killian."

"What I wanted to ask," the man broke in, "is

whether the foreign lady may have wine, and also a roast pigeon for which she longs. She will pay for it, she says, and indeed she is a very good little thing, and a pair of foreigners have been to pay her a visit in the tower and spent three hours there. The warder turned them away at night, but the lady was sadly put out, and she sent the warder to ask whether I would not pay her a visit, for she found the time hang heavy."

"She must conform to the regulations," growled the sergeant. "To-morrow she will be free, and then she can recommence her godless trade, as she too surely will so soon as she is beyond our jurisdiction. Good-night, Killian."

He turned to Frau Helena, who had gone to the door of the hall, and there in deep shadow leant against the wall. While he led her out, and on the way to her house, whither he accompanied her, he kept railing against the dissolute creature, who might well have the unfortunate dead on her conscience instead of throwing out baits for fresh victims before the earth had closed over the last. He protested it removed a stone from his heart to know that this Laporte was no Amthor, and he hoped that the real Andreas might yet live to make up to his mother for all that she had so christianly endured. The Council, however, was truly indebted to the worthy matron for having given herself the trouble of this late walk.

And so saying he took leave of the silent lady, and wished her a night of refreshing sleep.

That wish was most certainly not realised. A storm arose that filled the night with such wild uproar, that it seemed as if the very earth trembled. In the room which had once been that of Andreas, a window-shutter had been blown open, and now kept beating and flapping against the wall. Lisabethli, who had fallen asleep, woke up in terror at the sound. She saw her mother leave the room without a light, and heard her go upstairs, and there was an end to that source of disturbance as she fastened the shutter again. The young girl waited awhile for her return, but fell asleep before it, and indeed she would have waited in vain. For Frau Helena remained in the dark room above, as though it were more tolerable to her to listen to the storm than to the breathing of her child, who, in her happy dreams spoke of her Kurt, and called him loving names.

About dawn the wind went down, and in its place came a cold rain which got heavier and heavier, and at length veiled town and river in a grey mist. The sexton who, with two companions to help him, had by five o'clock dug a grave by the churchyard wall, and lowered a rudely-made coffin into it, was quicker than ever over his work, and the coffin rested slantingly in the shallow pit. Then, since the clergyman who was to have blessed it, omitted his duty in consequence of the terrible weather, the man of the spade himself said a Paternoster for the poor soul, and hastily shovelled in the coarse clods, leaving the rest to be finished by his companions. He was about to hasten home and catch a short morning-nap in his warm room, when he noticed a female figure kneeling by a head-stone not far from the new grave, her head, covered by a black veil, resting against the stone. That stone had long been deserted, the family of the one who slept there having removed to another country. What could the lady be doing there? As, however, she remained quite still, and spite of the rain seemed absorbed in her devotions, he did not venture to disturb her. For an instant it flashed across him that it might be the foreign hussy who had paid for the grave of the murdered man, but he heard afterwards that she had slept till a late hour, and had, indeed, only awaked when the beadle came to march her out of the town.

A few days later there reached him from an unknown source, a considerable sum of money, which purported to be payment for a forgotten burial. He for his part gave himself no thought about the matter, and pocketed the unexpected windfall as though it had dropped from the sky.

What follows is soon told. In the next spring the marriage of Kurt Brucker and Elizabeth Amthor was, according to custom, celebrated at the home of the bride, and the Augsburg relations came in great state to do all honour to the bride's mother, and the family of the Amthors. Nothing which could be looked for on such an occasion was left undone, and Lisabethli had no cause to complain of her dower, her outfit, or the wedding banquet. One thing only was lacking—the smile of joy on the face of the bride's mother. She was kind and courteous to all, to strangers and relatives alike, and bowed assent when the guests remarked to her how completely made for each other the young couple were, and that both houses might well be congratulated on so fitting and honourable an alliance. But amidst all the loud cheer of the bridal banquet, she sat pale and silent as a ghost, and though the rest of the family of the bridegroom who had not known her before, gradually grew reconciled to this, and whispered to each other that it was the sorrow for her absent son which pressed so hardly upon her on this joyous day— yet Kurt had not been wont to see his mother-in-law thus, and it struck him as strange that she never once gave him her hand, or pressed him in her arms as she had done the stranger-guest when, but half-recovered, he had ventured to woo her child. It was only when the youthful pair set out to their new home, that the mother kissed her daughter with such a violent burst of tears, it seemed as though her heart would break and melt away, and then laid her damp hand on her son-in-law's brow, murmuring words that no one could understand. Then she turned hurriedly away, and even before they left the house, locked herself up in the solitude of her own room.

There she spent the few years that she had to live, avoiding all society, reading religious books, and only opening her door to the poor and the sorrowful. When, in a year's time, letters came from Augsburg, pressingly inviting her to the christening of a grandson, she excused herself on account of her age and infirmities which un-fitted her to travel. Yet she was often seen to walk with vigorous step in solitary roads outside the town—old Valentin a few paces behind her. But she never ad-dressed him and seemed, indeed, almost to have lost the habit of speech. It was only on her death-bed, when she felt her end drawing near, that she sent for the parish priest, who spent some hours with her. What she then imparted was told by him to one of her daugh-ter's children who travelled to Berne to see his grand-mother's grave. That she had ordered to be dug by the churchyard wall, close to the long-ago-levelled mound under which her lost son had found his last resting-place.

END OF THE LOST SON.

THE FAIR KATE.

THE FAIR KATE.

"It is incontestably true," said the old landscape-painter B———, slowly stroking down his grey or rather mouse-coloured beard, "women will be women, that is, sex dominates in the best as in the worst; and though they are often obstinate enough in taking things into their head, yet after all it is but seldom a head with any special or original character, is only a feminine head. A genuine individuality that can be measured by itself alone is far more rare among them than among us men, and positively I do not know if the fact gives us anything to boast of. Very often our peculiarity is only peculiar folly—a departure from nature, whether through culture or mutilation; while women, for whose training or spoiling less is done from without, seldom become unnatural either in good or evil, seldom exceed the average. But when they do so I have always found something to marvel at.

"For instance one case remains indelibly fixed on my memory, when I actually witnessed a thing unheard of and unparalleled, a lovely girl who had an actual hatred of her own beauty, not merely a conceited, coquettish, pretended indifference to it, or even an over-strained, saintly, nun-like renunciation of it, but what one might call an honourable enmity against it, which had, indeed, its good grounds.

"I became acquainted with the story in question in the following way.

"At that time—it's now more than twenty years ago —I was very intimate with a long-forgotten Dutch painter, Jan van Kuylen or Kuyden—you will not find the name in any catalogue of known artists.

"In the course of the usual journey to Rome, he had remained hanging about Munich, the real reason being that Raphael and Michael Angelo were secretly oppressive to him, crushed his own small personality, and disgusted him with the neat Dutch style by which he made a good deal of money. He was a curious fellow, the oddest mixture of humour and phlegm, ideality and cynicism, sentimental tendencies and caustic irony. And so, too, in his studio you found the oddest medley; there were exquisite specimens of Venetian glass for which he had a great love, costly instruments inlaid with silver and mother of pearl, for he played the guitar and lute well; then again on some heavily embroidered cloth you would see a tin-plate with bits of cheese-rind, or a quart of beer in an ugly mug, and the room would be filled with thick, strong-smelling, cheap tobacco which he had sent to him from Holland, and smoked in a small black clay pipe the whole day through.

"In his pictures, however, everything was so neat, clean, and accurate that at the first glance there was not much to distinguish them from those of the old masters —Netscher, Mieris, and Gerard Dow. But when you looked closer you saw they betrayed a most eccentric vein, various displays of a humour, which, however, chiefly delighted to disport itself in caricature or parody. This was not the fashion then as now, and therefore in Munich, where the pathetic or the simply naïve was still in the ascendant, Jan van Kuylen's too often profane performances did not go down well. The first picture that he exhibited there was one of Paradise, where Adam, a gaunt, lean, yellow-visaged fellow, was digging the ground in the sweat of his brow, while Eve darned an old jacket, and glanced up in evident ill-humour at the forbidden fruit, while the first person of the Trinity looked smilingly over the hedge. The picture was at once removed, for naturally the clergy took umbrage at it. And indeed Jan did not fare much better with the second, which also showed the cloven foot. He called it the Temptation of St. Anthony. It is true that this new version widely departed from the simple honest absence of all propriety with which the worthy Teniers has illustrated the legend. A young peasant woman—evidently returning from a wedding or christening feast, as she was carrying a basket filled with meat, cakes, and a bottle of wine—had let herself be induced by the cool of the evening hour, and probably her own heavy head, to take a nap in the shade of the wood. St. Anthony, a very sturdy youth, with his cowl thrown back, had evidently been coming unsuspectingly along, and at the sudden sight stood rooted to the spot, looking now at the young woman, now at the basket of good things, and manifestly waging a violent warfare with his conscience, during which he scratched his head in absurd perplexity. The expression of his face was so irresistibly droll, that on this occasion even the clergy could not avoid winking at it with a smile.

"But I have not yet mentioned the strangest part of it all: this Saint in two minds, and the Adam in the picture of Paradise, were both exact portraits of the painter himself. And this added immensely to the drollery of the thing. For in point of fact my friend's appearance was a perfect study for a humorist. He might have been painted entirely in different shades of yellow, his complexion of the tender tone of a fresh Edam cheese, his hair and beard like overgrown dusty stubble, his grey eyes almost hidden by thick pale eyelashes. And to make the matter more complete he always dressed himself from top to toe in sand-coloured cloth for winter, in nankeen for summer, and was fond of bringing forward and ridiculing his own personal peculiarities by the most far-fetched comparisons. So, too, in his pictures, where he regularly and as prominently as possible introduced himself moderately caricatured, but always in positions that were half-comic and half-sad, half-expressive of self-contempt, and half of resignation. It seemed as if he wished to show that he did not take in ill-part, but rather was the first to laugh over, the practical joke played him by the step-dame Nature.

"Well, it was Whit Monday, my wife had a party of her friends to coffee, and the buzz and hum of female voices —which I could hear through double doors—drove me out. As it was a beautiful afternoon, with everything in its early freshness, and plenty for me to study on the banks of the Isar, I determined to invite Van Kuylen to take a walk. He was living at that time in Theresa-meadows, in a small house with a room to the north, that he had fitted up for a studio. You entered it by a little garden, in which of course the inevitable tulips were not now wanting, but which equally abounded with lilacs and jessamine. Next you turned into a small court where a fountain was playing, which the eccentric artist had adorned with a misshapen Triton, the work of his own hands, for he dabbled in modelling. Then you came to the studio door, which was seldom open, for Jan painted away with unwearied diligence from morning to night, and neither sought amusement nor society.

"I was, therefore, surprised on the present occasion, to find the door open, and for a moment thought he must have gone out, and that his maid might be busy arranging the room, when I heard his voice saying to some one, 'If you are weary, we will leave off for to-day, and besides it is a high festival. Let us hope your father confessor will not be angry at our being engaged with such worldly subjects, instead of keeping it holy!'

"No answer was returned, or at all events none that I heard. I was amazed. To have a model sitting with an open door was no more usual or befitting at that time than it is now. And that the strong smell of the Dutch tobacco should not come through that door, bordered on the miraculous.

"When, however, I drew a step nearer, I soon saw why my good Jan had given up smoking, and though I was only a landscape painter, I did not at all wonder at him. For such a model was worth while losing one's head for, to say nothing of one's pipe.

"The colours on the face of the young girl who sat there in the best light, as motionless as a picture, with a red damask curtain behind her, were really so brilliant, that they exceeded all probability, and made me perfectly stupid with amazement. Such a white satin-skin, just tinged with faintest rose-colour, and here and there with blue, such vividly red lips, such velvety brown eyes and silky hair of the same colour growing rather low on a superbly arched brow, I have never before nor since seen, except, indeed in pictures, where they make little impression because they are exaggerated. Nature can certainly venture upon much that Art can never safely aspire to. When I had somewhat got over the first shock of this sensational style of nature-painting, I saw that in the drawing, too, the very best possible had been done; done with a grandeur and solidity which were almost prodigal, for it is not wise to expend every resource, colour and form, both in perfection, on any one figure. Even a sculptor must have confessed that only in the best antiques had he seen anything of the kind. Above all I was amazed at the contour of the cheeks, the noble, massively-rounded chin, the half-opened lips that seemed to breathe out a very overflow of life, and the perfect shape of the straight, scornful little nose, which was just a trifle too broad, perhaps, for modern taste. It was only the eyes that afforded any room for fault-finding, if after seeing those calm and melancholy stars beaming on one, one had the heart for it. At least I found out later that the line of the eyelids might have been more curved, and they themselves a degree broader.

"For the first ten minutes I stood there actually spell-bound, did not even say 'Good-day,' and was—as people often stupidly call it—all eyes. And indeed no one spoke. Van Kuylen, his extinct pipe in his mouth, had merely given me a side nod, and continued painting hard. The motionless beauty queened it before her red curtain on an old satin ottoman with gilt lions' heads, her eyes fixed upon the great half-darkened window, her hands—which were very slender and white, but not small—carelessly folded on her lap. She wore a common dark-coloured cotton gown, with an old tulle frill crammed in at her throat, but had neither ear-rings, rings, nor ornaments of any kind.

"Beside her on a low stool, sat a little girl of about seven, slowly and reluctantly knitting away at a coarse blue stocking.

"At length I found it necessary to make some re-
mark.

"'I am disturbing you, Mynheer,' said I, though for a
quarter of an hour past I had seen that he did not per-
mit himself to be disturbed by me. We painters used to
call him Mynheer in jest.

"'Send me away at once,' I went on, 'if I am in
any way inconvenient either to you or the young lady.
Though indeed when one has hit upon such a discovery,
it is but a man's Christian duty to share it with his
neighbours.'

"Van Kuylen muttered a Dutch word or two between
his teeth; the girl looked gloomy as though I had said
something to offend her; the child with the stocking
yawned heartily, and dropped a dozen stitches.

"'My good friend,' I at length resumed in Dutch, in
which he had taught me to jabber a little, 'tell me
honestly whether you wish me at the Devil, or whether
I may remain a little longer to stare at this really quite
unreasonably exquisite face that your lucky star has led
you to—Heaven knows how—and which, to speak
plainly, is infinitely too good for you. Such a subject—
begging your pardon—is not appropriate for your foot-
square canvas, and your finickin genre-brush. Life-size,
indeed, and faithfully and humbly copied—as it pleased
God to make her—in the manner of the old Venetians,
that would be a different thing. But I know you too
well, with your worthy visage; you would want to be
peeping down upon her from some window-corner or
other, or giving scope to some of your antic humour,
and that would be an insult to such a paragon of Grecian perfection, with whose face that wretched cotton
gown is no more in keeping than a modern crinoline
with the Juno Ludovisi.'

"I had no scruple in thus crudely speaking my mind to him; he was rather fond of pungent personal remarks, and did not remain long in my debt.

"He rose to get something that he wanted for his work, and answered without removing his empty pipe from his lips: 'I can well imagine your mouth watering after such an exceptional morsel. You would like, perhaps, to paint her as another pigeon-breasted Diana emerging from a pool under a German oak-tree, and setting horns on the brow of an Acteon who has stolen his legs from the Apollo Belvedere? The girl seems to you good enough for that, does she not? But that's not to be done. You will never get her to consent to any mythological ambiguities. Do you suppose I have ever seen an inch more of her than what she is gracious enough to shew us both at this present moment? And even for this I have had to run after her long, and almost despaired of her ever sitting to me at all. But hunger is the best of go-betweens. And so I have had to give in to all her severe conditions. The door is always to stand open, the little school-girl is always to sit there, and if I ever venture to visit her at her own abode, there is to be an end of us both! Of course I agreed to everything she chose; I was so besotted by her face, I could have committed one of the seven deadly sins just to see her once in this light, sitting on that seat, and so to be able to study her to my heart's content. As to what I am to make of it afterwards that is immaterial. But if I secretly hoped gradually to melt the ice between us—at all events to a kind of brotherly friendship and regard—why, I was much mistaken. It is no great wonder after all. I am not to her taste, and I think none the worse of her for that. But there have been others who accidentally turned in—this is the third

sitting—who were thoroughly discomfited, very showy
audacious gentry—handsome Fritz, and Schluchten-
müller, and our Don Ramiro, with his languishing tenor
voice. They were all tinder at once, but after a little
burning and glowing had to retire, extinguished as if by
a gush of cold water. Is it not so, Miss,' said he suddenly in German to the silent beauty, 'it is perfectly
useless to pay you compliments? This gentleman—who
is only a landscape-painter it is true, but still a connois-
seur in women—would willingly express his wonder and
admiration. But I have told him that you would rather
not hear anything of the sort.'

"'You are right,' she replied with the utmost indifference. 'It is the fact, I know, and I cannot alter it.
But God knows if I had had anything to do with it, I
should never have chosen the face He has given me.'

"Her manner of saying this perfectly amazed me. It
had not a touch of that mock modesty, which says the
very reverse of what it thinks, in hopes of being contradicted. No, it expressed a weary, but unalterable con-
tempt for the gift of beauty; it was the tone of one who
has to drag a sack of gold through a desert, and sighs
from the very core of his heart, 'I would give it all for
one morsel of bread.'

"Then, too, her way of expressing herself, showed
more culture than you usually find amongst girls who
hire themselves out to be painted. It was easy to see
that the fair creature had some strange story connected
with her.

"'Nay, nay,' said I, 'if you had chosen your own
face you would not have shown bad taste in the matter.
And though, indeed, beauty is transient, while ugliness
endures, and there may be inconveniences, or even dangers in the impressions it makes on those who see you,

still you would hardly convince me, young lady, that you are seriously annoyed at having such a face. You would be quite unique if it were so.'

"'You may think what you like,' she replied negligently, and her lovely full upper lip assumed a scornful expression. 'I know perfectly well what men are. If a poor thing is vain of her little bit of pink and white, *that* does not suit them, and if she is not vain at all, but rather curses the beauty which has cost her so dear, why that will not please them either! But after all I have nothing to do with setting other people right, it is enough that I know what I know.'

"After this unflattering declaration came a long pause. Mynheer van Kuylen sat at his easel, and attempted by the tenderest glazing to convey the smoothness of that skin, and the lustre of those moist eyes; the child had laid down her stocking, and was turning the pages of a picture-book, and by way of putting a good face on my embarrassment I lit a cigar.

"'You have no objection, Miss?' I enquired in my most ingratiating tones.

"She slightly nodded, and in so doing gave a sigh, and her delicate nostrils quivered.

"'May one venture to ask your name, Fräulein?' I resumed after a while.

"'My name is Katharine,' she replied in the same curt, out-spoken way. 'But all who know me call me Kate. As to my parent's name that would not interest you.'

"'Miss Kate,' I said, 'I notice from your manner of speech that you do not belong to Munich."

"'No.'

"'Your accent has something Rhinelandish about it.'

"'Very possibly.'

"'Have you any reasons for objecting to speak of your home?'

"'Why do you ask?'

"'I should like one of these days to go and see whether there are many faces there like yours.'

"'Only one,' she replied in the most matter-of-fact tone. 'But that is painted on glass in St. Catharine's Church.'

"'Then you sat for it?'

"'No,' returned she; 'it was just the other way.'

"I looked at Van Kuylen to see whether he could make anything of this strange speech, but he seemed so taken up with his work as not even to hear our conversation.

"'You must not be offended with me, Miss Kate,' said I after an interval, 'if I put a few more questions to you. Your answers are so many riddles. I am not prompted believe me by mere curiosity, but by sincere interest in knowing what circumstances can have led you to leave your home, and after so good an education, and with so beautiful a face, to adopt here—'

"'You mean that I seem to have been brought up for something better than to make money of my looks. That may be. But this is what things have come to, and since it is my face that has brought me into trouble, it must help me out of it—at least so far as it can do creditably.'

"A cloud passed over her eyes; she looked before her even more steadfastly than her wont, with an expression between anger and sorrow that rendered her more enchanting than ever. We were silent. Suddenly she resumed—

"'I really do not know why I should make any mystery about my story. There is no disgrace in it, and you two gentlemen would only imagine something far worse. Besides you both look thoroughly good and trustworthy,' (Van Kuylen gave a short cough) 'and if you were ever to hear any slander about me I could appeal to you. Babette, dear,' turning to the little girl, 'go into the garden and make yourself a very smart wreath of lilac and jasmine—do not gather any tulips. It is only,' she went on in a low voice as soon as the child had left, 'because there is no need the people I lodge with should know everything, and that little creature—young as she is—has already very long ears, and repeats whatever she picks up. Not, indeed, that I need to be ashamed of my past, but that they would look upon me as crazy if they knew all its ins and outs, whereas as things stand now, they are sorry for me, believing that I have only had some common unfortunate love-affair, and therefore consider myself unworthy that the sun should shine upon me.'

"She was once more silent, and seemed to have forgotten all about her intended narration. There was a Sabbath stillness all around; we only caught through the open door the sound of little Babette's heavy shoes on the gravel walks, and the twittering of birds in the meadows. Van Kuylen had risen and gone to a carved cupboard, in which he had a habit of keeping all sorts of odds and ends; he now brought out of it a wicker-covered flask of curious shape, filled three small glasses from it, and presented them on an old china-tray, first to the young girl, then to me. After we had both declined, he tossed them all three off in succession, and then sat down before his easel, not painting, but resting his head on his hand.

"'What surprises me,' said I, breaking silence at length, 'is that I have never met you before, Miss Kate.

Yet I am a pretty constant lounger in our streets, and not unobservant; indeed, my dear wife reproves me for looking over-boldly under the bonnets of pretty girls. You must live like a mole in some underground dwelling, or you never could have escaped me.'

"'Nay,' said she with a slight smile, the first which had lit up her melancholy; 'I walk out every day. I cannot sit still. I find time hang so heavy, as I am not skilled in work. But then I wear a very thick veil, the everlasting staring is so hateful to me, particularly in a strange place. There was only one evening, when standing before a bright shop-window, that I did venture to throw back my veil—at that very moment Herr van Kuylen chanced to pass, and since then he has often and often recognized me, though I am wrapped up like a nun. Besides I always have Babette with me. I should be afraid of going out alone, for though it is now more than a year since I left home, I still feel so desolate and forlorn, and my heart aches so, that I am often tempted to jump into the first deep water I come across, and get rid of myself, and my whole useless existence.'

"Her smile had vanished, and instead, tears stood in her eyes.

"'Were you not then beloved in your home?' I enquired. 'So beautiful and sweet a child must—'

"'Loved! Yes, indeed, if only there had been sense in their affection. I was loved sometimes too much, sometimes too little. If I had had another face it would all have been right enough. But they expected all sorts of wonders, and out of sheer vanity must make me unhappy. There were six brothers and sisters older than myself—I am the youngest and last—and all the rest, who had quite common-place human countenances, are now contented and well provided for, married unnoticed folk of whom no bad or good is said, and about whom no one troubles himself to enquire. But as for me, no sooner was I out of my swaddling-clothes than I was pronounced a little wonder of the world, and all the aunts and cousins lifted their hands in amazement at the sight of me, and told my mother no princess need be ashamed of having brought such a child into the world. And there was something wonderful in it, too. My father was a poor schoolmaster, my mother a sexton's daughter, neither of them particularly handsome; only through my maternal grandmother, pretty hands and feet, and beautiful long hair, had come into the family. But as it happened, while I was coming into the world, Count F——, the patron of our church, put up a magnificent new window in St. Catharine's, representing the Saint kneeling by the wheel, a palm-branch between her folded hands, and painted in such beautiful vivid colours, people were never tired of looking at it. Our whole village, Catholics and Protestants, crowded to see it, and for weeks nothing else was spoken of, at least in our house. My eldest brother, who already drew very well, copied it at once, but my good mother especially saw the picture—as she afterwards told us—constantly before her day and night, whether her eyes were open or shut; and when I was born, she insisted upon it that I must be baptised by the name of Katharine. It was not long before they all took to calling me "the fair Kate," and all agreed that I had stolen my face from the picture on the window.

"'You may suppose that when I first came to understand this, trotting about as a little child, I had no cause to regret it. Everybody coaxed and praised me, and if the kissing and stroking was at times rather too much of a good thing, yet on the whole it had its advantages.

As the last of the batch, too, I was better treated in every way than my brothers and sisters, nor had I anything to endure from their jealousy, for they really, as well as my parents, did consider me a thing apart, a special gift and grace of God to the family, reflecting some glory on its other members. It was a thing, of course, that I—so far as our poverty permitted it—should be well dressed, have the best food kept for me, and receive more instruction than the rest. My father used to devote his two hours of leisure to me; I must needs learn French and pianoforte playing, and it was evident to all that not only must I take no share in the house-work, but that my delicate fingers must not be spoilt by sewing or knitting. I only wonder that I did not become more idle and vain than I actually was. But indeed to me, too, it seemed so much a thing of course that I did not give it any particular thought. Apricots have different flavours to wild pears, and cost different sums. That is all very natural. One man has a hundred thousand dollars, another a voice in his throat that bewitches people, a third is so learned that all take off their hats to him, and *I* was "the fair Kate," with whom everybody fell in love. What the exact value of *that* was—I mean the falling in love—I did not know; I had not found out that I too had a heart, I was not even very fond of my own family, because I found it tiresome to be always so much made of, and as to falling in love with myself, that couldn't well happen, as I had been used to my bit of red and white, and all the rest that people made such a fuss about, from a child.

"'I had only one playfellow that I cared at all for, and for the very reason that he was rather cross than kind to me; a youth different to the rest, but neither particularly handsome or lively, and one of the poorest.

His father shipped charcoal up and down the Rhine, and worked very hard; his mother was a quiet sickly woman, always at home or in the church, with a sorrowful face that made me feel ashamed of my smart clothes. Her son, too—he was about five years older than I, and had often to help his father—would look more crossly than ever out of his eyes if he met me on a Sunday, when my mother had decked me with all sorts of colours. He made no remarks, but he always avoided me on those occasions, and childish as I was, and vain, too, of being the fair Kate, this never failed to give me a pang. I would contrive to get into my every-day clothes to creep down about twilight to the banks of the Rhine where his cottage stood, and I was quite happy if Hans Lutz would only be good-natured to me and say, "Now you look like a human being again, and not like a doll." He had a way—silent as he was—of amusing me better than anybody else, would cut me out little boats of bark that rode at anchor in a little harbour that he built; he could play me my favourite airs on a reed-pipe, and it was often night, and I had to be scolded away before I would consent to part from him.

"'You see already what that was leading to. I could no longer do without him, although others held him cheap as being inferior to them all, because he had had the small-pox and went about in the coarsest and most thread-bare jacket. I almost think there was some vanity in it. I seemed to myself to be a princess condescending to the charcoal-burner; then again in my better hours I noticed that I had an especial respect for him, more indeed than for any other human creature, and that I never respected myself so much as when he had given me a kind word.

"'Our years of childish play were nearly over; he was

fifteen, I ten, when a legacy came to his parents, not, indeed, enough to set them up with carriage and horses, but to make them much more comfortable than before. The father gave up the charcoal-loading business, and became—I really do not quite know what—a sort of factor or agent. The eldest son, my Hans Lutz, was sent off to a school for artisans; he was to be an engineer, and was indeed made for it. His younger brother, who was about my own age, remained at home and took to violin playing, in hopes of gaining admission into the Ducal Chapel; they had a distant cousin there who played the bassoon.

"'Time went on: at first I missed my companion dreadfully, I did not know what to do with myself on Sundays, and found out fully how much he had been to me. However, I gradually got accustomed to his absence, to going about again dressed like a doll, to being serenaded by the students who passed through the town, or to reading poems and love-letters which were thrown in to me through the window, but which I never answered. For my mother was pretty strict with me, and after my first Communion, I was never allowed to leave the house alone. I believe she was afraid that one of the mad Englishmen, who stared at me worst of all, would carry me off, or that the Rhine water-sprites would draw me down out of envy and spite. Now and then real wooers would make their appearance, very respectable people, quite able to support a wife. But they had a pretty reception! My father was not going to part with me on such easy terms; he would hear of nothing under a Count, as I overheard him telling my mother, or else a man so rich as to be able to lay down my weight in money. It was all one to me, the privilege that I enjoyed of being the beautiful Kate, and treated as the most remarkable and important person in our district quite satisfied me, and since the departure of Hans Lutz I did not so much as know that I had a heart.

"'He never wrote to me, never sent me a message. It was only seldom that I heard from his mother how well he was doing, how industrious he was, and how much he was praised by his instructors. I used to wonder that he never came over for a visit. The distance from Carlsruhe was not so great after all, and however sparing of his time or his money, he might, I thought, have made the effort if he cared about seeing me again.

"'But the most wonderful thing of all, and to me wholly incomprehensible, was that he *did* once come over, spent a whole long day with his parents, and seemed to think that there was nothing else to be seen in the neighbourhood. I never so much as got a distant glimpse of him, nor did he leave a single message for me. Naturally I was very much offended, and determined if I ever saw him again to make him rue it. A year or so later there came an opportunity of doing this. I was just seventeen years old, he, therefore, was two-and-twenty, when it was rumoured that he had passed through all the schools with great honour, and was now looking out for some post or other which he was sure to get. That he should in the first instance pay a visit to his parents, stood to reason, but he had not fixed the day and hour. I was, therefore, not a little startled one afternoon, when sitting with my sister in the wood behind the old castle and sketching the view,—for I, too, took drawing-lessons, though I had no particular talent —just when I was about to pronounce his name and to ask Lina if she knew the day of his return, I saw a tall, slender, dark young man emerge from the bushes, take off his hat, and prepare to go down the hill without a word. I knew him instantly; he had still his old face, only with the addition of a dark beard, and he was much better-looking. The marks of the small-pox had almost disappeared. "Good Heavens!" cried I springing from my seat, "it is you, Hans Lutz! How can you startle one so!" "I beg your pardon," he said, in a formal polite way, "I had no idea that I should be disturbing young ladies here; I will no longer intrude upon them," and therewith he again took off his hat, the abominable man, and went straight away as if he had only met an old woman picking sticks, and not the playfellow of his childhood, the paragon of beauty whom other people took long journeys to admire, and who had such a fine lecture to read him, too.

"'I do believe I should have burst into tears if I had been alone, but before Lina I restrained myself, only saying, "He has indeed grown haughty and rude," and tried to go on with my drawing. To no purpose. I could not put in another stroke, my eyes swam so in tears.

"'And in the midst of all my disappointment and vexation, the worst part of it was that I could not be angry with him, that I would have done anything to get a friendly look from him; and my shame at this weakness made me so thoroughly unhappy, that at that moment, spite of my much-extolled beauty, I seemed to myself the most wretched human creature in the whole world.

"'I could not go on keeping up appearances much longer, but threw my arms round my good sister's neck, and with many tears confessed to her how deeply hurt I was, and that I must find out the reason of his estrangement, or my heart would break. The kind soul comforted me as well as she could, and when evening came, helped me to invent a pretext to induce our mother to let us both go down together to the river, to the very place where in former days our little harbour used to be. There Lina left me alone, found out that she had something to do at Hans Lutz's home, and whispered into his ear that I was waiting outside under the willow, and had something to ask him. At first, as she told me afterwards, he had looked very gloomy, and left her in doubt as to what he would do. Then he seemed to relent, and a little later I saw him coming down the road straight towards me, and I do not yet know how I had courage to stand still and wait for him.

"'But at least I was rewarded for my courage. For he was by no means as chilling as before, he even gave me his hand and said, "It is very kind of you, Katharine, still to remember an old playfellow, and what is it you have to say to me?" "Nothing," I said, "only that I wanted to know what I had done to offend him, or whether anybody had been gossiping about me that he should treat me as if I was not worth a word or a look. That was all I asked to know, and then I would go away again immediately." Upon which he told me in his quiet way as if it did not signify to *him* in the least, that he had heard I had grown into a vain conceited little princess, held my head very high, did nothing but look in the glass, or let myself be stared at by foreign fools, and as he was not the man to come in to that, and had, indeed, other things to do than to be always swinging incense before such a Madonna, he thought I should have no loss of him, and that it would be better for us both if he kept out of my way.

"'All that he said to me, and still more the way in which he said it, hurt me so cruelly that I had not a

word to answer, but burst into a flood of tears that I
could not check, that got worse and worse, till I was
shaken by such a convulsion of sobs that I thought I
must have died on the spot. When he saw this, he was
suddenly transformed; he embraced me, and in the tenderest voice said a thousand things that at first, owing
to the confusion in my head, I only half understood.
He told me he had behaved so rudely merely to guard
against his own heart, that through all these years he
had had no other thought but me, and had only kept
away in order not quite to lose his senses, and that if it
were true that I cared at all for him—well, you can
imagine the rest! That evening we pledged ourselves to
live only for each other, and when at last Lina came
and drew me away, that our parents need not scold, I
had quite forgotten that I was the *fair* Kate, and only
thought that a *happier* Kate was not to be found in all
Rhineland, or anywhere under the sun.'

"When she had got so far, she rose and went to the
door, as if to look after the child, who was quietly sitting on a garden-seat, and weaving her garland. When
Kate turned round to us again, I noticed the traces of
tears. Van Kuylen, however, did not seem to observe
them; he had got hold of an old cork and was carving
away at it, his cold pipe still in the corner of his
mouth.

"'And how was it,' said I after a while, 'that fortune
deserted you, and that what began so well had so melancholy an issue? I find it hard to believe that he was
not true to you!'

"'*He!*' returned she with an indescribable tone and
expression. 'If it had only all depended upon him!
But you see the misfortune was just this, that I was such
a wonder of the world they needs must make the most

of me, however unhappy I myself might be. My elder sisters—if Hans Lutz had taken a fancy to one of them, why he would have had her with all the pleasure in the world, and indeed the husbands that they did get were not fit to hold a candle to my lover. But *I*, that he should aspire to *me*, he who was neither a Count nor made of money, that was such audacity that he could hardly be supposed to be right in his mind. True he did not himself think of marrying at the present time, all that he wanted was our betrothal, and then a couple of years to try his fortune in, and I—to wait ten years for him would have been as nothing to me. But you should have heard my father! The Emperor of China, if some crazy sailor were to apply for his daughter's hand, could not put on a more majestic aspect, or pronounce a more compassionate "No." He was not even angry, he treated the whole thing as a mere stupid jest. It was only when my mother—who well knew how my heart stood—ventured to address him on the subject, and to represent Hans Lutz as not after all a *quite* despicable suitor, that he was roused to indignation and silenced her at once. As for me, when I declared that I never would have any one else for my husband, I was locked up, and sat for eight days like an imprisoned princess in the best room, only visited by my mother and sister. To be sure I still had my pretty face, but what was that to me, I was made to feel that I myself had no right to it.

"'I sent through Lina, a letter to Hans Lutz, declaring that I would remain true to him, and begging for God's sake, that he would not punish me for my father's vengeance and anger. To which he wrote me back word that he had no hope, that he was going far away, perhaps to America, and did not know that he should ever return. I was to give up all thought of him, and he formally returned both my word and my ring. For well he knew what would be the end of it all; my parents would look me out some husband after their own heart, and at last I too should get tired of waiting, and so he would not bind me, and add to all other sorrow, the weight of a broken promise on my heart. You may well imagine with how many tears I read that letter, when Lina told me that the writer was already no one knew how far away, and had not wished her to give it me till after his departure.

"'After this all went on apparently in the old way, with this exception, that though I was still "the fair Kate," and estimated as such, there stole over me a silent and unconquerable detestation of my own face, since it had cost me my dearest happiness. But for my father, who was bent upon cutting a figure with me, I should never have come down from my upper room, and as it was I only did so when I could not possibly help it. I never sat in the open window except with my back turned, no power on earth could get me on a steamer where the English stared so, and when artists came to draw or paint me, I never *would* sit still, let my father be as angry as he liked.

"'But all my indoor life, and fretting and grieving did nothing for me; I grew handsomer day by day, and since I had become indifferent to what I wore, I seemed to be more admired than ever, most people having probably thought before with Hans Lutz that I was an over-dressed doll. But no letter came from the one I loved best, and no news of any kind; and so from three to four years passed by, and I found that life is a most wretched pastime when one has not got one's heart's desire.

"'Then, besides, there were constant disputes at home, for every fresh offer of marriage was a new bone of contention. There were many of these suitors—though, indeed, none of them were Counts—to whom my father would most willingly have given me; there was a rich Russian, who swore he would jump into the Rhine if he did not get me, but afterwards preferred to drown himself in Champagne, and went about Wiesbaden with ladies of all kinds. Then there was a young baron, who was master of the horse to some prince, and was wild about horses as well as about me, and there were numbers of worthy well-to-do people who were all intolerable to me because I secretly compared them with my Hans Lutz. My sister Lina was long ago married and happy, and I still sat useless at home, and as my father was not the best of managers, and my mother was sickly, we were often straitened enough, and while one rich suitor after another went away rejected, want began to stare us in the face. Now nothing sours the temper so much as not having enough to eat, and what with unkind words and spiteful remarks, you may believe I spent wretched days, and cried my eyes red at night.

"'At last my father lost all patience, and when another suitor appeared who seemed to him worthy to carry away the jewel of beauty, since he was able to bid high for it, he declared to me either I must consent, or he would make me feel the whole weight of his anger. What he exactly meant by that I really did not know, but I was glad of a change myself, for I could no longer endure my father's anger and my mother's grief. So I said that I would give my hand to Mr. So-and-so, provided no message came from Hans Lutz in the course of the next three months. This contented my parents, and made the bridegroom more than blessed; he was actually idiotic with rapture, said the craziest things to me, and in spite of my misery, it made me again feel proud and childish to find that I had such power over any human being. He was a young and very rich tanner from the neighbouring town of M——, not so bad as to face or figure; indeed he passed for a handsome man; but it made me positively ill if I had to sit by him longer than a quarter of an hour, first because his love rendered him so silly and mawkish, and then because he had a habit of deluging himself with scents, probably to get rid of the smell of the tan-yard. I will not weary you with the history of this horrible engagement. I get goose-skin all over at the very recollection of it; the visits here, there, and everywhere; the congratulations at which I had to smile when I would much rather have cried; the day when he took me over his house and factory, and I thought the smell of the dyes and skins would have suffocated me. Well, it went on as long as it could go on, that is till it came to the point. On the day before the wedding day, my bridegroom gave a party to my favourite friends and my parents at his own house; the actual marriage was to be solemnized at my parent's house. He was so inordinately happy, foolish, and scented, that I suddenly said to myself, "Better suffer anything than please such a simpleton as this," and that very night when they were all asleep, I actually left the house, only taking with me a few necessaries in a bundle, and leaving behind a letter to my parents saying they must forgive the sorrow I had caused them, but that marry I could not and would not, and so in order to be no longer a burden to them, I had gone off to my aunt at Speyer, and would see whether I could not do something to support myself.

"'I was helped in my flight by the brother of my Hans Lutz, who happened to be on a visit to his parents at the time, and would have gone through fire and water for me. He took me safely to where I wanted to go, to my aunt Millie's, her real name was Amelia, but so we children always called her. She was an old widow-woman, lived upon her small means, and had always been very fond of me, though she used to shake her head at the way in which my family idolised me. When I told her all that had happened she neither praised nor blamed me, but wrote to my parents and tried to bring them round. That, alas, was in vain. My father answered very curtly that if I did not marry the young tanner I was no child of his; my mother tried persuasion. I now found out that it was only my unfortunate beauty that they had really loved, that a red-and-white mask stood between my own parents' hearts and that of their child. Out of sheer admiration and worship, they had less fondness for me than for any of their other children.

"'But for this would they not have found time in the course of the whole year since I have left them, to comprehend that what I had run away from could not have made me happy, and that I was not necessarily a bad daughter, because unable to gratify them in that respect? But no, they have remained as hard as stone, hard as no one could be to any living creature who had a soul, but only towards a soulless picture such as they had long considered me, and as such set me up for show. It is true that while I remained at Speyer they might have hoped that I should change my mind. But my stay there was but short. My old aunt was accustomed to a very quiet life. Now when a beauty suddenly made her appearance in the house, whom all young men followed, and that visits and enquiries became incessant, and this person and that were always bringing me an offer from some one or other, it was too much for the good woman to bear. She told me one day that I could not remain any longer with her, but that she had found me a very good situation with a baroness who lived on her estates near Munich, and wanted a governess for her two little daughters; and as I had been well educated, could speak French and play the pianoforte, my aunt had arranged it all, and I was to set off the next day but one.

"'I was very much pleased at this; I longed to begin life on my own account, and earn my own bread. But this too was to be a failure, and again there was no one to blame but this hateful face that I cannot get rid of. Well, to make a long story short, the baroness and the children took to me and I to them, and during the first days when we were alone, everything went well. Then came the baron from the city to pay us a visit, and instantly the sky changed; he behaved, indeed, very politely, only that he made the usual face of amazement which I am so sick of, and that all people make who see me for the first time. I, indeed, am accustomed to it, take no notice, and go my way quietly, but the gracious lady, who had not seen that expression on her husband's face before, could not take it so easily, and the end of the matter was, that on the following day, after a very lively discussion between the master and mistress of the house, I was sent for to her boudoir, and told that she much regretted being unable to keep me, but needed the room that I occupied for a young relative who had suddenly announced herself for the whole winter. However, she was conscientious enough to give me, without my demanding it, my salary for that whole winter.

15 *

"'There I was again on the wide world! I had a great mind to buy myself a black mask, like the lady with the death's head, and hide my face once for all, that it might not get me into any further trouble.

"'And indeed if I could only have foreseen what I had yet to endure I should have done so, or something madder still. I should have become a Catholic just to go into a nunnery.

"'Three times in this town I have had to change my rooms because people would not leave me alone. I can assure you, if I had stolen or forged, or done any other disgraceful thing that I feared might come out, I could not live in greater anxiety and uncertainty than now, when I have no one to stand by me in the right way and guard me from wicked men and my unfortunate fate: but I will spare you all details; you can imagine them. And then to have nothing to do, and not rightly to understand anything, to read half the day, the other half to wonder what is to become of me when my money and my patience come to an end, as they must. The people with whom I lodge at present—Babette's parents—have all been sorry for me since they saw that I was no worthless runaway creature, but had only been afflicted with that church-window face. But what can *they* do? I help a little in the house, I have learnt some sewing, as the man is a regimental tailor; I teach Babette to read and write, but the good souls are too poor to keep a governess. So this last March when I had had to give up a situation in a jeweller's shop—of course on account of my face—I was obliged to write again to my parents, and ask them to take me back. No doubt they thought they need only remain hard for a little time in order perfectly to soften me. They wrote me word, therefore, that the tanner was still waiting for

me, and that all would be forgiven if I came to my
senses at last, but if I did not do so, I might just remain where I was. My aunt Millie sent me a little
money, but not much; she has herself been swindled lat-
terly out of great part of her means. And so there I
had to sit again, my hands in my lap; and if I accidentally saw myself in the glass, I was so angry and
wild with the unlucky face that looked back at me, that
I should have scratched my eyes out if only my nails
and my courage had had strength for it.

"'Meanwhile the tailor's wife had often advised me
to make a maintenance by sitting as a model. A relation of hers lived that way, who was no real beauty, but
only well-grown. Looks were a gift of God like everything else, and if a singer hired out her beautiful voice
for gold, why should not I let the same face that had
brought me into trouble help me out of it again? But
to all such propositions I always returned the same answer; I knew that nothing could be so bitter to my
lover as to hear that I had let myself be looked at for
money like a show at a fair, and had gone to serve as
lay figure first to one and then to another. That I knew
he would never forgive. "*He* forgive, indeed," said the
woman, "he ought to think himself very happy if you
forgive him for having taken himself off, and never
making a sign since." However, I remained quite resolute, till at length I was at the last gasp, and did not
know how I was to pay my next month's lodgings. If
Herr van Kuylen had not come forward—whom I could
trust to have no bad intentions—God knows I have
many a time walked through the English garden, and
thought if I took a cold bath there, it would be the best
and quickest way of escape!

"'And now forgive me for telling you such a long

story from beginning to end. But you have done me a real kindness by listening without laughing or shaking your heads. For most people will not believe that one can be unhappy except through his own fault, and least of all unhappy through what is considered the greatest good fortune. Babette,' said she to the child, who just then brought in her wreath, 'take up your knitting and put the book back in its place. We must go, it has struck five, and your mother will be waiting.'

"Van Kuylen jumped up as if some one had shaken him out of sleep.

"'Will you come to-morrow at the same time, Miss Kate?' said he, without looking at her.

"'To-morrow my landlady goes to a wedding,' she replied, tying on a little black bonnet that framed her face most exquisitely. 'I must stay at home with the children, but the day after to-morrow if it suits you—'

"He silently bowed, and prepared to help her on with her dark woollen shawl, which, however, she declined. She muffled herself up so completely in it that her slender form was hardly apparent, even to an artist's eye; then she tied on an almost impervious black veil, and curtsied to me with a bewitching blush. I smiled and heartily shook hands with her. 'I am much indebted to you, my dear young lady,' said I, 'for having acquainted me with your singular story. I am a married man, and, thank God! still in love with my wife, so that there can be no fear of jealousy in our case; therefore, if ever you need counsel or help, my house is—so-and-so—and I should be delighted if you had confidence in us and allowed us to render you some slight service. For the rest I cannot look upon the matter so despairingly. Who knows whether you will not have to apologise to your face for all the hard words you have be-

stowed upon it? He who wins the first prize in a lottery
may have indeed some perplexities in consequence, but
for all that the first prize is no bad thing, and makes
up to us for many a drawback. Everywhere there is
light and shade'—and so forth, for I do not suppose
that the cheap wisdom with which I sought to console
the poor child would be tolerable repeated.

"Indeed I was aware even at the time that it did not
produce much effect. On the contrary the beautiful face
grew sad and weary, as if she was at confession, and
she went away without saying another word; only I heard
a sigh under the thick veil, which fell, and produced a
total eclipse.

"I was alone with Van Kuylen, and for a short time
we each went on silently puffing out thick clouds, for
the little Dutchman lit his clay-pipe the moment the
beautiful girl disappeared.

"'Well, Mynheer,' said I at last, 'I must congratulate
you; you are a lucky dog.'

"'I!' he returned, with a short ironical laugh. 'Through
what sort of glasses do you look upon the world that you
can utter such a prophecy?'

"'Through my own unaided eyes,' returned I. 'Are
you not indeed enviable enough in this, that you have
caught in your net the shy bird after which so many
have followed in vain. If you only set about it rightly,
the bird will grow so tame that you will be able to cage
it at last.'

"He turned away: he did not wish me to see the vivid
red that suffused his yellow face.

"'You don't know her,' he muttered, 'she is quite
different to all others, and if I were the fool you take
me to be—'

"'You would be no fool at all,' I continued, exciting

myself as I went on. 'You need not of course repeat it to my wife, but by St. Katharine I swear to you, Master Jan, that were I in your place I should not long play St. Anthony's part. I would do everything on earth to deliver that poor child from her purgatory—'

"'And to lead her into a Paradise where such an Adam —get off with you,' said he, with a very unpolite gesture.

"But I knew how to take him; I drew nearer and placed my hand on his shoulder.

"'If it is disagreeable to you, I will not say another word, but can you suppose that a certain Hans Lutz—'

"He sprang from his low seat and ran distractedly up and down the studio.

"'Don't make me mad,' he cried. 'If you have noticed that I am over head and ears in love with the girl—as far as *that* goes there is no disgrace in it; but I am not such an insane idiotic ape as to imagine for a moment that my respectable visage will drive the sweet child's first love out of her heart, and that a mere settlement in life will not decoy her you have yourself heard. Why then come and blow upon the coals with the bellows of your common-place philosophy? Am I not already wretched enough, in that I plainly see how hopeless the whole matter is, and yet cannot leave off gazing at her by the hour, just to burn in that cruel face of hers upon my memory? And now, forsooth, you must come and prate of solid possibilities, and congratulate me, and— the devil take it! It is just as if you were to hold the pin on which a living cockchafer is impaled in a candle, and make it red-hot.'

"He threw himself down on a low ottoman in the corner with such vehemence, that he broke off the neck of a costly Florentine lute lying there, without even noticing it.

"I would now gladly have recalled my thoughtless words.

"'If the case is really so, Mynheer,' said I, 'I own there *is* nothing to congratulate you upon. But I do not understand why a man like you should so utterly despair. You have no tannery, but you are a famous artist; you do not smell of scents, but as a man should, of strong Porto Rico; and all the rest is mere matter of taste. Women are women, and it is impossible to reckon upon their fancies. That she is not exactly set upon an Adonis is evident—'

"I might have gone on for some time putting forth these platitudes, with the best intentions, if he had not suddenly turned upon me with a quite phlegmatic air, and asked me—not without a quiver in his voice—what o'clock it was, and whether the 'Muette de Portici' was not going to be performed that night. I then saw plainly how things stood, swallowed down my annoyance at having so stupidly interfered in so tender a matter, and took leave under the pretext that my wife was waiting for me to pay a visit.

"A visit on Whit Monday afternoon when no one is at home! but so one stumbles on from one discrepancy to another.

"Accordingly the series of my mortifications was not yet over for that particular day; for when I had got home to my good wife, and given her a true and faithful account of where I had been, and what I had seen and heard, and finally (though indeed her silence in listening foreboded no good), added: 'It would be a real comfort to me if I could do something for the pretty child, and might it not be as well to offer her our spare room as it chanced to be empty,'—a small matrimonial tempest burst at once, which I had passively to endure. My wife had, indeed, long been upon the point of telling me that this Van Kuylen exercised the worst influence over me, and was the most unfit companion; a frivolous bachelor who had no respect for holy things, and had already infected me with his mocking and blasphemous spirit. She had supposed, when she married a landscape painter, that her house would at least be free from such a disreputable set as models generally are, lost to all sense of decency and shame, and of whom the most horrible stories were heard. And now I had returned from that trumpery Dutchman, not only with my clothes reeking of the very worst tobacco-smoke, but in such a wholly perverted state of mind, and with such entire forgetfulness of what was due to a virtuous young wife, that I could actually propose to her to receive into our family this suspicious person, who had turned my head with her bit of prettiness and her dubious adventures. Rather than consent to such a step, she would take her innocent children in her arms, and at once leave the field clear; for it was too plain to see from the fervour with which I had proposed this fine plan, what must eventually come of-it. And so saying, she caught up our little Christopher who had tripped in, with such a passionate burst of tears, and pressed his small fair head so closely to her breast, it seemed as if she would fain save the poor harmless child from the evil eye of a sinful father who had irrevocably made over his soul to him who shall be nameless.

"I had no small difficulty in allaying the excitement of my dear better-half; she was generally patience and self-abnegation itself, but there is one point on which women are not to be trifled with, which makes hyenas of them, as Schiller says, and I inwardly called myself a confounded ass for having displayed my æsthetic enthusiasm for the beautiful girl in so wrong a quarter.

"Of course I took good care not to revert to the dangerous subject, but remained at home the whole of the next day, and devoted myself to painting an old oak-forest, as if the riven and rugged bark of the secular trees was far more bewitching than the smoothest satin-skin of a maiden of twenty, and a gnarled oak-branch more ensnaring than the exquisite little Venus-like nose of our poor persecuted beauty.

"The next day I even accomplished a greater triumph over myself, in that I withstood the temptation of looking in—quite accidentally, of course—at Van Kuylen's studio, there to play the part of comforter to a distressed child of humanity. I was certainly a little absent-minded all the afternoon, and as we walked to Nymphenburg, our children pushed along in the perambulator by the maid, failed to get up any very animated conversation. I apologised somewhat lamely for it, on the plea that I was studying atmospheric effects, though indeed there was nothing very noticeable in the sky. But my wife found it much pleasanter than if I had indulged my bad habit of too earnestly studying the faces of the girls and women we passed. There is indisputably about the sex this one weakness, that they have themselves no conception of a purely artistic standpoint, and therefore never allow for it in others.

"At last after four or five days, I found it intolerable to my manly self-respect, thus suddenly to withdraw from my worthy Dutchman, merely because he was in my wife's bad books. Consequently, after washing my brushes, I set out just about twilight, when I knew that though he could paint no longer, he was sure to be at home; and in this was most perfectly justified in my own eyes, since I could not possibly be expecting to find the fair Kate there, but only my small and unjustly calumniated friend.

"And to be sure I saw from a distance the shining of his lamp through the window: nevertheless I had to be told by the old servant that her master was gone out. Neither did I fare any better on the following day when I knocked at his studio during his hours of work. I called out my name as loud as I could, but he wouldn't open. When I enquired from the old servant whether he was occupied with a model, she shook her head, and shrugged her shoulders; then tapping her forehead with a very significant gesture, she sighed and said, 'Things had not been right with the good gentleman for some days past; he ate and drank nothing to speak of, walked up and down his bed-room half the night, and spoke to no one.' I asked whether the young lady who was with him on Whit Monday had been there since. The answer was that she had not, but that he still went on painting her, out of his head, and the good woman herself had already thought that love might have something to do with her master's silence and absence of mind.

"The truth flashed in upon me too plainly, and I tacitly reproached myself with having poured oil on the flame by speaking of his attachment to the lovely being as something quite reasonable and by no means hopeless. Truly, if we always reflected the serious mischief our jesting words might make, we should be at least as cautious in uttering them, as we are in ascertaining upon what we are about to throw the burning end of our cigar.

"Meanwhile there was nothing to be done. I knew my eccentric Mynheer Jan too well. If he had taken it into his head to eat a whole Edam cheese for his breakfast, no one could have dissuaded him. I made two other attempts to get at him, but in vain; and one evening when I accidentally met him by the 'Aukirche'—we had almost run up against each other—he was off like a shot, and all my calling, and scolding, and running after him did no good; he *would* not have anything to do with me.

"By-and-bye I came to take the matter more quietly, and to say to myself, 'If he can do without thee, thou canst get on without him.' This mood of mine won me approving looks from my dear wife. I willingly allowed her the triumph—of which, by-the-way, she did not boast ungenerously—of believing that her remonstrances had weaned me from that soul-destroyer, Jan, and brought me back to the paths of virtue and landscape-painting. When my oak forest was done, we broke up our tent in the town, to pitch it, as we annually did, in the mountains. I wrote a kindly note to wish my friend good-bye, but got no answer in return. And so most of the summer passed away without my knowing whether he were dead or alive. The fair Kate seemed to have been swallowed up by an earthquake. Of all my friends and colleagues, who were generally not long in tracking out anything rare, none had discovered the slightest trace of our poor wonder of the world.

"When, however, the middle of September came, and I had got a little tired of painting studies, and perhaps, also, of the monotonous fare of our country abode, and began to long for a return to the amenities of town life, I became conscious of a lively desire to know what had become of my Dutchman and his beauty. My first walk in Munich was to his studio, where I found the nest empty indeed, but left upon his little slate my name and a hearty greeting. After that I went with my wife

to the exhibition, for where one has been so long face
to face with nature, it is a pleasure to see how art has
been getting on in the meantime. But what was my
amazement, when the first picture my eyes fell upon,
was nothing else than an unmistakable genuine Van
Kuylen, in which his unfortunate studies of Kate were
turned to account in his well-known manner, and certainly so questionably, that I at first pretended not to
notice it, in order to get my wife safely past. But she
with her lynx-eyes instantly made out the whole story.

"'But do look,' she said, in a tolerably calm voice,
in which, however, I could detect a satirical tone; 'here
is a picture by your Dutch painter of holy subjects, and
on a larger scale than any we have seen before. I must
say, if the subject were not so objectionable, it would go
far to reconcile me to him. It seems to me that he has
made great progress: one might almost call this picture
beautiful; not only the colouring, but the whole composition has something grandiose, historical as you call it,
a style—' (You may see that the little woman had not
consorted with artists for the last six years for nothing,
and could deliver her art-criticisms as confidently as any
newspaper writer, only rather more intelligently.) 'But
I believe,' she continued, 'that the Bathsheba who is
there undressing to take a bath in a very shallow reser-
voir, is your marvellous creature from the Rhine. At all
events, she does not look like any of the other studies
in the room, and the little King David who peeps from
an upper window, and naturally shows us the beautiful
cheese-coloured face of the painter, looks at the lady
with a genuine artist's eye, such as I have seen in other
people's heads when staring under the bonnets of pretty
girls,' (with that, a side glance at her faithful husband.)
'Well! I must say she is not bad-looking, if he has not

idealised his model too much; but was I not right to refuse to take that persecuted innocence into our house? A pretty snake, indeed, I should have warmed in my breast! *She* helpless! I think one who lets herself be painted thus, knows very well how to help herself. And really I do not know which I ought to wonder at most, at my good unsuspicious husband, who was so easily taken in by an experienced adventuress, or, if indeed he were not so entirely harmless in the matter, at his sanguine hope of humbugging me. At all events I am very glad that things have taken this turn.'

"After this attack and these imputations clothed in the most discreet and proper language, to which I had not so much as a word to answer, my domestic guardian angel drew me hastily away, as if fearing that dangerous person might even in her picture exercise some witchcraft over me. And really there was nothing out of the way in the idea, for all that my eccentric friend possessed of taste and love of beauty, had been expended on the figure of the young woman, who, already undraped to the hips, sat on a low stool in the act of taking off her little shoe. While so doing she turned to the left the well-remembered profile, which was drawn with the tenderest contour, not a single feature altered, and a striking likeness; her hair, which seemed to have been just loosened, fell in bewitching confusion over her lustrous neck. Her back and arms were so beautifully drawn, that I knew not how to give the good 'genre' painter credit for them. But what specially attracted me was the sad impassive expression with which the fair being bent her head, and cast her long-lashed eyes on the ground. King David up there in his balcony did not appear to me at that moment to be such a great sinner after all; or at least the extenuating circumstances under which that abominable letter anent Uriah was written, came before me more impressively than they had ever done in the presence of any painting of the subject before.

"I confess that I spent the rest of the day in a somewhat perturbed mood; my old creed, namely, that women *were* women, was once more confirmed, and the apparent exception turned out to be an illusion. Whether it were through vanity, or distress, or mere apathy, the beautiful girl had not maintained her inviolability. But although it is very pleasant to be proved right, and though I ought, besides, to have rejoiced that the poor *innamorato* should in this not unusual way be healed of his madness, and probably at this moment happily betrothed, if not already a husband, there nevertheless lurked a certain uncomfortable feeling in my mind, and I caught myself involuntarily shaking my head as though there were something not quite right about it. My quick-witted wife seemed to discern what was going on within me, but as though the subject of my musings were too low and common to bear discussion, she never referred to the picture, and treated me with a gentleness and consideration befitting a penitent; in the spirit, in short, of the beautiful axiom, 'If a man have fallen, let love bring him back to duty.'

"On the following morning I was anxious to go to work, with fresh energies, at a new picture which I had already mentally composed; but I discovered that there was something wrong with me—there was still that story to unravel. What I should have liked best would have been to have gone at once to Mynheer Jan, and heard the truth, but he never got up before ten o'clock in the morning; so I lounged off again to the exhibition, that I might study the picture I had too hurriedly looked at the previous day, and was not a little annoyed at being reminded by the closed door that it was Saturday, the day when the pictures are hung and the public excluded. The official told me that Herr van Kuylen's picture had been taken back to his studio in the course of the previous evening.

"To while away the hours till ten, I turned off through the arcades, and betook myself to the English garden, where I never found time long. It is so celebrated that I need not praise it; but I venture to say there are not many, even among our good old Munich inhabitants, who know it at the time of its very greatest beauty, and that is early on an autumn, or late-summer morning, when it is as solemn and deserted as a primeval forest, and you can wander along the lofty avenues of shade without meeting a human creature. The gold-daisied meadows are luxuriant in the sun, the trees have lost none of their gorgeous foliage, the sun-light falls, I might say, in *pasto* on the mirror-like ponds, and the magical dreamy silence thrills with the quiet rushing of the Isar, and the light and noiseless hopping of birds and squirrels from branch to branch. There was no one to be seen on the lonely benches, unless, perhaps, a student preparing for his examination, or some poor poet meditating his love-songs. As to my colleagues the landscape painters, I have never met one of them here.

"Accordingly as I said, I was lounging on this parti-cular morning in the well-known paths, but not in a particularly good mood for making studies, for Van Kuylen's picture, and what could have happened to enable him to paint it, was constantly running in my head. When I had dreamingly sauntered on to the vi-

cinity of the famous waterfall, which the grateful inhabitants prepared at so much expense as a surprise for
King Ludwig, I saw a lady on the bench upon the little
hill overlooking it, sitting motionless, and having nothing about her to excite my interest, till all at once
it struck me that she had a black veil down. I thought,
however, 'she has some reason for not wishing to be
recognized except by the one for whom she is waiting,
and I will pass quickly by,' when a strange impulse led
me to turn round and give her another look. The
veiled figure made a little start, as though it recognized
me, but the next moment sat as motionless as before.
But there was a something in the turn of the head
which seemed to me so familiar, that I involuntarily
turned back a step or two, and—'Good Heavens! It is
you, Miss Kate,' I cried, 'and what brings you here?'
and I held out my hand in cordial greeting. But she
did not take it, and seemed on the point of running off.
'Stop,' said I, 'I have not bargained for this,' and in a
friendly way I detained her. 'One is not to fly from an
old friend in this manner, but to tell him where one has
been for so many months past.' Meanwhile some uncomfortable terror was creeping over me, partly by reason of her strange silence and her looking about her
as if for a way of escape, and partly because I had seen
her hide a bottle under her shawl. It was, therefore, so
plainly my duty not to leave her, that even my wife
must have allowed it.

"'I shall not go away, Miss Kate,' I began, 'till you
restore me a little of that confidence you showed at our
first interview. You know I have only friendly intentions. You have something on your mind; it is vain to
deny it; and I believe there is no one who can be so
unselfish a confidant and adviser as I. Come, my dear

young lady, let us seat ourselves on this bench. And now tell me why you seemed so shocked at seeing me again, and what sort of a cordial you are carrying there, and hiding from me. Fie, fie, Miss Kate, are you going to take to drinking secretly in your early youth?'

"She made no reply, but allowed herself to be led back to the bench, where I seated myself beside her.

"In order to give her time to compose herself, I began to talk of quite indifferent subjects: of the weather, and how beautiful it was here by the waterfall, and of how I had spent my summer, purposely dwelling a good deal upon my wife and children, as it always makes a good impression when doctors and spiritual pastors are affectionate husbands and parents.

"She seemed to be deaf to everything. There was no help for it, then, I must take the bull by the horns.

"'Miss Kate,' I said, 'is it long since you have seen Herr van Kuylen? My first expedition yesterday was to his house, but as I found no one at home—'

"She started at the sound of his name. Aha! I thought, there is something wrong here.

"'He must have been very industrious these last months,' I continued, as unconcernedly as I could; 'I myself have only seen one picture of his in the exhibition, but—'

"No sooner were the words spoken than from beneath the veil of the silent girl beside me, there burst such heart-rending sobs that I jumped up in horror.

"'For God's sake!' I cried, 'what is the matter with you? Here is a secret that will break your heart if you don't give it words. Tell me—explain to me—'

"'Let me go,' she cried out passionately, and again tried to make her escape. 'I am so unhappy that nobody can help me, and even if you do really wish me well—still it is too late. Nothing remains for me now but to—'

"Die—she would have said, but her sobs choked her. Meanwhile I had availed myself of the opportunity to get hold of the bottle, which she had put down on the bench beside her. With one quick gesture I at once hurled it into the little cascade below us.

"'So then,' said I, 'that was it! You are a little fury, Kate, and in your present heroic frame of mind, you were on the point of drinking off that little bottle, and making me your executor!'

"She shook her head. 'You are mistaken,' she said, 'it was not poison, it was only common *aquafortis*, not intended for internal use. If you must know everything, I was only going to wash my face with it.'

"'Kate!' I cried in horror. 'Are you mad?'

"'Not at all,' she gravely replied. 'The expedient would be rather rough, but efficient. I should then get rid of this accursed face which has been the cause of all my misery, and now, too, at length—of my shame.'

"These last words were scarcely audible, her face being hidden in her hands. I misunderstood their purport, and consequently did not at once know what to reply.

"It was she who solved my perplexity.

"She suddenly left off sobbing, and looked me full in the face with a singularly resolute expression.

"I could therefore contemplate her at my leisure, and found that if possible she was more beautiful than ever, her features still more delicate and refined, the tears on her fair cheeks—altogether she was the most enchanting and touching spectacle that a man could behold.

"'You think a good deal of what you have done,'

she said in her quietest tones. 'However if it is not in this hour it will be in some other; carried out my purpose will surely be, for I am sick of life. If you knew all you would certainly not blame me, but in the main you do know; you have been yourself at the exhibition, you have there seen how a wicked and cruel-hearted man has dared to behave to a poor, virtuous, unhappy girl who would have nothing to say to him.'

"'What!' I cried, and the solution of the mystery flashed across me; 'he has then—you have not sat to him once for it?'

"'I!' she cried, with all the offended dignity of a little queen. 'I do not so much as know what it looks like. I have only been told of it by my landlady, who has not herself seen it, but an officer, to whom she carried back a uniform yesterday evening, said to her: "Your lodger, the pretty girl, who is so vastly coy whenever one comes to propose anything to her, and always locks herself up, does not seem to be so inaccessible to civilians; there she is at the exhibition, painted just as God made her; to be sure Dutch ducats are more valuable than our uniform buttons." At this the tailor's wife asked further questions, and told me again all that she learnt. She herself is quite furious, and never would have believed it of Herr van Kuylen. And all because I had refused to go again to his studio after he had come the third day of Whitsuntide to pay me a visit, when he knew I should be alone with the children, and made me an offer of marriage in French that Babette might not understand him; for which very reason I answered in German that I did not mean to marry, and that he knew very well why, and that now after his declaration I could no longer sit to him as he must perfectly understand. But he seemed to understand nothing, he was like a maniac, and I had great difficulty to get him out of the room at all, for he always broke out anew, now with jests, now with the most fearful adjurations. Since then I have never spoken a word to him, nor let him in when he knocked at my door, and in the street I always got out of the way so speedily, that he could have no hope at all. And then what does he go and do? Out of revenge and wickedness he puts me as it were in the pillory, so that every one may point their finger at me, and I no longer dare look up in the presence of respectable women. Oh, what men are! And I had thought that he, at least, was an exception, because he did not prate, and had a kind of appearance which was not likely to lead any one into folly and shame for his sake. Now I have had to pay for my stupid confidence by the misery of my whole life.'

"Then again she burst into tears.

"I now attempted to comfort her, and also to defend my friend Jan, by representing to her that painters think very differently on these matters to what ladies do; that he had most certainly not done it out of revenge; and that she could lose nothing in the eyes of any rational beings if this picture—like all the rest of Van Kuylen's —were destined for the gallery of some Amsterdam merchant, who knew as little of the existence of 'the fair Kate,' as she did of his.

"But it was all in vain. With the active imagination of all self-torturers, she pictured to herself that the picture might be engraved or lithographed, and then hung up in the windows of all the print-shops, and in all the public-rooms of the hotels along the Rhine, and that then everybody would say, 'Only see what our coy little schoolmaster's daughter has come to! A pretty face may lead a person great lengths indeed!' and what would her parents and sisters think of her —and suppose that such a print ever got as far as America, and came one day to the eyes of Hans Lutz. No, no, she would much rather—having rendered herself unrecognizable so far as she could—leap into the Isar, than day and night imagine such fearful things.

"'Do you know what?' said I at length. 'All these desperate lamentations and resolutions have no practical sense in them, and do not lead us any nearer the goal that you wish to reach—the nullifying as much as possible the mischief done. Be reasonable, Miss Kate, and accompany me at once to our common friend, who has certainly no idea how evil-disposed you are towards him. There you can at all events obtain a written assurance from him that he painted the picture in question entirely out of his own head, that you never sat to him except for a most unexceptionably decorous portrait, and even then were not alone with him. I will also try to induce him either to remove the likeness of the lady Bathsheba to you, or to put an honest drapery over her back. Come now, will not this be much more to the purpose than your spoiling your complexion either with the water of the Isar, or *aquafortis?* Only think what people would say about it; that you had done yourself a mischief out of an unfortunate attachment to our little Dutchman to whom you had sat!'

"This last quite too appalling idea seemed to remove all her objections; she saw that a rational measure taken now, need not prevent her doing the most despairing things by-and-bye, and as an empty cab happened to be coming up the great avenue, we both got into it, with the intention of at once bringing Van Kuylen to book.

"During the whole of the way she was silent, only

answering Yes and No to my questions. Indeed I did not say much either, and pushed myself back as far as I could into the corner of the half-open vehicle; for we had to pass through the street in which I lived. If my good wife should chance to be looking out of the window, or were out walking, and met her husband driving with a veiled lady! As I have said she is one of the best of women, but all have a spot where they are vulnerable, and appearances would have been decidedly against me; for what could induce a landscape-painter to engage a female model in the English garden, and to get into a cab with her?—his own family may well suffice *him* as lay figures!

"Meanwhile we had safely arrived at Van Kuylen's house in the meadows.

"An empty cab waiting in the street showed we had been preceded by some other visitor. As we passed through the little garden and approached the studio, we plainly heard the sound of voices within.

"'Sit down for a few moments on this bench, Miss Kate,' said I, 'I will just listen whether I know the other voice, and whether there seems any prospect of the person soon going away.'

"So saying, I went up to the door, which certainly was closed, but as it was only a very thin one—in winter another door was added—one could distinctly hear every word, unless, indeed, the speakers lowered their voices intentionally.

"The girl was far too excited and impatient to think of sitting down; she came and stood immediately behind me.

"'I have already explained to you,' we now heard Van Kuylen say, 'that I am not going to sell the picture, and as for the copy you wish for, I never copy any of my pictures. I am only too glad when I have once got myself expressed, however poorly it may be, and I lack the mercantile genius necessary for picture-multiplying.'

"'If you yourself do not intend to repeat it,' said a rather rough manly voice which was entirely strange to me, 'perhaps you will allow another to copy it for me, or at least let me have a photograph of it.'

"'I am sorry,' repeated Van Kuylen, 'that I cannot consent to have that picture reproduced in any way. The circumstances are quite peculiar,' and then he murmured something that we did not catch.

"'He is making short work of him,' said I, turning round to the girl. 'It is our time to appear on the scene,' I was going to add, but the words stuck in my throat. Pale as death, with wide-staring eyes, as though she saw a spectre, I do believe the poor child would have fallen if I had not thrown my arm around her and supported her in the very nick of time.

"'What is it? What is it?' I cried. 'Let me take you in to Van Kuylen's sofa. Are you ill?'

"She, however, shook her head in silence, and made a sign signifying, 'Hush! I must listen,' and now we heard the stranger speak again. 'I must request you at least to answer me one more question. Had you a model for the female figure?'

"'Certainly,' replied Van Kuylen, 'I never paint a stroke but from nature.'

"'Then you must know this girl intimately; you know where she lives, and can tell me—'

"'Give yourself no further trouble, sir,' interrupted Van Kuylen. 'I can well understand that this picture may excite other than artistic admiration, but as for telling who sat to me for it—no, sir. My studio is no bureau of enquiry, and besides—' then came some more muttered words.

"'Forgive me,' said the stranger, his voice all the more raised; 'I can comprehend that under the peculiar relation in which you seem to stand to your model—'

"At this moment the girl tore away from me like lightning, rushed to the door, and before I could try to hold her back, had burst in, and now stood—the most exquisite little fury that ever defended her good name—between the two men.

"I followed her instantly, and was just opening my mouth to interpose, when I heard the stranger give a hollow groan, and saw him reel back a step or two. I looked at him more closely. He was really a fine-looking man, remarkably well-dressed in black, with a resolute somewhat sunburnt face, in which I at once detected a few slight marks of small-pox.

"'Excuse me,' I stammered out in much embarrassment; 'I have the honour, Mr. Hans Lutz—'

"But Kate did not let me finish my speech; one quick glance at the picture, which stood on an easel in the middle of the studio, had sent all the blood back to her face. 'That is scandalous,' said she, going straight up to Van Kuylen, who with his straw-coloured face and nankeen attire cut a most unfortunate figure on this occasion. '*That*, then, is your gratitude to me for making an exception in your case, and consenting to sit for my portrait to you; and because I would consent to nothing else, you would degrade me in this way before the whole world, and represent me as a bad bold girl who lets herself be seen for money, and has no objection to her shame being openly exhibited! Declare now once for all before these two witnesses, whether you have ever seen me as I am painted there, whether I was ever alone with you, whether I did not show you the door when you came to me at my lodgings and begged and entreated me to be your wife.'

"Her eyes flashed, and now that she was silent, her nostrils quivered, and I noticed that she pressed her clenched fist closely to her side, as though she feared she might be tempted to commit an assault upon the little yellow man.

"I for my part, marvelled that he took it all so calmly.

"'I find out now,' he said at length with the utmost phlegm, and laying down his pipe, 'who it is I have before me. You are no doubt the engineering gentleman of whom the young lady has already told us. I congratulate you on your return, which will probably set all things to rights. If they went wrong it was your own fault. A person who allows so long a time to pass without being heard of, cannot be surprised at others coming forward in his absence. For the rest, I am prepared to give the lady whatever spoken or written assurance she may require. The best explanation, perhaps, will be found in *this*.'

"So saying he went to a corner of the room, where all sorts of sketches and unfinished pictures were heaped up together, and after a short search, produced a study painted on paper, a female figure in the precise position of Bathsheba, and although the face was merely an outline, one saw at a glance that a quite different model must have sat for it—a coarse common-place person with black hair whose back and shoulders were widely celebrated amongst artists.

"'I thank you,' said the stranger, who seemed somewhat to have recovered the unexpected meeting. 'I believe every word you have said, but I hope you will not consider me too importunate if I repeat the request that the picture may be mine. You understand—'

"'I understand it all,' drily returned Van Kuylen, while lighting his clay-pipe with a large match; 'and as I have something to apologise for, and very much wish that the lady should not eternally resent my inconsiderate freak, I give you the picture for your new establishment. And now—you will excuse me. I have some business which cannot be postponed. A good journey to you.'

"Before one of us could find a word to reply, he made us an abrupt bow, and passed through a door leading into the interior of the house.

"We three who remained behind stood there in utter helplessness. I felt that I was one too many, and was planning how best to leave the pair alone, when suddenly the lovely girl came up to me, held out her hand, and with apparent composure said:

"'Farewell, dear sir; I thank you for all the kindness you have shown me. I will now go home and trouble you no further.'

"With that she turned round without casting one glance at her sun-burnt lover, and moved towards the door.

"'Katharine!' cried the young man, rushing towards her.

"'Leave me!' said the incensed beauty. 'We have no longer anything to do with each other. One who could believe *that* of me—who could suppose that I should ever degrade myself so far—'

"'Listen to me, dear Kate,' I interposed, for I saw that both the proud high-tempered creatures were just in the mood to part as suddenly as they had met; 'if you really believe that I am a friend to you, do try to follow me and consider the question more calmly. Just put yourself in the place of your Hans Lutz, (you will forgive me', my dear sir, for using your Christian name though we have not even been introduced,) and ask yourself whether a lover is very likely to retain his five senses, when he chances to enter a picture-gallery, and sees the girl of his heart turn her back upon him in that fashion. And yet supposing you had really been Frau van Kuylen, and your husband *had* painted you behind your back, as our greatest artists have been wont to do with their wives and mistresses, that would have been nothing so very out of the way either. Instead, therefore, of treating the matter so tragically, you ought rather to thank God for having brought things so happily round; to be reconciled to your lover; to my poor friend, who after all is the one to be pitied, for he goes empty away; and to your own face with which you were so very angry. It has, indeed, been an infliction to you, but at last it is to it that you are indebted for the happiness of having Mr. Hans Lutz again. For if Mrs. Bathsheba had not stolen your bewitching profile, who knows whether your lover would ever have come on your track here in Munich, and finally carried off picture and original both!'

"Such was the gist of my address, and my eloquence had the happiest results. There ensued a most affecting reconciliation, an embracing, kissing, and handshaking, whereof—as regards the last at all events—I had my due share, and in another five minutes I saw the happy pair drive off in the cab, radiant with delirious bliss, and had scarcely time to invite them to pay a visit to my house, and to call after the driver to go through the English garden, that being the best scene for such an idyll.

"Van Kuylen did not show himself again. But as I

slowly followed the cab, and turned round once more, I thought I saw from the upper window of the small house, a resigned cloud of smoke eddy up from a white clay-pipe. He had not spared himself the pain of looking after the lovers from his lonely watch-tower.

"I need not say that I instantly went home, and accurately repeated the whole remarkable story to my dear wife. Alas! I failed to produce the desired effect thereby. There lurked in the soul of that excellent woman a prejudice against a girl who presumed to be so beautiful that all men ran after her, and even the steadiest landscape painters took in her an interest—fatherly, indeed, but dangerously warm. The suspicion that all might not have been so very right after all, seemed to gain confirmation, when day after day passed without bringing the happy pair to pay their promised visit. My wife went about again with a well-known air of magnanimously suppressed triumph, and treated me with such compassionate indulgence, that it almost drove me wild. But what was to be done? I must needs put up with it, and had only the choice of passing as a bad judge of character, or a secret sinner.

"However, in a fortnight's time the tide turned. I was sitting quietly over my work about noon, when in ran my little Christopher, and called out to me that I was to come instantly to mamma, that there was a most beautiful lady there with a gentleman, and that they had asked for me. There they were then, husband and wife, on their marriage trip through Italy to New York. On the day I had last seen them they had set out homewards to present themselves to their parents, and as Hans Lutz—his real name was Johann Ludwig Weinmann—was making a quantity of money over there in America, it was probably much the same to the father of the fair Kate, whether the result was attained by railway-making and bridge-building, or the tanning of leather. My good wife had at first—she afterwards confessed to me—sat rather monosyllabically there, but when I came in, and neither the young woman nor I blushed, nor exchanged any sign whatever of a private understanding, she finally resumed her equipoise, and was obliged to believe in me: more—in the course of the next half-hour she fell so completely in love with the beautiful world's wonder, she did not know how to let her go, and finally parted from her with the tenderest embraces. Later she said to me, 'It really *is* a very good thing she is gone to America.'

"The same evening brought another leave-taking, but only in the form of a letter. My good mynheer sent me a note, in which he after his own fashion, and with divers humorous marginal illustrations, announced his journey to Italy. He enclosed a small pen-and-ink drawing as a keepsake; which was very highly finished and in all respects a genuine Van Kuylen. Before a hut in a primeval forest sat a young pair under the shade of palms, bananas, and bread-fruit trees, a couple of fine children playing about their feet, the wife occupied with needle-work, the husband reading to her. Above them on the branch of a majestic tree squatted a small thin ape who was just about to throw a date into the beautiful young woman's lap. Whom the faces of the wedded pair resembled, and who had sat to the artist for the odd, pinched, resigned countenance of the ape it were needless to particularise."

END OF THE FAIR KATE.

GEOFFROY AND GARCINDE.

GEOFFROY AND GARCINDE.

About the time of the second crusade, there lived near Carcassonne in Provence, a nobleman, Count Hugo of Malaspina, who after the death of his fair and virtuous wife, sent his only daughter Garcinde, then ten years old, accompanied by her foster-sister Aigleta, to be educated at the convent of Mont Salvair, and recommenced himself, spite of grizzling hair, a wandering bachelor life. He was a stately knight, and popular both with men and women, so he had no lack of invitations to merry-making tournaments, and banquets at the castles of the wealthy nobles, far and near. But, however, his delight in military exercises and minstrelsy grew cool with years, so that he left the palm in both to be carried off by younger aspirants, developing, at the same time, an increasing love for wine and dice, and falling from his former character of a wise manager of himself and of his substance, to that of a degraded night-reveller, who even occupied the castle of his fathers as tenant to his creditors, and had nothing left to call his own but his unstained knightly courage, and the heart of his child. In order not to grieve that child, Count Hugo took the greatest care to prevent the rumour of the low state of his finances reaching the convent. He was in the habit of twice a year visiting his daughter, and the young girl, who up to this time had devoted all the power of loving she as yet had to her father, and admired him as the ideal of every human and knightly virtue and perfection,—did not fail to notice that the eyes of the fast aging man, had for some time back lost their open and joyous expression, that his cheeks were sunk, and his lips habitually compressed. But as she knew the way to cheer him, and for the time to make him forget the world outside the cloister-walls, she naturally attributed his depression to his solitude, and lovingly urged him to take her back, and keep her near him. At which the Count would sigh, gloomily shake his head and declare that it would not be consistent with her fair fame to live in a castle inhabited by men only, without better protection than he could offer. He could not, therefore, remove her from the cloister until she should exchange the companionship of the pious sisters for that of some worthy husband. This was not pleasant hearing to the intelligent girl, for although her life had not been otherwise than happy with the nuns, who were cheerful and busy, and though she had had, moreover, the companionship of the bright-eyed Aigleta—a lively girl and full of whatever fun was possible in a convent—yet Garcinde yearned to know and enjoy something of the world without, and above all to devote her loving heart entirely to her father. But he persisted that the honour of his house allowed of no other arrangement than the present, and after every conversation on the subject—as though stung by some secret vexation—he would abruptly take leave of his lovely child, who on such occasions sat in the turret of the convent-garden wall, lost in thought, and gazing on the road her father had taken.

Thus year after year passed by: the Count's daughter had long out-grown childhood, and the good nuns, reluctant as they might have been to part with their

charge, yet began to wonder that nothing was said about
marrying her. For they had no idea that Count Hugo,
shrinking from confessing to a son-in-law that he was a
beggar, spoke as little about his daughter as though she
had been changed in her cradle, and a fairy bantling
placed there in her stead.

Now it happened that early one morning, when no
one was expecting him at his own castle, the Count returned quite alone on his roan mare, and gave a faint
knock as a man mortally sick might give at a hospital-gate.
The porter, growling over the untimely guest who roused
him from his morning sleep, looked through the grating
in the iron court-door, and was so startled by what he
saw, that his trembling hands could scarcely draw the
heavy bolt in order to admit of his master's entrance.
For the face of the Count was pale as that of the dead,
and his eyes hollow, fixed, and expressionless, as if,
instead of having returned from a merry-making at
the castle of his rich neighbour, the Count Pierre of
Gaillac, he might have been emerging from the cave
of St. Patrick, or from a still more terrible place where
he had spent the night with spectres. He threw the
bridle of his horse (the animal was covered with foam,
and greedily drank the rain-water on the ground,) to the
alarmed domestic, and uttered one word only, "Geoffroy." Then he ascended the winding-stair to his lonely
room, shaking his head when the servant enquired whether the Count would have any refreshments, and whether
he should wake up the other retainers.

The porter, who had never seen his master in such
a plight, would have been slow to recover from the
shock he had received, had not the horse, with a shrill
neigh of distress, sunk on the ground. With some difficulty he got it to its feet again, and led the utterly ex-

hausted animal to the stable, where he rendered it every care; then still talking to himself, and calling upon all saints and angels, he ran to the Geoffroy whom the Count had demanded.

The youth who bore this name dwelt in a lonely ivy-grown turret close to the moat, and as the dawn had hardly broken, he still lay in the sound sleep beseeming his health and early years. He was only twenty, a nephew of the Count's, the offspring of the unfortunate love between the high-born Countess Beatrix and a wandering minstrel, who knowing the proud spirit and the customs of the house of Malaspina, had no way of winning, except persuading her to elope with him. Count Rambaut her father, when he discovered the disgrace that had befallen his family, took no one into his counsels but his son Hugo; and father and brother rode forth by night to follow the track of the offenders. In seven days time they returned, walking their horses, a closed litter between them, in which the young Countess lay with snow-white face, more like a waxen form than a living woman. Her brother had killed her lover, her father had cursed the dying man. From that time she never spoke another word to either of them, but lived a widow in a detached turret, where she brought her boy into the world. She made no complaint, but resisted all attempts at reconciliation, though on their father's death', her brother, who had always been deeply attached to her, endeavoured by all the means in his power, to conciliate her. He himself bore her son to the font, and when he married, he imposed upon his wife the duty of daily visiting the lonely one, who never of her own accord left her self-elected prison. Both ladies had now departed this life; the young man Geoffroy—he was named after his father—was brought up

almost as the Count's own son, and truly the proudest
might have gloried in such a son. He was a beautiful
youth, broad-shouldered, dark-complexioned, with great
earnest eyes, and a sweet sad mouth almost feminine in
form, which seldom smiled. For although he had in
abundance all that a young heart could desire, gay gar-
ments, finely-tempered weapons, horse, falcon, and leisure enough for every knightly practice, and though, too,
from his earliest infancy no one had ever spoken an unkind word to him, or reproached him with his birth, yet
for all that a shadow hung over him. Unless he were
wandering in the forest—which bordered on the moat,
and was reached by a narrow bridge in ten paces or so
—he would keep himself apart from all joyous company,
in the same room where his mother had brought him
into the world, as though there were no other place on
earth where he had a right to be. In his mother's life-
time he had planted the little tower about with roses,
and he still kept her chamber, bed, and wardrobe, just
as she had liked them to be. He for his part had but
few wants, and always held himself prepared to leave
even this corner where he was tolerated, at the first insulting word. However, no one thought of such an
event less than did Count Hugo, whose heart the boy
had entirely won, for he had transferred his love for his
sister, to her fatherless child. But as spite of all the
kindness and care shown him, the son could never force
himself to return the friendly grasp of the hand that had
slain his father, all that the Count could do was to leave
his nephew in perfect freedom. He never required any service from him, thanked him as for a favour conferred if
Geoffroy tamed a falcon, or broke a horse for him, and
when his means began to fail, he would rather himself
dispense with a necessary than that Geoffroy should be

disappointed of a wish. However, he never took him
with him on a visit, not that he wished to deny this
illegitimate sprout of the family tree—especially since
his unfortunate mother was no longer there to blush for
him—but rather that he did not wish the youth to witness his own reckless mode of life, or to be corrupted
by the loose manners and dissolute society of the neighbouring nobles.

Therefore it was that the nephew, who had never
received an order from his uncle, was surprised to be
thus suddenly disturbed at so unusual an hour by the
porter, who breathlessly told him what had happened,
and summoned him to the castle. He did not, however,
delay to dress and obey the call. When he entered the
chamber, dimly lighted by the dawning day, he saw the
Count sitting at a table with a taper before him, by the
aid of which he had evidently been writing a letter. He
now sat motionless, his head resting on his hands, which
were buried deep in his grey hair. Geoffroy had to call
him three times before he could rouse him from his
trance, then when he saw the haggard face and lifeless
eyes he, too, was shocked, although he did not love his
uncle. But he made an effort, enquired whether he was
ill, and whether he should ride to Carcassonne to fetch
a leech.

"Saddle a horse, Geoffroy," returned Count Hugo,
slowly rising, folding the letter he had written, and seal-
ing it with his signet-ring. "You must take this letter
to-day to the Lady Abbess of the Convent of Mont Salvair, and to-morrow she must send me off my daughter
Garcinde, for I have something to say to her. And as I
myself cannot reach her—my ride this night has done
me harm, and my gout admonishes me to get into bed
rather than into the saddle—I could wish that you

should escort your cousin, and see to her safe journey hither. Take a servant with you who will bring back, on a baggage-horse, whatever may be personally needed, till the abbess can send the rest. The convent will lend Garcinde a horse. I have requested this to be done in my letter. You will rest for a night half-way, at the farm of La Vaquiera, my daughter being unaccustomed to riding, and the summer heat great. On the evening of the third day I shall expect to see you here."

The youth received the letter, lingered for a moment on the threshold as though some question were burning on his lips, then merely said, "It shall be done, my lord," and with a slight inclination, took his departure. When he got outside the door, he fancied that he heard himself recalled, and stood still a moment to see whether it really were so, but hearing nothing further he ran down the winding-stair, got his horse out of the stable, gave the requisite orders to one of the few servants that remained about the fallen house, and as the man was sleepy and slow in his movements, ordered him to follow after, while he himself sprang through the gate past the wondering porter, to whose questions as to what the Count wanted, and whether it really were all over with him, he merely replied by a shrug of the shoulders.

The reason of his haste in fulfilling his mission, was a fear that the Count might change his mind and call him back, for during the eight years that his cousin had been away from her father's house, whenever a message had to be sent to her, he was never the one appointed to carry it, and there seemed to be a deliberate purpose to prevent their meeting. It is true that when they were both children there had been no one of whom the little

Countess was so fond as of her silent, proud-spirited playfellow, the wandering minstrel's son, who at that time already led a strange and solitary life in the small tower where his mother had died. The servants had concluded that it was on account of young Geoffroy that Sir Hugo had sent his daughter to a convent, instead of taking a duenna into his house as many a widower had done, so as not to be separated from his child; and now here was the cousin sent to bring back the young lady, who had meanwhile, according to common report, grown up into unparalleled beauty. Had some suitor made his appearance on the previous evening, so that it was no longer necessary to guard the girl against an unsuitable attachment? Or had Death on his spectral horse accompanied the Count on his last night's ride, so that all earthly considerations having now fallen off from him, he merely thought of making his peace with God, and leaving his child free to be happy or unhappy in her own way? There was no solving the mystery.

As soon, however, as the turrets of the Castle of Malaspina were out of sight, Geoffroy threw away all care and sadness, and only suffered pleasant thoughts— rare guests in his mind—to go forth to meet the playfellow of his childhood, whose delicate face with its laughing white teeth and large dark eyes, shone out as plainly before him as though he had seen them but yesterday. The day was cloudless, the woods resounded with the song of birds, the beautiful fields of Provence spread before him golden with the ripening corn, and for the first time life appeared to him to be indeed a heavenly boon. He took to singing the song with which his father had won his mother's heart; he had found it in a music-book with the words written in the margin by her own hand.

> "Le douz chans d'un auzelh,
> Tue chantava en un plays,
> Me desviet l'autr'ier
> De mon camin—"

He knew not why this particular song should come to his mind: he had never till now thought of it but with sorrow, but to-day he sang it with clear voice and joyous heart.

As he approached the convent at evening, his mood became quieter, and his brow clouded. With fast beating heart he knocked at the gate, and delivering the letter through a grating to a lay-sister, awaited a message from the abbess. Before long the answer came, saying the command of the Count would be obeyed, that with the dawn of morning both the young girls would be given over to the messenger's charge, and that meanwhile he might spend the night at the house of the convent bailiff, who was accustomed to receive strangers, and dwelt in the vineyards of Mont Salvair.

The night, however, seemed long to the youth, for his trusty friend sleep came not as usual to speed it away; he envied the servant (who had only arrived about midnight with the baggage-horse,) the influence of the strong convent wine, and the deep unconsciousness that followed. In Geoffroy there was something awake which was stronger than wine or fatigue.

Once more it was day: they saddled their horses, took leave of the bailiff, and rode to the gate of Mont Salvair, there to await the youthful Countess. They were not there long before the door opened, the abbess came out, her train of nuns behind her, and in their midst the young Garcinde and her foster-sister, who were about to enter upon life and liberty, while the sisters returned to their pious bondage. There were so many tears and sighs, embraces and benedictions, that Geoffroy had still to wait some time before he could see the face of his cousin, now lost to him under one veil after another. But one glance of her black eyes, and the sheen of her fair hair, had wrought such an effect upon him, that he stood by his horse in utter confusion of mind, and hardly heard the abbess, who enquired in evident wonder whether he were really the messenger who yesterday brought Count Malaspina's letter, and to whom his daughter was to be confided. The servant, who was standing by with folded hands and open mouth, staring at the holy women, had to nudge the youth with his elbow before he came to himself, and reverentially bowed assent to what he had only imperfectly heard. "Sir Hugo himself," he said, his eyes still fixed on his cousin's fair hair, "had been prevented coming. He had charged him to ride slowly, and to spend the night at La Vaquiera." By mentioning this prudent plan, he hoped to remove any scruple the abbess might have in confiding the maiden to so young an escort. He seemed however, to have produced a quite contrary effect, for after one perturbed heavenward look, the noble lady turned away to some of the older nuns, and began in a low voice to take counsel with them. Then when the bailiff had led out the horses for the young women, and while some of the lay-sisters helped the servant to load the baggage horse with clothes and provisions, a lively face emerged from the living hedge of black and white veils. It belonged to Aigleta, the child of Garcinde's nurse, who had grown up to be a blooming maiden, and who now approached the mute messenger, holding out a small but vigorous hand, and exclaiming, "In God's name be welcome, Sir Geoffroy! Is it you?" After which she went up to the abbess and whispered a word or two in her ear which seemed to dispel all anxiety.

The pious lady depended too fully on the lessons of wisdom and virtue, which her charge had imbibed with conventual milk, to hold it possible that she should give her heart to a nameless illegitimate cousin, especially at a time when, in all probability, a distinguished alliance awaited her. Accordingly she clasped Garcinde—who burst into tears—in her motherly embrace, herself helped her to mount the old convent grey, while Aigleta was lifted by Geoffroy on to a spirited pony, and with much sobbing and waving of hands and handkerchiefs, the small cavalcade was at last sent off from the old arched gate of Mont Salvair, through which the band of the Brides of Heaven slowly and mournfully returned.

But the young travelling-companions, too, proceeded on their way more silently and thoughtfully than might be expected, when a knightly youth, on the fairest of summer days, guides two fair maidens mounted on fresh horses upon their first expedition into a smiling world. After a hasty question as to how her father was, Garcinde had not again addressed Geoffroy, influenced, perhaps, by the curt although reverential manner in which he had seemed to avoid entering into further details. But Aigleta, who for her part had not allowed the departure from Mont Salvair to weigh the least upon her spirits, took up a livelier tone, and after a sigh of gratitude for being at last delivered from the pious monotony of cloistered life, began to give Geoffroy an amusing account of its course from day to day. She was an excellent mimic, and counterfeited the voices of the different sisters, their mild whispers, and downcast eyes, their unrestrained laughing and screaming as soon as they were unobserved, their petty spiteful quarrels, their cloying affectionateness to each other, ready at a moment's notice to turn into deadly enmity. In the midst

of all this she introduced the solemn bass voice of the
abbess, exhorting to peace, and painting the dangers of
the world; and finally she concluded with a wild medley
of pious and godless speeches, in which the nuns were
supposed to express their feelings on the departure of
the young Countess, their envy, their fear that Satan with
all his crew might be waiting for them outside the gates;
lastly the prayer of the abbess for their deliverance from
all dangers, especially from the temptations of bold
knights, and suspicious young cousins.

Garcinde who had been riding a yard or two in advance, now cut short this burst of spirits, and with her
gentle voice—without, however, turning towards Aigleta
—rebuked her frivolous tone. It was sinful, she said,
after all the love and kindness they had enjoyed, to ex-
pose to view the weaknesses of the poor and sadly
limited life, and she at least should never forget that
when orphaned, she had found there a second home.
Whereupon the pert girl, who in Geoffroy's presence
did not at all approve of having this well-merited sermon addressed to her, only replied with a couple of
proverbs, "Each bird sings according as it is fed,"
and—

> "To tell the simple truth I ween,
> May be unwise, but 'tis not sin."

But she was all the more vexed and put out because
the handsome youth by her side treated her as so perfect a stranger, while she for her part remembered him
so well, and how glad she used to be when their childish
games were so arranged that "Jaufret"—so they called
him then—should be on her side to deliver her from a
dragon, or to wake her by a kiss out of magic sleep.
And while she now engaged the servant in common-
place talk, she could not help stealing frequent glances

at her other companion, noticing how handsome and
manly he had become; how with a slight turn of the
wrist he could rein in a fiery horse, and yet had such a
sad and earnest beauty in his eyes as would have become the very saints in the church of Mont Salvair.
What could make him so silent, she kept wondering;
and if she were below the attention of so noble a gentleman, how was it that he abstained from all attempt
to find favour in the eyes of his lady-cousin? All this
perplexed her so much that she gradually left off talking,
and entirely forgot the slight anger she had felt at the
admonition received. Meanwhile the youth on his side,
who had so impatiently watched for this day, wished, as
the sun rose higher, that it had never dawned upon him
at all, instead of looking down on his joy and sorrow
with so heartless a splendour. It is true that from his
boyish years he had preserved the image of his cousin
as his ideal of all beauty and loveliness, but the spark
had smouldered on as a quiet memory in a well-guarded
portion of his heart; but now at the first greeting from
her lips, at the perfume that floated over to him from
her hair, this spark burst out into a mighty flame, and
he suffered tortures such as he had never known before.
And then her apparent estrangement from him increased
his anguish, for although he did not know whether it
were disinclination to him personally, or the calm con-
tempt of the Count's daughter for her father's poor re-
tainer which closed her lips and kept her eyes averted,
he had leisure enough in these silent hours to estimate
with miserable accuracy the social gulf between them,
and the duty of crushing every foolish hope. Then, again,
his thoughts turned to conjectures as to what posses-
sor he would have to make over the jewel entrusted to
him, whether her hand would be given away without her

heart, or whether her father in the gloom of sickness had so yearned for his only child, as suddenly to recall her to his deserted home. Even were it so, would his case be less hopeless if he had longer time to learn the full preciousness of the treasure which must at length be surrendered to another?

Thus he sank more and more into a profound melancholy, so that even Garcinde, who was not herself joyous, remarked it, and asked him whether he were suffering, whether he would rest and refresh himself with a draught of wine? Geoffroy, crimsoning to the roots of his hair, excused himself for his absent mood, accounted for it by a sleepless night, and did all he could to appear more cheerful. And at noon when they halted in a wood beside a spring to recruit themselves with the provisions with which the pious sisterhood had laden the baggage-horse, his spirits in a measure revived, while Aigleta, who had long got over her fit of sullenness, recovered the audacity of her mood, and flavoured the mid-day meal with the drollest freaks of fancy. Garcinde sat in the shadow of a tall black-thorn, and patiently endured that the little witch who could not rest a moment, should adorn the whole party with garlands, even to the servant and the grazing horses, singing merry songs the while, not always of spiritual import, at which even the servant laughed, so that the young Countess rose with a grave air, removed the wreath from her brow, and proposed that they should ride on again. The last to rise from the green grass was Geoffroy; to him the spot seemed a Paradise where he would willingly have dreamed his days away, yet when he lifted his cousin into her saddle, he did not dare to bestow on the little foot that she placed in his hand, anything more than the very slightest pressure. She turned her face

away from him, and he was for an instant's space veiled
in the flow of soft tresses that fell down to her girdle.
Then she put her horse into a gentle canter. Thus they
all rode on for a while, men and beasts refreshed by
their hour's repose, and even Geoffroy carried his head
higher, as though the red wine that Aigleta had given
him in a cup garlanded with flowers, had put new life
into his veins, and inspired him with energy to enjoy the
bliss of the present hour.

La Vaquiera, which they reached early in the afternoon, was a dairy-farm, beautifully situated between
richest pastures and wooded grounds; until late years in
the possession of the house of Malaspina, but staked
and lost at play by the Count to a neighbouring noble,
Pierre de Gaillac, who had, however, something else to
do than to look after herds of cattle and flocks of
sheep in this quiet corner. The farmer himself and his
wife, who lived here with a troop of shepherds and milk-
maids, and whom Sir Hugo greeted as usual whenever
he rode past, had not a notion that they no longer held
under him, and they received his daughter—whom they
well remembered in her childhood—with all the re-
verence and attention due to their young mistress. They
had only a small house, as the servants slept in the
stables, but they at once gave up their one sleeping-
chamber to the two girls, and themselves found a resting-place in the kitchen. Geoffroy had to put up with
a loft reached by a ladder, fortunately an airy one
having plenty of fresh hay. It was late, however, when
he betook himself to it, for the best part of the starry
night had been spent in such earnest and serious converse, that his impetuous feelings were somewhat sub-
dued, and spite of the vicinity of Garcinde, he made up
for the lost sleep of the night before. The two girls, on

the contrary, although they too—what with the long ride and the strong wine—owned to being very tired, yet enlivened themselves during their unrobing, by much of that seeming confidential talk common to maidens who share the same couch, and yet would fain conceal their heart's secrets from each other. For girls believe there is no better way of holding their tongue on one subject than letting it run on unguardedly on every other. "Why have you been so little glad all day long, and are you sure you are not still angry with me for all the nonsense I have talked, out of sheer delight at getting back into the world?" said Aigleta to her friend, while helping her to braid and bind her hair. "Not so, dear heart," replied her thoughtful companion, letting her delicate arms drop into her lap. "I envy you your light-heartedness, I do not censure it. But my heart is heavy. Oh, Aigleta, I used to have such happy dreams of returning to my father, of breathing free air, and seeing the world as it lay beyond the hill of Mont Salvair. And now—"

"Does not the world seem to you fair enough, the sky blue enough, the meadows green enough, the stream clear enough to reflect back your beauty?" laughed Aigleta.

"How can you mock at my anxiety and gloom?" returned the Count's daughter. "Just think—on the very day when I re-enter the world, my dear father is absent from me. I cannot grasp his hand or hear his voice. Oh believe me, there is something mysterious, dark, perhaps appalling, that is kept back from me, the foreboding of which has—spite of all the sunshine—darkened for me this much longed for day."

"Nonsense!" said Aigleta. "Shall I tell you where the cloud lay that threw its dull shadow over you? On the brow and in the eyes of that simple Sir Jaufret.

Deny it as you will I know what I know, and have
not got eyes in my head for nothing. And have you
not, indeed, every right to be offended with his un-
courteous, indifferent manner? Fie! To make such a
melancholy face when one has the good fortune to serve
as knight to two sweet young ladies, one of whom, moreover, is a high-born countess and his own first cousin!
And this evening, too, when we walked round the pastures, could he not have found something more lively to
talk of than the stars above us, and whether we went to
them after death, and horrid subjects of that kind? I
think he might have found some stars nearer at hand,
and only to talk about dying we need not have left
Mont Salvair! He is certainly—as one can see—likely
to die of love, but that is no excuse. Such gloom may
do very well for poems when he writes you them, but
while you were together and alone—for as for me, I
closed my eyes and pretended to be asleep—"

"What art thou prating about, foolish one?" said
Garcinde, trying to look angry, although a sweet emotion
sent the blood tingling to her cheeks. "Dost thou not
know why he is so grave and sad, and never, indeed,
will be quite happy all his life long? Not though that
he *need* take his birth thus to heart. If he would only
go to the court of some foreign prince, and there gain
renown, no one would reproach him with what he could
not help; and he might win wealth, and land, and fame,
and be a fit wooer for any count's daughter. But even
though he be a dreamer, and does not understand his
own advantage, he is not so foolish as to turn his
thoughts towards me, for well he knows my father would
never give me to him. Nay I rather think that he hates me
as being my father's daughter—above him in position—
though I for my part would always behave to him as in

our childish days, and do everything in my power to
renew the old intimacy."

"Hm," said Aigleta, as she unlaced her bodice, "it
may be that you are right, and yet I wish he hated *me*
in the way he hates *thee*. I should desire nothing better,
but I am a servant's daughter. Who would give himself
the trouble to look and see whether I deserve love or
hate? And yet I think," and so saying she shook her
thick hair over her white shoulders, "it might be well
worth their while too, and whether high-born or not, you
shall see, *Domna Comtessa*, in the net of these black hairs.
I shall catch gay-plumaged birds as well as you with
your gold threads, and even if that black crow Jaufret
keeps out of them—"

"Any one who heard you speak," interposed Garcinde, "would think that you came from some quite other
place than a convent. But now we will go to sleep. I
wish morning were come and that I had embraced my
father."

They lay quiet for an hour, yet neither of them
closed an eye; the bed at the farm was certainly harder
than their Mont Salvair couch, but that alone would not
have troubled the repose of girls of eighteen. They both
held their breath, and kept motionless, till Aigleta suddenly sat up and said, "I never believed the nuns when
they said the outer world would steal away our rest; and
now see, we have hardly put our foot outside their gates,
and already sleep flies from us. And yet we are not
even in love, I at least am not. Oh, Blessed Lady of
Mont Salvair, what *will* happen when it comes to that!
You of course will have some distinguished husband,
and then lovers as many as you will, but I—suppose
one took my fancy whom I could not have—I believe I
should set a wood on fire and jump into the midst of it!"

"What are you dreaming about?" answered Garcinde, without raising her head from the pillow. "Do you suppose that I would take a husband whom I did not love, or that my father would give me to any one against whom my heart rebelled? Do you not know that he loves nothing on earth so well as me, and could have no greater sorrow than to see me suffer? Go to sleep—the wine has got into your head. I think you have been let out of the convent too soon."

"Amen," said the merry girl in the deep voice of the abbess; then she laughed out loud, but left off talking, and was asleep before her young mistress.

The next morning the horses had stood saddled and pawing the ground in the courtyard, for a good hour before the girls appeared on the threshold. They nodded familiarly to Geoffroy, and chatted a little with the good people of La Vaquiera. Then they spurred their horses in order to get over the four hour's ride to Malaspina, before the mid-day heat.

Again but little was said on the way; the youth, spite of his sound sleep, was still paler and sadder than on the previous day; even Aigleta seemed lost in thought, bit her full lip, and now and then sighed. Moreover they had difficulty to keep up with the young Countess, who urged her horse as though the wild huntsmen were on her track. Once she turned to Geoffroy, who kept near her for fear the over-urged palfrey should make a false step. "Do you think my father will ride to meet us?" she enquired, and anxiously waited for his answer. "I should think so," replied the youth without daring to look at her, for his mind, too, was full of gloomy forebodings.

When they first came in sight of the Castle of Malaspina, Garcinde suddenly drew bridle, and shading her eyes with her hand gazed for several moments at the well-remembered ancient pile. The road wound like a bright narrow ribbon through the short-cut grass, and they could see every pebble on it. But of any horseman crossing the drawbridge and hastening to meet them, nothing was to be seen; even when they came so near that the warder blew his horn, everything remained unchanged, and there was no sign of the festal reception of which the girl had dreamed. The porter appeared in the open gateway, and behind him a few shabby-looking retainers, who stood round as if confused, and for the first time aware how high the grass and nettles grew between the flags in the courtyard. Geoffroy had made some pretext for remaining behind, for his heart bled at the idea of witnessing such a return home. For although the innocent, inexperienced girl could not take in the whole extent of the change—as she had only a childish recollection of the place, and it was not written over the gateway that scarcely the bare walls remained in her father's possession—yet the paucity of domestics, and their thread-bare attire, might well startle her; and above all, that her own parent had not the heart to welcome his beloved child in front of the ancestral dwelling!

"Is my father ill?" she cried, as without awaiting help she leapt from her saddle.

"It is only a sharp attack of gout, lady," replied the porter, glancing up at an arched window that looked into the court, as if expecting that at least his master would beckon from thence to his daughter, even though his ailments might prevent his descending the stairs. But the window was empty, and a blush suffused Garcinde's face as her glance, which had taken the same direction, came back unsatisfied and distressed. "I will go upstairs to him, Aigleta," she whispered, "wait here till I call you."

She went, the others descended from their horses and made them over to the servants. Geoffroy after exchanging a few rapid words with the porter: "Anything new?" "All as it was," took his own horse to the stable, unbridled him, and then crossed the courtyard on his way to his little turret without taking any notice of Aigleta, who, lost and forsaken, sat on a stone bench amongst the menials, and could have wept heartily over so disappointing a return to the much desired home, had there not been too many lookers on. She saw the young man take his way to the well-known rose-embowered tower, but his head hung down so dejectedly that she did not venture to address him, or ask him to let her go with him to their old play-ground. As for him, he seemed to have forgotten that he was in the world, or that he walked among men. Although he had only had a little bread and wine in the early morning, and it was now past noon, he had no thought of eating or drinking, but sat in his turret-chamber on his mother's bed, motionless like one struck by lightning, his widely-opened eyes fixed on his father's song-book, which on his entrance he had taken down from the shelf and opened out on his knee. Yet he did not seem to be reading, but rather listening to some words that his own heart was setting to the music, whether glad or sorrowful none could have guessed from his stony aspect. All at once, however, he started back into life, and his dark face flushed deeply; he sprang so hastily from the bed that the song-book slipped from his knee and fell open upon the flags, then he held his breath, and listened to some sound in the garden of roses below. Yes, it was her step, no other human being's was like it, and now her hand was upon the turret-door, now she crossed the dark and narrow hall, now she opened the inner door and stepped over its threshold into his small chamber.

As she entered, his eyes involuntarily fell, and he sought to disguise his emotion by lifting from the floor the parchment-book that lay between her and him, and now that he raised his eyes to her he started, horror-stricken. For her face but lately blooming with youth and health, had so changed in one short hour that she seemed to have traversed years of hopeless grief.

"I disturb you, cousin," she said in a voice from which the music had fled, "but I come to you because I think you are my friend—perhaps the only one I have. Let me sit down, I am mortally weary. No, not on the bed; my dear aunt died there. Oh, Jaufret, if I only knew that it would be my death-bed too—and that my heart would grow still the moment I lay down there— God is my witness I would throw myself upon it at once!"

She sank down on the seat that he offered her, hiding her face in her hands, and tears streaming between her white fingers. "For God's sake, cousin," he cried, "you break my heart. What has happened? What has your father said?"

Then she removed her hands from her face, pressed back her tears, and looked steadfastly at him. "I will not weep," she said, "it is childish. If all is true that I have heard, tears are too weak for such sorrow. But I want to hear it from you, cousin. Is it indeed the case that the Count of Malaspina is a beggar, and that his daughter has nothing to call her own except the clothes she wears? You are silent, Jaufret. Be it so then; what should I care for that? I have long had a foreboding that there was trouble before me, and as to poverty, I have seen *that* in the convent, and know it, and it does not affright me. But shame, Jaufret, shame—"

"By the blood of our Lord," he exclaimed. "Who dares to say that shame threatens you so long as I can bear a sword, and lay a lance in rest?"

She did not appear to hear him. Then after a pause in which she, as if unconsciously, drew her rosary through her hands, she shudderingly enquired, "Do you know the Count de Gaillac?" The youth started as though he had trodden upon a snake, he muttered a curse between his teeth, and convulsively clutched the silken coverlet.

"You seem to know him," the maiden continued, "and I know him too. About two years ago a hunting-party came to Mont Salvair, a great gathering of knights and fair dames. They all sat themselves down to feast in the wood that bordered the convent garden, and we from our shrubbery could see what was going on; the drinking, the banqueting; and could hear the songs that the Count's mistress—a tall, proud-looking woman—sang to her lute. Oh cousin, what dreadful human beings there are! Even then I felt a terror come over me, and was glad when the abbess came to drive us out of the garden, and set us down in the refectory to our spinning-wheels. There nothing was heard but the whispering of the nuns, every one of whom knew something of the wildness and godlessness of the Count de Gaillac. For they know everything in the convent, know all about the outer world and its ways, otherwise they would die of tedium. Then the abbess came in, told me that the Count was standing at the grating, and desired to see me, as he was the bearer of a message from my father. I do not know how I had strength enough to rise, and walk across the long hall to her; then, however, she took my hand in her mother-like clasp, and whispered, 'Remember that thou art here in a consecrated place; here the evil one himself could have no power over thee.' So saying she led me to where the godless man with his hawk's eyes in his wolf's face, was waiting behind the grating, the handsome, bold-looking woman by his side. They were laughing loud when we appeared, but suddenly grew silent. I heard the Count say something in Italian to the lady that I perfectly understood, but could not contradict. What his message to me was I never knew, but it cut me to the heart to hear him name my father, and call him his best friend. A cloud darkened my eyes,—when I came to myself again, they were gone. The abbess never alluded to this visit, and forbade the nuns ever to name Pierre de Gaillac before me. Thus I never heard of him again, till to-day, when my own father has told me that on one wretched night, after gambling away the remnant of his possessions to this man, he had staked the hand of his daughter upon the last throw of the dice, and lost that too."

A sound forced its way from the young man's breast, a hollow cry of horror and of rage, but his limbs seemed paralysed, and his tongue bound, for he did not speak a word, and there was such stillness in the small chamber, that the grinding of the sand beneath his feet was plainly heard.

"You hate my father," the girl at length continued with downcast eyes but calm voice. "Oh, Jaufret, I have known this for many years, and it has grieved me enough. But what I have now told you ought not to increase your hatred, for if there be one miserable being on earth, who in the burning torture of his soul already endures hell-fire, and expiates his sins, believe me, cousin, it is the Count of Malaspina, who would gladly

change places with the dropsical cripple at his castle
gate, if only he could undo what he has done. He
writhed as though impaled at the stake, and buried his
face in the pillows that I might not see him while he
told me how it all came about; how they clouded his
mind with hippocras; how at every throw they pressed
the goblet into his hand, till at length the mocking
laughter of the Count seemed to awake him from a
dream, and he gazed with sheer horror at the abyss into
which he had hurled his last possession, the happiness
of his child. He did everything he could to propitiate
his malicious enemy and conqueror, nay he offered to be
his serf, his bondservant, if only he might pay the fearful
debt thus. But the Count had merely laughed and said,
'A Jew's bargain indeed you would make with me, my
friend, to offer me a plucked old cock for a plump
young hen. I have more servants to feed than I care
for, but a young wife I do want, for you know that I
am getting old, and I am not so fond of my mistress as
to wish to leave her my lands and castles after my
death. Moreover, I fear she might make me a very bad
return, and before my eyes were closed, drink with some
younger fellow to my approaching end. But your daughter has been chastely and piously brought up, and will
convert me—grey in sin as I am—to an orderly life.
Therefore I would not take all the treasures on earth in
exchange for her small hand, which can alone open the
door of Heaven to me; and so I charge you by your
honour that within three weeks you bring her to celebrate the marriage here in Gaillac. I on my part, as my
gift on the morning after the nuptials, will make over
to you all the woods and lands that I have won from
you of late years, in order that your child need not pro-
vide for you like a beggar, but that you may live out

your old age in state and comfort.' And so saying he called for his servants to light him to bed, and left my father alone."

At this moment Geoffroy made a gesture as though about to speak; but she rose quickly, advanced towards him, and laid her small, cold, trembling hand beseechingly on his clenched fist. "Cousin," said she, "do not speak yet. I know what you would say: that it would be better to go forth as a beggar from home and hearth, and to wander through the wide world, than to endure disgrace, and give up body and soul to a demon. But consider that my father has nothing on earth besides his honour, his sacred, inviolable, knightly word, and that it would ill become me, his daughter, to counsel him to break it. At the same time, I feel that if there were no other means of fulfilling the pledge given, and paying this debt than by giving my hand to this abhorred suitor, I should prefer what is honourable in the sight of God, to what men call honour. But let us hope, my friend, that this last alternative may be spared me. I propose to write a letter to the man who has us in his power, and you—if you are really my friend— you must take it this very day to Gaillac, for until I know the answer I cannot lay me down to sleep. But do you rest here awhile and take some food. I will go and write the letter; they always commended my skill in writing at the convent; God grant that it may stand me in good stead now! See, I leave you much calmer than I was when I came, although you have not spoken one word of comfort to me; but here in this place where we were so happy as children, here where it seems as if no bad spirits had power over me, here—I cannot persuade myself that the hideous dream is true, and the father's honour pledged to the child's disgrace."

She paused for a moment, but when the youth bent before her with a deep sigh, and pressed her hand to his lips in token that she might depend upon him, she laid her other hand affectionately on his shoulder, and took leave of him, saying, "Aigleta will bring you the letter. Farewell, dear friend, and God go with you," and then on the threshold of the door, folding her hands after kissing the image of the Virgin on the wall, she repeated in a low voice the following prayer:

"Maires de Crist, ton filh car
Prega per nos, quens ampar
E quens gardo de cazer
A la fin en desesper. "

Then she left him alone.

A day and night passed away, and yet another day and night.   Geoffroy did not return.

Sir Hugo never missed him; he was, indeed, accustomed to the youth going his own way, and weeks often passed without his seeing him, and at the present time he hated the sight of any human being. He would sit for hours in one place in his room. The food carried in to him remained untouched, but he drank wine greedily, as though seeking forgetfulness from it; forgetfulness of himself, of the past, and the future.

On the evening of the first day, when Garcinde had gone to see him, he could not even face his own child, but when she approached him, and gently threw her arm over his shoulder, his whole frame was convulsed, and slipping from his chair on to the stone floor, sobbing he clasped her knees and pressed his brow against her feet, so that she had difficulty in raising him and leading him back to his couch. Since then she avoided

his chamber, for if she had tried to comfort him by telling him the reason of Geoffroy's absence, her own de-
sponding heart would have contradicted her words.

The third morning she woke early out of a painful
dream, and called to Aigleta who shared her couch:
"Do you hear nothing, dear? I thought I caught the
sound of horses' hoofs beyond the drawbridge—no, I
was only dreaming. Oh, Aigleta! if I have also made
him unhappy—sent *him* to his ruin. But hark! the
sound comes nearer—I hear the gate creak on its hinges
—it is he. Mother of God! What does he bring—Life
or Death!"

She had sprung up and thrown a cloak around her.
Aigleta, too, hastily rose and bound up her hair; the
rosy morning light shone into the room, and coloured
the pale, worn face of the Count's daughter. She would
have gone to meet Geoffroy had her knees supported her;
as it was she was standing in the middle of the room when
he entered. He, too, was pale, and as he bent before
her, it struck Aigleta that he did not raise the leathern
cap which covered one-half of his brow. But Garcinde
saw nothing but his eyes which sought to avoid hers.

"You bring no comfort?" she said. "I knew it."
Then seating herself on a bench in the window, she
listened impassively to what he narrated with a faltering
voice.

He reached Gaillac that same evening, for he had
not spared his horse. When he was ushered into the
hall where the Count was, he found him at supper, a
couple of his riotous companions with him, and the one
of his mistresses who just then was highest in his favour.
On a low stool at his feet crouched a mis-shapen dwarf,
who played the part of fool and fed his dogs. The
beautiful bold woman sat by his side, and poured him

out red wine into a silver goblet, putting her lips to it before he drained it at a draught. "They all looked at me," said Geoffroy, "as though I arrived very opportunely to divert their dulness by some novelty or other, for none of them appeared in spirits except the fool, who with shallow jests that waked no laughter, went on throwing fragments of food to the dogs. I delivered your letter without speaking a word, and while the Count unfolded and read it, I could not but think how she who wrote it would have been received at such a table. The thought made the blood rush to my head, and such a giddiness came over me that I was obliged to lean upon my sword. One of the guests who noticed this ordered that wine should be brought me, for I must be weary and thirsty after my rapid ride, but I shook my head and said I would only await the answer, and then return at once. Meanwhile the Count had read the letter, and made it over in silence to his neighbour; she had scarcely run her eyes over the first few lines before she burst out into loud laughter. 'A sermon!' she cried, 'God's death! You are going to get a saint for a wife,' and then she began to read the letter aloud, line for line; and the words that would have made stones weep and moved the gates of hell, waked only mocking echoes here. Blasphemies and impious jests broke out, interrupting the reading. Then the woman rose, and casting a proud look upon the Count, said with curled lip, 'The saint may come and welcome. I was averse to her, thinking she might turn your heart from us all and rule here alone, but now that I have read her letter I am not afraid of her. You, Pierre de Gaillac are not the man to wear a hair-shirt and a prickly girdle. You are accustomed to the fires of hell, and the air of heaven would but chill you. In hell, however, there is more joy over one who sickens of penance and returns to his evil ways than over ninety-and-nine lost souls. Whereupon I empty this goblet to the last drop, and call upon you to pledge me.' She drank, the Count drew her closer to his side, and whispered something into her ear that made her laugh loud. They all seemed to have forgotten the messenger who had brought the letter; the letter itself was handed to the others, and when it came back to the Count, the dwarf snatched at it and cried, 'You have not read it rightly, godmother. Now listen how it ought to be sung to move you all to laughter,' and he began to read it once more aloud in the manner in which they chant litanies in church, wagging head and hands like a preacher giving out the blessing, and if they had all laughed the first time, they knew not now what to do, they held their sides and groaned out responses. At last rage got the better of me. I sprang upon the shameless fellow, tore the letter from him, and struck him such a blow that he rolled over backwards, and upset the silver vessel that held the food for the dogs. 'If I am to obtain no answer,' I cried, 'worthy of the lady who has sent me here, I will at least silence the daring mouth that has mocked at a noble virgin, and dragged the words of a pure and lofty soul through the mire!'

"For a moment there was silence. I even thought I might pass through the hall unhindered, but I had reckoned without my host. Servants rushed in, the guests raged and railed at me, the dogs howled, but the Count still sat in his place, pale as death, and motionless with fury, and the woman by his side shot fiery looks at me. When—a quarter of an hour later—I found myself on damp straw behind a bolted door, a wound in my head, and darkness before my eyes, I thanked my Saviour that I was delivered from the neighbourhood of those brutal men, and could no longer hear them blaspheme the name dearest to me. I do not know how I passed the night and the following day. I think I must have slept through them, but about the middle of the second night, I was gently waked by a soft hand passing over my face, and the light of a small lamp shone into my eyes. It was the Count's mistress who stood before me there, and signed to me to be silent; gently she led me up the broken stairs, through empty passages and halls to a narrow door of which she had the key. 'I cannot let you starve to death in unbroken darkness down there,' said she. 'Outside you will find your horse and something to eat at the saddle-bow. Fly! if ever thou needest a friend come to Carcassonne, and ask for Agnes the Sardinian. You will easily find me out.' She waited an answer, perhaps she had even dreamed of a tenderer farewell, but as I was silent she opened the door, and again passed her hand over my blood-stained hair. 'Poor youth,' said she, 'thou deservedst a better fate.' Then I leapt into the saddle, and spurred my horse hard, and thus I rode on without stopping, for in the night air my senses gradually awoke and the fever of my wound left me. And here I am— and this is all the answer that I bring back."

So saying he bared his head, and showed his brow —a thick curl of his hair lay upon the wound and seemed to have stanched its bleeding.

Then Garcinde rose from her seat and advanced towards him as though she had something to say, but she stopped short and remained speechless with downcast eyes before him. Aigleta was the one to speak. "I will go and bring linen and salves to dress the wound properly," said she; then she looked at her friend as though

she had some quite other thought, secretly sighed, and
left the two alone. And scarcely had she turned away
when Geoffroy fell on his knees before the fair and
silent mourner, and cried as he seized her hands and
pressed them passionately to his heart: "Command me
—what shall I do? For my life is worthless to me unless I can offer it up to thee. Never should I have betrayed the sweet pangs I endured, if sorrow had not
overshadowed thee. But now thou art no longer the
Countess, the proud daughter of Malaspina, at whom I
gazed as at a star far above me. Thine is a poor unfortunate tortured heart which will not despise another
heart which devotes itself to thee for life and death.
Oh, cousin! loveliest love, say but one word, and I
mount again the horse that still stands saddled in the
courtyard, to ride back to Gaillac, and plunge this
dagger into the breast of the enemy of thy honour and
peace, in the midst of all his boon companions, even
though his dogs should tear me to pieces the next moment!"

Then she bent down towards him, and for the first
time a smile played over her pale face. "Jaufret," said
she, pressing her lips to his blood-stained brow; "the
fever of thy wound shows in thy speech. Go and lie
down, and let Aigleta—who understands such tasks—
wash away the blood and dress thy wound, and then refresh thyself with sleep and food. For by our dear lady
of Mont Salvair I accept the life you offer me. I am no
rich countess to disdain such a gift, and yet I am rich
enough to repay it. While you were relating your adventure—hideous and cruel enough to destroy all hope—
I was considering what I would and could do. But this
is not the time for talking. See, here comes your doc-
tress, I make you over to her, and you must do all she

tells you, and if you are tractable and obedient, be sure, cousin, you shall not rue it! See that he sleeps and gets strong, Aigleta," she said to her friend, who nodded, and looked as though she understood more than was uttered. Meanwhile, the youth who still gazed at Garcinde in utmost perplexity, had risen from his knees, and loosed her hands. He could not understand how she could be so composed since he had brought her no hope. But half from the exhaustion of his wound, and half from his blind confidence in her strong and lofty nature, he parted from her with a lightened heart, and followed Aigleta who had now lost all her gaiety. "What can she be planning?" said he to the girl, as they both went down the stair together. "Who can tell — obey and sleep," said Aigleta with a quick hoarse voice, and then turning her head away, she added, "The Lord gives to those He loves in sleep."

She led him into his turret hermitage; she saw to his wound, which was indeed but slight, and already disposed to heal; she furnished him with all that he could need for refreshment, and then seeing that his eyes were growing heavy she left him.

She herself, however, did not instantly return to Garcinde; she still lingered among the roses, made a nosegay, pulled it to pieces again, and when at last she returned to the castle, her eyes were red, and she washed them long with cold water that no one should observe it.

Geoffroy only slept a few hours: then he awoke a new man, with brow cool, thanks to Aigleta's salve, and heart on fire, thanks to the mysterious hope-encouraging words of his cousin. Like a wanderer on whom the fairy of the woods has bestowed the wishing-rod, by which at the hour of midnight he may find and possess himself of a treasure, and who dreams away the intervening time, so the youth sat hour after hour, gazing only at the sunbeam which slowly moved along the stone floor, and listening only to the song of the birds around his turret. No one came to disturb him: the servants lay yawning in shady corners of the court, the horses were stamping in the stable to shake off the flies; both girls had locked themselves up in their castle chamber, and did not appear all day. Once only through his narrow window did he catch sight of Sir Hugo, who stepped out on the balcony before his chamber, and looked down into the castle moat as though considering whether it would not be better for him to dash himself to pieces there. His hair and beard had become white as snow, his face was worn to a shadow; soon he vanished again like a restless ghost. And now the sun went down, and the moon rose above the wood, and silvered the rose-garden around Geoffroy's tower. The birds were silent, but the bull-frogs in the moat seemed to croak the louder, and in the distance a nightingale's song was heard. It was so light in the tower that the youth could read every letter in his parchment book, but he knew not what he was reading.

Another hour passed away, and yet another, and then light and rapid steps along the narrow path woke the listener out of his trance. He rushed to the door and threw it open wide, and saw with amazement not only the one that his heart foretold, but her friend also beside her on the threshold. They greeted him with a silent nod, and it was only when they had passed into his narrow chamber that Garcinde shyly spoke, "You see that I keep my word, cousin, but have you not in the course of the day changed your mind? Do you not regret what you said to me this morning?" and as he looked at her with mute enquiry she blushingly continued: "That you loved me, Jaufret, loved me more than your life, and would devote that life to me in sorrow until death. You may speak out your heart openly, this faithful friend knows all. She knew even earlier than I did myself that my heart belonged to thee, as thine to me. Oh, Jaufret, even at La Vaquiera, when we spoke by night about the stars, what made me so still and so sad was that I kept saying to myself, Is there no place amongst those countless orbs where he and I may belong to each other? Must I lose him whom I have only just regained? For I foresaw too clearly that my heart and my hand would not long remain my own. And God is my witness I was resolved to obey my father, had he betrothed me to any worthy husband, however distasteful he might have proved. But to fall a victim in an unholy hour to the mere chance of the dice, that cannot be God's will, though he has commanded us to honour father and mother; for I have in dreams seen my mother weeping over me, and I know that were she still living, she would go with me into poverty rather than give me to such a husband. And therefore am I come to thee, my beloved, and if thou art in earnest as I believe and know thou art, I will in this very hour before God and this witness, take thee for my husband, and fly forth with thee into the wide world. And sure am I that when our flight is discovered, my father will not mount his horse and follow us to punish the son as he did the father; he knows that he dare not judge, that a judge should have a guiltless heart. But we—where shall we fly? Are not all places home to us, so I am with thee, Jaufret, and thou with thy Garcinde?"

With these words she gave him her little hand, but while he, in a transport of silent rapture, took it and held it fast, Aigleta stepped forward and said in her lively way, and with a smiling face. "Just look at this coy gentleman, Garcinde. Can this be the son of the man whose lips overflowed with sweetest sayings, and not a single poor word falls from *his* mouth; even when one brings him the fairest of count's daughters, who whistles all the castles and lands of Gaillac down the wind, in order to beg her way through the world with this helpless lover. But come, come, we cannot wait till a miracle is wrought, and the dumb regains his speech. You must exchange rings, and pronounce the marriage-vow, and then go forth and far away, and I—poor forsaken one—have only to make the sign of the cross behind you; for to me you are dead and buried, that I know all too well. I shall—"

Her voice broke down, spite of all her self-control and her effort to smile, and she had to stoop and pretend to adjust her shoe, that her tears might drop unnoticed. Geoffroy, meantime, had collected himself and now drew a ring from his finger.

"Do you know it?" he said to Garcinde. "With this little ring my father betrothed himself to my mother, and as in his case it betokened the firmest constancy—a constancy that was sealed by death—I now give it to thee, my passionately loved bride, and swear in presence of the Holy Trinity, and before our true friend, I will never be the husband of any other woman than Garcinde of Malaspina."

"And I will never be the wife of any other man than my Geoffroy," said the bride.

"Amen. So be it," said Aigleta, in corroboration of their vow, laying—after the exchange of rings—their hands together. Then the pair knelt down before the picture of the Mother of God, and remained for a short season, in silent prayer. But when they rose again and sank into each other's arms, and with heart on heart, and mouth on mouth, ratified their holy vow, the witness slipped softly away. By-and-bye, they found her outside amongst the roses, of which she had woven two garlands. "No wedding without a garland," said she, and smiled, though her eyes were wet, while she crowned them both. Then the youth hurried to the stable and noiselessly saddled his horse and led him to the garden, where Garcinde lay on the breast of her friend, and whispered amidst her tears: "I know why thou weepest. God make thee as happy as thou hast been brave, and true to me."

They set off quietly, Geoffroy leading the horse, who with dilated nostrils snorted at the moonlight, the girls following him over the bridge; then he lifted his young wife into the saddle, sprang up himself behind her, and waving his hand to Aigleta, spurred his faithful charger on. It did not feel the weight it bore too heavy, for with the exception of his sword and dagger, Geoffroy had taken nothing with him but his father's song-book, and Garcinde only a few ornaments which she had inherited from her mother, and which her father had never touched. Thus, then, they rode through the moonlit forest. They did not say much: every now and then when the horse was slowly crossing boggy ground, she would turn half round to him, and then he kissed her cheek, and her black eyes smiled while she whispered, "My dearest husband."

She rested in his arms so sweetly, and the good horse trod so securely, that they hardly realised their circumstances—a hasty flight by night—a dark future before them—but enjoyed their bliss as though no shadow of care and danger hung over their love.

But when they got out of the wood and reached the hill from whence Garcinde a few days ago had first beheld again her father's castle, she suddenly pulled the rein and turned the horse round.

"What ails thee, sweet wife? And why dost thou halt here?" asked Geoffroy.

She did not reply, but gazed over the wide plain towards the dark pile with its leaden-roofed turrets that shone in the moonlight.

"What is it that you see, dearest?" asked the youth, who felt her tremble on his breast, as though a frosty chill had overtaken her on the warm summer night. "Let us look forwards, not back. Our happiness lies before us." But she only shook her head sorrowfully, turned away when he wished to kiss her, and said not a word. All of a sudden she had seemed to see in the deserted castle her father with a taper in his hand wandering from room to room, and crying, "Where is my daughter Garcinde? I have pledged my honour, she must redeem my pledge. Where is my child, and where is my honour? I was a beggar. I had nothing but my unstained name, and now that is lost. The last of the Malaspina has destroyed the good fame of the house, for she knows that I can no longer pursue her as in former years I should have done. I am old and sick, and a sinful man. Now, therefore, I must go down disgraced to the grave, for mine enemy will say I have connived at this, and that to avoid paying my debt, I have preferred even to give my last jewel to a beggar, than to the creditor I hated!" Then again this image vanished, and she now saw herself and her lover pursued on strange roads by an angry band, Pierre de Gaillac at their head, resolved to claim his bride from her ravisher. She saw her Jaufret fight with the energy of a despairing man, and yet at length conquered by numbers, shed his life's blood on the green grass, and

she heard the mocking conqueror laugh, "So thou en-
viest me my gains at play, thou player's son; the creditor
reclaims the debt the debtor would have withheld from
him!" Then a deadly shudder passed over her; she
thought for a moment that her heart had ceased to beat.
All the joys of her young love seemed crushed by an
icy hand. She knew now that what had appeared to
her in her trouble a way of escape and an immeasurable bliss was a false dream; that she should but bring
death and ruin to both the beings whom she supremely
loved!

"For the love of the Saints!" cried Geoffroy, who
felt her cherished form grow heavy as a lifeless body in
his embrace, "come to thyself again. What fearful
thoughts hast thou in thy mind that thus thy lips move
silently as though speaking with the departed? Give me
the bridle and let us turn to life, to liberty. The spirits
that hover over those towers will have no power over
thee when once thou art the other side of this hill. Wilt
thou make us both wretched? Wilt thou even—"

He stopped when he saw the stony eyes of his young
wife from which every beam of hope and joy had utterly vanished. But this did not last long, the convulsion was now over. She gave a deep sigh, turned on
him eyes of yearning love, and said, while endeavouring
to smile:

"I have scared thee; forgive me, my beloved. What
have we two to fear from any spirits that may hover
over that house and envy us our bliss. Thou, my husband, and I, thy wife, eternally one, body and soul! But
I have been thinking about our flight, that it is not the
will of Heaven; and if we persisted, Jaufret, against my
conscience, we should be punished, and should end as
miserably as did thy father and my dear aunt. Trust

to me, I have another idea which thou shalt know to-morrow early. Thou wilt praise thy wife when thou seest how she has contrived both to pay the debt to the creditor, and yet to be the wife of no man except her dearest cousin, to whom she has given herself in the presence of God. Lift me down from the saddle, I do not wish to ride any longer. If it pleases you, my husband, let us walk back through the wood, there are still many hours before day, and a fairer wedding-night no count's daughter could ever wish for. And now kiss me, so that I may again see a smile on thy lips; for truly this poor life is too short for us to spoil even one moment of it by care and gloom." He reluctantly did what she required of him; but when he took her into his arms and their lips met, he could not refrain from asking, "Oh Garcinde! What art thou thinking of? Hast thou not too much confidence in thyself, and wilt thou not if thy plan fails make us both eternally wretched?" But she smiled at him with bright eyes, laid her finger on his mouth, and said, "You are the happiest married man on earth, Sir Geoffroy; you have a wife who knows how to keep a secret. But now do not press me any further. What have we to do with the morrow? To-day are we already such old married people that we can find more important subjects to speak of than our love? Say, Jaufret, do I really please thee better than Agnes of Sardinia, and was her hand when she stroked thy hair not softer than mine? Nay, but thou must not embrace me so ardently here, the moon looks too boldly down, and after all she does not know that thou art my dear husband. Come into the wood, I am weary with our ride and would fain rest awhile. I know a bank where a brook runs through the moss, numbers of flowers bloom there, and I will weave them into fresh garlands, for those

Aigleta made are quite crushed. Poor Aigleta! Dost
thou know that she loved thee too well? But that cannot be helped now: no one can be the husband of two
women; that is against God's law. And I, though I be
not indeed better than she, I am the more unhappy of
the two, or at least I should have been if thy heart, my
beautiful love, had not been mine."

With such words as these, which intoxicated the
youth like strong wine, they went down the hill and entered the wood. Their gentle horse followed them of
his own accord, and peacefully grazed near them in the
flowery glade where they laid them down. Through the
whole of the night the brook rippled and the nightin-
gales sang, and the moon shone so brightly that no one
could have thought of sleep, not at least two who had
so much to confide to each other, and knew not whether
there would be time for it on the following day. When
the morning drew near, and the dew began to fall, and
a cooler air swept through the wood, Garcinde arose
and said, while a shudder passed over her, "It is growing cold, my husband. I think we ought to go home."
"Where?" asked he, looking at her in amazement, but
she smiled.

"Only come," said she, "I will show you. Can I
have any other home than thine?" With that she took
his arm and led him out of the wood, and over the
bridge back into his tower.

"Here let me rest," said she, as she seated herself
on his mother's bed. "Here I would fain sleep for an
hour until the sun rises. But leave me alone, my beloved, otherwise we shall go on talking, and I shall not
be able to close an eye. And give me your song-book
too, I should like to read a verse or two before I fall

asleep. And now, one good-night kiss, and then go! Oh, Jaufret, I love thee more than my life! Are we not two happy beings to have enjoyed such bliss that nothing can trouble us. And if we lived a hundred years, could time make us richer in joys when we have drunk from the cup of eternal blessedness?" Once more he embraced the lovely one, and kissed her long and fervently on her mouth. Then he left her alone.

An hour later the cock crew. But it did not wake the youth who lay in the rose-garden, his cloak thrown over him, smiling in his dream as though he were inwardly happy, and murmuring the name of his young wife. Neither did it wake the sleeper in the turret-room, whose lips were half-open as though they, too, would pronounce a name, but all was still as death in the dim chamber.

It was only when the sun had already risen over the tops of the trees, that Aigleta came by with weary eyes and pale face, listless and absorbed in her own thoughts. When she saw Geoffroy lying in the garden, she was horror-stricken as though she had seen a ghost, and it was only when she ascertained that he was breathing that she bent down to wake him. "You still here?" she whispered. "And where is—your wife?"

He sprang up in haste, and without answering a word, rushed to his turret. When he opened the door, he gave a cry like a man mortally wounded, and fell upon the bed. There lay his young bride, one hand pressed to her heart, from which a little stream of blood still flowed, her other hand rested on the song-book, which was open at its last page, and the white fingers pointed to a newly written line that ran thus in the language of Provence:

Lo deuteire paqua al crezedor tot lo deute.
The debtor pays to the creditor all the debt.

It was noon before the servants ventured carefully
to apprise Count Hugo of the heart-rending truth. He
listened to the tidings as though he did not rightly understand their purport; even when they led him down to
where his child, like á proud and beautiful statue of
whitest marble, lay outstretched on the bed he knew so
well, he gave no token of what he felt, spoke not a
word, shed not a tear. All night he shut himself up
with the dead. The next morning he ordered a bier to
be prepared. He would redeem his word, he said, and
carry the bride to her bridegroom. The servants silently
obeyed. Geoffroy—who might else have put in his
claim—lay in a raging fever, tended by Aigleta; his
wound on the forehead had burst open afresh, and no
salve availed to close it.

When the procession came to Gaillac, Count Hugo
at its head, the dead bride on a high bier borne, by his
servants, a great crowd of peasants and retainers behind,
the bride's father sent a herald in advance to blow his
trumpet three times, and cry with a loud voice, "The
debtor pays to the creditor all that he owes him!" At
this cry, Count Pierre de Gaillac appeared on the balcony of his castle; but when he saw the lamentable
spectacle he turned away horrified, and violently signed
to them to go back, that he would have no such wedding. Then he flung himself on his horse and rode far
away, and only returned after many days a broken-down
man who had forgotten how to laugh.

Count Hugo, however, without giving one sign of grief, next ordered the bearers to carry the bier to a chapel that stood in the open country, and was dedicated to the blessed Lady of Mont Salvair. There on the land and property belonging to the Count de Gaillac, to whom he had to pay his debt, he buried the beautiful body of his child. And no one dared to touch a spade, for he determined with his own hands to prepare her last resting-place. When this ceremony had been performed amidst the tears of the crowd, all went away and left him. He remained alone in the chapel; no one knew whether he was praying or speaking with the dead. But when they went to look after him the next day, and to offer him food and drink, he was no longer living, and they buried him beside his child.

Of Geoffroy the chronicle tells nothing further, except that in the autumn of the same year he joined the crusaders, and travelled towards Jerusalem, from whence he never came back. But any one turning over the old records of the Convent of Mont Salvair would there find that towards the end of the century, there was an abbess of the name of Aigleta von Malaspina—in religion named Sor Sofrenza (in modern French Sœur Souffrance,)—who only at an advanced age entered into eternal rest.

THE END.